Agatha Christie®

By the Pricking of My Thumbs

HarperCollins*Publishers*

HarperCollins*Publishers* Ltd
1 London Bridge Street
London SE1 9GF

www.harpercollins.co.uk

HarperCollins*Publishers*
Macken House, 39/40 Mayor Street Upper
Dublin1, D01 C9W8, Ireland

This paperback edition 2015
13

First published in Great Britain by
Collins 1968

A catalogue record for this book is
available from the British Library

ISBN 978-0-00-759062-9 (PB)
ISBN 978-0-00-825556-5 (POD PB)

Set in Sabon by FMG using Atomik ePublisher from Easypress

Printed and bound in the UK using 100% renewable
electricity at CPI Group (UK) Ltd

BY THE PRICKING OF MY THUMBS

ALSO BY AGATHA CHRISTIE

Mysteries
The Man in the Brown Suit
The Secret of Chimneys
The Seven Dials Mystery
The Mysterious Mr Quin
The Sittaford Mystery
The Hound of Death
The Listerdale Mystery
Why Didn't They Ask Evans?
Parker Pyne Investigates
Murder Is Easy
And Then There Were None
Towards Zero
Death Comes as the End
Sparkling Cyanide
Crooked House
They Came to Baghdad
Destination Unknown
Spider's Web *
The Unexpected Guest *
Ordeal by Innocence
The Pale Horse
Endless Night
Passenger To Frankfurt
Problem at Pollensa Bay
While the Light Lasts

Poirot
The Mysterious Affair at Styles
The Murder on the Links
Poirot Investigates
The Murder of Roger Ackroyd
The Big Four
The Mystery of the Blue Train
Black Coffee *
Peril at End House
Lord Edgware Dies
Murder on the Orient Express
Three-Act Tragedy
Death in the Clouds
The ABC Murders
Murder in Mesopotamia
Cards on the Table
Murder in the Mews
Dumb Witness
Death on the Nile
Appointment with Death
Hercule Poirot's Christmas
Sad Cypress
One, Two, Buckle My Shoe
Evil Under the Sun
Five Little Pigs
The Hollow
The Labours of Hercules
Taken at the Flood
Mrs McGinty's Dead
After the Funeral
Hickory Dickory Dock
Dead Man's Folly
Cat Among the Pigeons
The Adventure of the Christmas Pudding
The Clocks
Third Girl
Hallowe'en Party
Elephants Can Remember
Poirot's Early Cases
Curtain: Poirot's Last Case

Marple
The Murder at the Vicarage
The Thirteen Problems
The Body in the Library
The Moving Finger
A Murder Is Announced
They Do It with Mirrors
A Pocket Full of Rye
4.50 from Paddington
The Mirror Crack'd from Side to Side
A Caribbean Mystery
At Bertram's Hotel
Nemesis
Sleeping Murder
Miss Marple's Final Cases

Tommy & Tuppence
The Secret Adversary
Partners in Crime
N or M?
By the Pricking of My Thumbs
Postern of Fate

Published as Mary Westmacott
Giant's Bread
Unfinished Portrait
Absent in the Spring
The Rose and the Yew Tree
A Daughter's a Daughter
The Burden

Memoirs
An Autobiography
Come, Tell Me How You Live
The Grand Tour

Play Collections
Akhnaton
The Mousetrap and Other Plays
The Floating Admiral †
Star Over Bethlehem

* novelized by Charles Osborne † contributor

This book is dedicated to the many readers in this and in other countries who write to me asking: 'What has happened to Tommy and Tuppence? What are they doing now?' My best wishes to you all, and I hope you will enjoy meeting Tommy and Tuppence again, years older, but with spirit unquenched!

Agatha Christie

Contents

Book 1: Sunny Ridge

1.	Aunt Ada	3
2.	Was It Your Poor Child?	13
3.	A Funeral	29
4.	Picture of a House	34
5.	Disappearance of an Old Lady	51
6.	Tuppence on the Trail	63

Book 2: The House on the Canal

7.	The Friendly Witch	73
8.	Sutton Chancellor	93
9.	A Morning in Market Basing	127

Book 3: Missing—A Wife

10.	A Conference—and After	143
11.	Bond Street and Dr Murray	157
12.	Tommy Meets an Old Friend	176
13.	Albert on Clues	203

Book 4: Here is a Church and here is the Steeple
Open the Doors and there are the People

14.	Exercise in Thinking	225
15.	Evening at the Vicarage	239
16.	The Morning After	259
17.	Mrs Lancaster	270

By the pricking of my thumbs
Something wicked this way comes.

—*Macbeth*

BOOK 1

Sunny Ridge

CHAPTER 1

Aunt Ada

Mr and Mrs Beresford were sitting at the breakfast table. They were an ordinary couple. Hundreds of elderly couples just like them were having breakfast all over England at that particular moment. It was an ordinary sort of day too, the kind of day that you get five days out of seven. It looked as though it might rain but wasn't quite sure of it.

Mr Beresford had once had red hair. There were traces of the red still, but most of it had gone that sandy-cum-grey colour that red-headed people so often arrive at in middle life. Mrs Beresford had once had black hair, a vigorous curling mop of it. Now the black was adulterated with streaks of grey laid on, apparently at random. It made a rather pleasant effect. Mrs Beresford had once thought of dyeing her hair, but in the end she had decided that she liked herself better as nature had made her. She had decided instead to try a new shade of lipstick so as to cheer herself up.

An elderly couple having breakfast together. A pleasant couple, but nothing remarkable about them. So an onlooker would have said. If the onlooker had been young he or she would have added, 'Oh yes, quite pleasant, but deadly dull, of course, like all old people.'

However, Mr and Mrs Beresford had not yet arrived at the time of life when they thought of themselves as old. And they had no idea that they and many others were automatically pronounced deadly dull solely on that account. Only by the young of course, but then, they would have thought indulgently, young people knew nothing about life. Poor dears, they were always worrying about examinations, or their sex life, or buying some extraordinary clothes, or doing extraordinary things to their hair to make them more noticeable. Mr and Mrs Beresford from their own point of view were just past the prime of life. They liked themselves and liked each other and day succeeded day in a quiet but enjoyable fashion.

There were, of course, moments, everyone has moments. Mr Beresford opened a letter, glanced through it and laid it down, adding it to the small pile by his left hand. He picked up the next letter but forbore to open it. Instead he stayed with it in his hand. He was not looking at the letter, he was looking at the toast-rack. His wife observed him for a few moments before saying,

'What's the matter, Tommy?'

'Matter?' said Tommy vaguely. 'Matter?'

'That's what I said,' said Mrs Beresford.

'Nothing is the matter,' said Mr Beresford. 'What should it be?'

'You've thought of something,' said Tuppence accusingly.

'I don't think I was thinking of anything at all.'

'Oh yes, you were. Has anything happened?'

'No, of course not. What should happen?' He added, 'I got the plumber's bill.'

'Oh,' said Tuppence with the air of one enlightened. 'More than you expected, I suppose.'

'Naturally,' said Tommy, 'it always is.'

'I can't think why we didn't train as plumbers,' said Tuppence. 'If you'd only trained as a plumber, I could have been a plumber's mate and we'd be raking in money day by day.'

'Very short-sighted of us not to see these opportunities.'

'Was that the plumber's bill you were looking at just now?'

'Oh no, that was just an Appeal.'

'Delinquent boys—Racial integration?'

'No. Just another Home they're opening for old people.'

'Well, that's more sensible anyway,' said Tuppence, 'but I don't see why you have to have that worried look about it.'

'Oh, I wasn't thinking of that.'

'Well, what *were* you thinking of?'

'I suppose it put it into my mind,' said Mr Beresford.

'What?' said Tuppence. 'You know you'll tell me in the end.'

'It really wasn't anything important. I just thought that perhaps—well, it was Aunt Ada.'

'Oh, I see,' said Tuppence, with instant comprehension. 'Yes,' she added, softly, meditatively. 'Aunt Ada.'

Their eyes met. It is regrettably true that in these days there is in nearly every family, the problem of what might be called an 'Aunt Ada'. The names are different—Aunt Amelia, Aunt Susan, Aunt Cathy, Aunt Joan. They are varied by grandmothers, aged cousins and even great-aunts. But they exist and present a problem in life which has to be dealt with. Arrangements have to be made. Suitable establishments for looking after the elderly have to be inspected and full questions asked about them. Recommendations are sought from doctors, from friends, who have Aunt Adas of their own who had been 'perfectly happy until she had died' at 'The Laurels, Bexhill', or 'Happy Meadows at Scarborough'.

The days are past when Aunt Elisabeth, Aunt Ada and the rest of them lived on happily in the homes where they had lived for many years previously, looked after by devoted if sometimes somewhat tyrannical old servants. Both sides were thoroughly satisfied with the arrangement. Or there were the innumerable poor relations, indigent nieces, semi-idiotic spinster cousins, all yearning for a good home with three good meals a day and a nice bedroom. Supply and demand complemented each other and all was well. Nowadays, things are different.

For the Aunt Adas of today arrangements have to be made suitable, not merely to an elderly lady who, owing to arthritis or other rheumatic difficulties, is liable to fall downstairs if she is left alone in a house, or who suffers from chronic bronchitis, or who quarrels with her neighbours and insults the tradespeople.

Unfortunately, the Aunt Adas are far more trouble than the opposite end of the age scale. Children can be provided with foster homes, foisted off on relations, or sent to suitable schools where they stay for the holidays, or arrangements can be made for pony treks or camps, and on the whole very little objection is made by the children to the arrangements so made for them. The Aunt Adas are very different. Tuppence Beresford's own aunt—Great-aunt Primrose—had been a notable troublemaker. Impossible to satisfy her. No sooner did she enter an establishment guaranteed to provide a good home and all comforts for elderly ladies than after writing a few highly complimentary letters to her niece praising this particular establishment, the next news would be that she had indignantly walked out of it without notice.

'Impossible. I couldn't stay there another minute!'

Within the space of a year Aunt Primrose had been in and out of eleven such establishments, finally writing to say that she had now met a very charming young man. 'Really a very devoted boy. He lost his mother at a young age and he badly needs looking after. I have rented a flat and he is coming to live with me. This arrangement will suit us both perfectly. We are natural affinities. You need have no more anxieties, dear Prudence. My future is settled. I am seeing my lawyer tomorrow as it is necessary that I should make some provision for Mervyn if I should pre-decease him which is, of course, the natural course of events, though I assure you at the moment I feel in the pink of health.'

Tuppence had hurried north (the incident had taken place in Aberdeen). But as it happened, the police had arrived there first and had removed the glamorous Mervyn, for whom they had been seeking for some time, on a charge of obtaining money under false pretences. Aunt Primrose had been highly indignant, and had called it persecution—but after attending the Court proceedings (where twenty-five other cases were taken into account)—had been forced to change her views of her *protégé*.

'I think I ought to go and see Aunt Ada, you know, Tuppence,' said Tommy. 'It's been some time.'

'I suppose so,' said Tuppence, without enthusiasm. 'How long has it been?'

Tommy considered. 'It must be nearly a year,' he said.

'It's more than that,' said Tuppence. 'I think it's over a year.'

'Oh dear,' said Tommy, 'the time does go so fast, doesn't it? I can't believe it's been as long as that. Still, I believe you're right, Tuppence.' He calculated. 'It's awful the way one forgets, isn't it? I really feel very badly about it.'

'I don't think you need,' said Tuppence. 'After all, we send her things and we write letters.'

'Oh yes, I know. You're awfully good about those sort of things, Tuppence. But all the same, one does read things sometimes that are very upsetting.'

'You're thinking of that dreadful book we got from the library,' said Tuppence, 'and how awful it was for the poor old dears. How they suffered.'

'I suppose it was true—taken from life.'

'Oh yes,' said Tuppence, 'there must be places like that. And there are people who are terribly unhappy, who can't help being unhappy. But what else is one to do, Tommy?'

'What can anyone do except be as careful as possible. Be very careful what you choose, find out all about it and make sure she's got a nice doctor looking after her.'

'Nobody could be nicer than Dr Murray, you must admit that.'

'Yes,' said Tommy, the worried look receding from his face. 'Murray's a first-class chap. Kind, patient. If anything was going wrong he'd let us know.'

'So I don't think you need worry about it,' said Tuppence. 'How old is she by now?'

'Eighty-two,' said Tommy. 'No—no. I think it's eighty-three,' he added. 'It must be rather awful when you've outlived everybody.'

'That's only what *we* feel,' said Tuppence. '*They* don't feel it.'

'You can't really tell.'

'Well, your Aunt Ada doesn't. Don't you remember the glee with which she told us the number of her old friends that she'd already outlived? She finished up by saying "and as for Amy Morgan, I've heard she won't last more than another six months. She always used to say I was so delicate and now it's practically a certainty that I shall outlive her. Outlive her by a good many years too." Triumphant, that's what she was at the prospect.'

'All the same—' said Tommy.

'I know,' said Tuppence, 'I know. All the same you feel it's your duty and so you've got to go.'

'Don't you think I'm right?'

'Unfortunately,' said Tuppence, 'I do think you're right. Absolutely right. And I'll come too,' she added, with a slight note of heroism in her voice.

'No,' said Tommy. 'Why should you? She's not your aunt. No, I'll go.'

'Not at all,' said Mrs Beresford. 'I like to suffer too. We'll suffer together. You won't enjoy it and I shan't enjoy it and I don't think for one moment that Aunt Ada will enjoy it. But I quite see it is one of those things that has got to be done.'

'No, I don't want you to go. After all, the last time, remember how frightfully rude she was to you?'

'Oh, I didn't mind that,' said Tuppence. 'It's probably the only bit of the visit that the poor old girl enjoyed. I don't grudge it to her, not for a moment.'

'You've always been nice to her,' said Tommy, 'even though you don't like her very much.'

'Nobody could like Aunt Ada,' said Tuppence. 'If you ask me I don't think anyone ever has.'

'One can't help feeling sorry for people when they get old,' said Tommy.

'I can,' said Tuppence. 'I haven't got as nice a nature as you have.'

'Being a woman you're more ruthless,' said Tommy.

'I suppose that might be it. After all, women haven't really got time to be anything but realistic over things. I mean I'm very sorry for people if they're old or sick or anything, if they're nice people. But if they're not nice people, well, it's different, you must admit. If you're pretty nasty when you're twenty and just as nasty when you're forty and nastier still when you're sixty, and a perfect devil by the time you're eighty—well, really, I don't see why one should be particularly sorry for people, just because they're old. You can't change yourself really. I know some absolute ducks who are seventy and eighty. Old Mrs Beauchamp, and Mary Carr and the baker's grandmother, dear old Mrs Poplett, who used to come in and clean for us. They were all dears and sweet and I'd do anything I could for them.'

'All right, all right,' said Tommy, 'be realistic. But if you really want to be noble and come with me—'

'I want to come with you,' said Tuppence. 'After all, I married you for better or for worse and Aunt Ada is decidedly the worse. So I shall go with you hand in hand. And we'll take her a bunch of flowers and a box of chocolates with soft centres and perhaps a magazine or two. You might write to Miss What's-her-name and say we're coming.'

'One day next week? I could manage Tuesday,' said Tommy, 'if that's all right for you.'

'Tuesday it is,' said Tuppence. 'What's the name of the woman? I can't remember—the matron or the superintendent or whoever she is. Begins with a P.'

'Miss Packard.'

'That's right.'

'Perhaps it'll be different this time,' said Tommy.

'Different? In what way?'

'Oh, I don't know. Something interesting might happen.'

'We might be in a railway accident on the way there,' said Tuppence, brightening up a little.

'Why on earth do you want to be in a railway accident?'

'Well I don't really, of course. It was just—'

'Just what?'

'Well, it would be an adventure of some kind, wouldn't it? Perhaps we could save lives or do something useful. Useful and at the same time exciting.'

'What a hope!' said Mr Beresford.

'I know,' agreed Tuppence. 'It's just that these sort of ideas come to one sometimes.'

CHAPTER 2

Was It Your Poor Child?

How Sunny Ridge had come by its name would be difficult to say. There was nothing prominently ridge-like about it. The grounds were flat, which was eminently more suitable for the elderly occupants. It had an ample, though rather undistinguished garden. It was a fairly large Victorian mansion kept in a good state of repair. There were some pleasant shady trees, a Virginia creeper running up the side of the house, and two monkey puzzles gave an exotic air to the scene. There were several benches in advantageous places to catch the sun, one or two garden chairs and a sheltered veranda on which the old ladies could sit sheltered from the east winds.

Tommy rang the front door bell and he and Tuppence were duly admitted by a rather harassed-looking young woman in a nylon overall. She showed them into a small sitting-room saying rather breathlessly, 'I'll tell Miss Packard. She's expecting you and she'll be down in a minute. You won't mind waiting just a little, will you, but it's old Mrs Carraway. She's been and swallowed her thimble again, you see.'

'How on earth did she do a thing like that?' asked Tuppence, surprised.

'Does it for fun,' explained the household help briefly. 'Always doing it.'

She departed and Tuppence sat down and said thoughtfully, 'I don't think I should like to swallow a thimble. It'd be awfully bobbly as it went down. Don't you think so?'

They had not very long to wait however before the door opened and Miss Packard came in, apologizing as she did so. She was a big, sandy-haired woman of about fifty with the air of calm competence about her which Tommy had always admired.

'I'm sorry if I have kept you waiting, Mr Beresford,' she said. 'How do you do, Mrs Beresford, I'm so glad you've come too.'

'Somebody swallowed something, I hear,' said Tommy.

'Oh, so Marlene told you that? Yes, it was old Mrs Carraway. She's always swallowing things. Very difficult, you know, because one can't watch them all the time. Of course one knows children do it, but it seems a funny thing to be a hobby of an elderly woman, doesn't it? It's grown upon her, you know. She gets worse every year. It doesn't seem to do her any harm, that's the cheeriest thing about it.'

'Perhaps her father was a sword swallower,' suggested Tuppence.

'Now that's a very interesting idea, Mrs Beresford. Perhaps it *would* explain things.' She went on, 'I've told Miss Fanshawe that you were coming, Mr Beresford. I don't know really whether she quite took it in. She doesn't always, you know.'

'How has she been lately?'

'Well, she's failing rather rapidly now, I'm afraid,' said Miss Packard in a comfortable voice. 'One never really knows how much she takes in and how much she doesn't. I told her last night and she said she was sure I must be mistaken because it was term time. She seemed to think that you were still at school. Poor old things, they get very muddled up sometimes, especially over time. However, this morning when I reminded her about your visit, she just said it was quite impossible because you were dead. Oh well,' Miss Packard went on cheerfully, 'I expect she'll recognize you when she sees you.'

'How is she in health? Much the same?'

'Well, perhaps as well as can be expected. Frankly, you know, I don't think she'll be with us very much longer. She doesn't suffer in any way but her heart condition's no better than it was. In fact, it's rather worse. So I think I'd like you to know that it's just as well to be prepared, so that if she did go suddenly it wouldn't be any shock to you.'

'We brought her some flowers,' said Tuppence.

'And a box of chocolates,' said Tommy.

'Oh, that's very kind of you I'm sure. She'll be very pleased. Would you like to come up now?'

Tommy and Tuppence rose and followed Miss Packard from the room. She led them up the broad staircase. As they passed one of the rooms in the passage upstairs, it opened suddenly and a little woman about five foot high trotted out, calling in a loud shrill voice, 'I want my cocoa. I want my cocoa. Where's Nurse Jane? I want my cocoa.'

A woman in a nurse's uniform popped out of the next door and said, 'There, there, dear, it's all right. You've had your cocoa. You had it twenty minutes ago.'

'No I didn't, Nurse. It's not true. I haven't had my cocoa. I'm thirsty.'

'Well, you shall have another cup if you like.'

'I can't have another when I haven't had one.'

They passed on and Miss Packard, after giving a brief rap on a door at the end of the passage, opened it and passed in.

'Here you are, Miss Fanshawe,' she said brightly. 'Here's your nephew come to see you. Isn't that nice?'

In a bed near the window an elderly lady sat up abruptly on her raised pillows. She had iron-grey hair, a thin wrinkled face with a large, high-bridged nose and a general air of disapprobation. Tommy advanced.

'Hullo, Aunt Ada,' he said. 'How are you?'

Aunt Ada paid no attention to him, but addressed Miss Packard angrily.

'I don't know what you mean by showing gentlemen into a lady's bedroom,' she said. 'Wouldn't have been thought proper at all in my young days! Telling me he's my nephew indeed! Who is he? A plumber or the electrician?'

'Now, now, that's not very nice,' said Miss Packard mildly.

'I'm your nephew, Thomas Beresford,' said Tommy. He advanced the box of chocolates. 'I've brought you a box of chocolates.'

'You can't get round me that way,' said Aunt Ada. 'I know your kind. Say anything, you will. Who's this woman?' She eyed Mrs Beresford with an air of distaste.

'I'm Prudence,' said Mrs Beresford. 'Your niece, Prudence.'

'What a ridiculous name,' said Aunt Ada. 'Sounds like a parlourmaid. My Great-uncle Mathew had a parlourmaid called Comfort and the housemaid was called Rejoice-in-the-Lord. Methodist she was. But my Great-aunt Fanny soon put a stop to that. Told her she was going to be called Rebecca as long as she was in *her* house.'

'I brought you a few roses,' said Tuppence.

'I don't care for flowers in a sick-room. Use up all the oxygen.'

'I'll put them in a vase for you,' said Miss Packard.

'You won't do anything of the kind. You ought to have learnt by now that I know my own mind.'

'You seem in fine form, Aunt Ada,' said Mr Beresford. 'Fighting fit, I should say.'

'I can take your measure all right. What d'you mean by saying that you're my nephew? What did you say your name was? Thomas?'

'Yes. Thomas or Tommy.'

'Never heard of you,' said Aunt Ada. 'I only had one nephew and he was called William. Killed in the last war. Good thing, too. He'd have gone to the bad if he'd lived. I'm tired,' said Aunt Ada, leaning back on her pillows and turning her head towards Miss Packard. 'Take 'em away. You shouldn't let strangers in to see me.'

'I thought a nice little visit might cheer you up,' said Miss Packard unperturbed.

Aunt Ada uttered a deep bass sound of ribald mirth.

'All right,' said Tuppence cheerfully. 'We'll go away again. I'll leave the roses. You might change your mind about them. Come on, Tommy,' said Tuppence. She turned towards the door.

'Well, goodbye, Aunt Ada. I'm sorry you don't remember me.'

Aunt Ada was silent until Tuppence had gone out of the door with Miss Packard and Tommy following her.

'Come back, *you*,' said Aunt Ada, raising her voice. 'I know you perfectly. You're Thomas. Red-haired you used to be. Carrots, that's the colour your hair was. Come back. I'll talk to you. I don't want the woman. No good her pretending she's your wife. I know better. Shouldn't bring that type of woman in here. Come and sit down here in this chair and tell me about your dear mother. You go away,' added Aunt Ada as a kind of postscript, waving her hand towards Tuppence who was hesitating in the doorway.

Tuppence retired immediately.

'Quite in one of her moods today,' said Miss Packard, unruffled, as they went down the stairs. 'Sometimes, you know,' she added, 'she can be quite pleasant. You would hardly believe it.'

Tommy sat down in the chair indicated to him by Aunt Ada and remarked mildly that he couldn't tell her much about his mother as she had been dead now for nearly forty years. Aunt Ada was unperturbed by this statement.

'Fancy,' she said, 'is it as long as that? Well, time does pass quickly.' She looked him over in a considering manner. 'Why don't you get married?' she said. 'Get some nice capable woman to look after you. You're getting on, you know. Save you taking up with all these loose women and bringing them round and speaking as though they were your wife.'

'I can see,' said Tommy, 'that I shall have to get Tuppence to bring her marriage lines along next time we come to see you.'

'Made an honest woman of her, have you?' said Aunt Ada.

'We've been married over thirty years,' said Tommy, 'and we've got a son and a daughter, and they're both married too.'

'The trouble is,' said Aunt Ada, shifting her ground with dexterity, 'that nobody tells me anything. If you'd kept me properly up to date—'

Tommy did not argue the point. Tuppence had once laid upon him a serious injunction. 'If anybody over the age of sixty-five finds fault with you,' she said, 'never argue. Never try to say you're right. Apologize at once and say it was all your fault and you're very sorry and you'll never do it again.'

It occurred to Tommy at this moment with some force that that would certainly be the line to take with Aunt Ada, and indeed always had been.

'I'm very sorry, Aunt Ada,' he said. 'I'm afraid, you know, one does tend to get forgetful as time goes on. It's not everyone,' he continued unblushingly, 'who has your wonderful memory for the past.'

Aunt Ada smirked. There was no other word for it. 'You have something there,' she said. 'I'm sorry if I received you rather roughly, but I don't care for being imposed upon.

You never know in this place. They let in anyone to see you. Anyone at all. If I accepted everyone for what they said they were, they might be intending to rob and murder me in my bed.'

'Oh, I don't think that's very likely,' said Tommy.

'You never know,' said Aunt Ada. 'The things you read in the paper. And the things people come and tell you. Not that I believe everything I'm told. But I keep a sharp look-out. Would you believe it, they brought a strange man in the other day—never seen him before. Called himself Dr Williams. Said Dr Murray was away on his holiday and this was his new partner. New partner! How was I to know he was his new partner? He just said he was, that's all.'

'Was he his new partner?'

'Well, as a matter of fact,' said Aunt Ada, slightly annoyed at losing ground, 'he actually was. But nobody could have known it for sure. There he was, drove up in a car, had that little kind of black box with him, which doctors carry to do blood pressure—and all that sort of thing. It's like the magic box they all used to talk about so much. Who was it, Joanna Southcott's?'

'No,' said Tommy. 'I think that was rather different. A prophecy of some kind.'

'Oh, I see. Well, my point is anyone could come into a place like this and say he was a doctor, and immediately all the nurses would smirk and giggle and say yes, Doctor, of course, Doctor, and more or less stand to attention, silly girls! And if the patient swore she didn't know the man, they'd only say she was forgetful and forgot people. I never forget a face,' said Aunt Ada firmly. 'I never have. How is your Aunt Caroline? I haven't heard from her for some time. Have you seen anything of her?'

Tommy said, rather apologetically, that his Aunt Caroline had been dead for fifteen years. Aunt Ada did not take this demise with any signs of sorrow. Aunt Caroline had after all not been her sister, but merely her first cousin.

'Everyone seems to be dying,' she said, with a certain relish. 'No stamina. That's what's the matter with them. Weak heart, coronary thrombosis, high blood pressure, chronic bronchitis, rheumatoid arthritis—all the rest of it. Feeble folk, all of them. That's how the doctors make their living. Giving them boxes and boxes and bottles and bottles of tablets. Yellow tablets, pink tablets, green tablets, even black tablets, I shouldn't be surprised. Ugh! Brimstone and treacle they used to use in my grandmother's day. I bet that was as good as anything. With the choice of getting well or having brimstone and treacle to drink, you chose getting well every time.' She nodded her head in a satisfied manner. 'Can't really trust doctors, can you? Not when it's a professional matter—some new fad—I'm told there's a lot of poisoning going on here. To get hearts for the surgeons, so I'm told. Don't think it's true, myself. Miss Packard's not the sort of woman who would stand for that.'

Downstairs Miss Packard, her manner slightly apologetic, indicated a room leading off the hall.

'I'm so sorry about this, Mrs Beresford, but I expect you know how it is with elderly people. They take fancies or dislikes and persist in them.'

'It must be very difficult running a place of this kind,' said Tuppence.

'Oh, not really,' said Miss Packard. 'I quite enjoy it, you know. And really, I'm quite fond of them all. One gets fond of people one has to look after, you know. I mean, they have their little ways and their fidgets, but they're quite easy to manage, if you know how.'

Tuppence thought to herself that Miss Packard was one of those people who would know how.

'They're like children, really,' said Miss Packard indulgently. 'Only children are far more logical which makes it difficult sometimes with them. But these people are illogical, they want to be reassured by your telling them what they want to believe. Then they're quite happy again for a bit. I've got a very nice staff here. People with patience, you know, and good temper, and not too brainy, because if you have people who are brainy they are bound to be very impatient. Yes, Miss Donovan, what is it?' She turned her head as a young woman with *pince-nez* came running down the stairs.

'It's Mrs Lockett again, Miss Packard. She says she's dying and she wants the doctor called at once.'

'Oh,' said Miss Packard, unimpressed, 'what's she dying from this time?'

'She says there was mushroom in the stew yesterday and that there must have been fungi in it and that she's poisoned.'

'That's a new one,' said Miss Packard. 'I'd better come up and talk to her. So sorry to leave you, Mrs Beresford. You'll find magazines and papers in that room.'

'Oh, I'll be quite all right,' said Tuppence.

She went into the room that had been indicated to her. It was a pleasant room overlooking the garden with french windows that opened on it. There were easy chairs, bowls of flowers on the tables. One wall had a bookshelf containing a mixture of modern novels and travel books, and also what might be described as old favourites, which possibly many of the inmates might be glad to meet again. There were magazines on a table.

At the moment there was only one occupant in the room. An old lady with white hair combed back off her face who was sitting in a chair, holding a glass of milk in her hand, and looking at it. She had a pretty pink and white face, and she smiled at Tuppence in a friendly manner.

'Good morning,' she said. 'Are you coming to live here or are you visiting?'

'I'm visiting,' said Tuppence. 'I have an aunt here. My husband's with her now. We thought perhaps two people at once was rather too much.'

'That was very thoughtful of you,' said the old lady. She took a sip of milk appreciatively. 'I wonder—no, I think it's quite all right. Wouldn't you like something? Some tea or some coffee perhaps? Let me ring the bell. They're very obliging here.'

'No thank you,' said Tuppence, 'really.'

'Or a glass of milk perhaps. It's not poisoned today.'

'No, no, not even that. We shan't be stopping very much longer.'

'Well, if you're quite sure—but it wouldn't be any trouble, you know. Nobody ever thinks anything is any trouble here. Unless, I mean, you ask for something quite impossible.'

'I daresay the aunt we're visiting sometimes asks for quite impossible things,' said Tuppence. 'She's a Miss Fanshawe,' she added.

'Oh, Miss Fanshawe,' said the old lady. 'Oh yes.'

Something seemed to be restraining her but Tuppence said cheerfully,

'She's rather a tartar, I should imagine. She always has been.'

'Oh, yes indeed she is. I used to have an aunt myself, you know, who was very like that, especially as she grew older. But we're all quite fond of Miss Fanshawe. She can be very, very amusing if she likes. About people, you know.'

'Yes, I daresay she could be,' said Tuppence. She reflected a moment or two, considering Aunt Ada in this new light.

'Very acid,' said the old lady. 'My name is Lancaster, by the way, Mrs Lancaster.'

'My name's Beresford,' said Tuppence.

'I'm afraid, you know, one does enjoy a bit of malice now and then. Her descriptions of some of the other guests here, and the things she says about them. Well, you know, one oughtn't, of course, to find it funny but one does.'

'Have you been living here long?'

'A good while now. Yes, let me see, seven years—eight years. Yes, yes it must be more than eight years.' She sighed. 'One loses touch with things. And people too. Any relations I have left live abroad.'

'That must be rather sad.'

'No, not really. I didn't care for them very much. Indeed, I didn't even know them well. I had a bad illness—a very bad illness—and I was alone in the world, so they thought it was better for me to live in a place like this. I think I'm very lucky to have come here. They are so kind and thoughtful. And the gardens are really beautiful. I know myself that I shouldn't like to be living on my own because I do get very confused sometimes, you know. Very confused.' She tapped her forehead. 'I get confused here. I mix things up. I don't always remember properly the things that have happened.'

'I'm sorry,' said Tuppence. 'I suppose one always has to have something, doesn't one?'

'Some illnesses are very painful. We have two poor women living here with very bad rheumatoid arthritis. They suffer terribly. So I think perhaps it doesn't matter so much if one gets, well, just a little confused about what happened and where, and who it was, and all that sort of thing, you know. At any rate it's not painful physically.'

'No. I think perhaps you're quite right,' said Tuppence.

The door opened and a girl in a white overall came in with a little tray with a coffee pot on it and a plate with two biscuits, which she set down at Tuppence's side.

'Miss Packard thought you might care for a cup of coffee,' she said.

'Oh. Thank you,' said Tuppence.

The girl went out again and Mrs Lancaster said,

'There, you see. Very thoughtful, aren't they?'

'Yes indeed.'

Tuppence poured out her coffee and began to drink it. The two women sat in silence for some time. Tuppence offered the plate of biscuits but the old lady shook her head.

'No thank you, dear. I just like my milk plain.'

She put down the empty glass and leaned back in her chair, her eyes half closed. Tuppence thought that perhaps this was the moment in the morning when she took a little nap, so she remained silent. Suddenly however, Mrs Lancaster seemed to jerk herself awake again. Her eyes opened, she looked at Tuppence and said,

'I see you're looking at the fireplace.'

'Oh. Was I?' said Tuppence, slightly startled.

'Yes. I wondered—' she leant forward and lowered her voice. '—Excuse me, was it your poor child?'

Tuppence slightly taken aback, hesitated.

'I—no, I don't think so,' she said.

'I wondered. I thought perhaps you'd come for that reason. Someone ought to come some time. Perhaps they will. And looking at the fireplace, the way you did. That's where it is, you know. Behind the fireplace.'

'Oh,' said Tuppence. 'Oh. Is it?'

'Always the same time,' said Mrs Lancaster, in a low voice. 'Always the same time of day.' She looked up at the clock on the mantelpiece. Tuppence looked up also. 'Ten past eleven,' said the old lady. 'Ten past eleven. Yes, it's always the same time every morning.'

She sighed. 'People didn't understand—I told them what I knew—but they wouldn't believe me!'

Tuppence was relieved that at that moment the door opened and Tommy came in. Tuppence rose to her feet.

'Here I am. I'm ready.' She went towards the door turning her head to say, 'Goodbye, Mrs Lancaster.'

'How did you get on?' she asked Tommy, as they emerged into the hall.

'After *you* left,' said Tommy, 'like a house on fire.'

'I seem to have had a bad effect on her, don't I?' said Tuppence. 'Rather cheering, in a way.'

'Why cheering?'

'Well, at my age,' said Tuppence, 'and what with my neat and respectable and slightly boring appearance, it's nice to think that you might be taken for a depraved woman of fatal sexual charm.'

'Idiot,' said Tommy, pinching her arm affectionately. 'Who were you hobnobbing with? She looked a very nice fluffy old lady.'

'She was very nice,' said Tuppence. 'A dear old thing, I think. But unfortunately bats.'

'Bats?'

'Yes. Seemed to think there was a dead child behind the fireplace or something of the kind. She asked me if it was my poor child.'

'Rather unnerving,' said Tommy. 'I suppose there must be some people who are slightly batty here, as well as normal elderly relatives with nothing but age to trouble them. Still, she looked nice.'

'Oh, she was nice,' said Tuppence. 'Nice and very sweet, I think. I wonder what exactly her fancies are and why.'

Miss Packard appeared again suddenly.

'Goodbye, Mrs Beresford. I hope they brought you some coffee?'

'Oh yes, they did, thank you.'

'Well, it's been very kind of you to come, I'm sure,' said Miss Packard. Turning to Tommy, she said, 'And I know Miss Fanshawe has enjoyed your visit very much. I'm sorry she was rude to your wife.'

'I think that gave her a lot of pleasure too,' said Tuppence.

'Yes, you're quite right. She does like being rude to people. She's unfortunately rather good at it.'

'And so she practises the art as often as she can,' said Tommy.

'You're very understanding, both of you,' said Miss Packard.

'The old lady I was talking to,' said Tuppence. 'Mrs Lancaster, I think she said her name was?'

'Oh yes, Mrs Lancaster. We're all very fond of her.'

'She's—is she a little peculiar?'

'Well, she has fancies,' said Miss Packard indulgently. 'We have several people here who have fancies. Quite harmless ones. But—well, there they are. Things that they believe have happened to them. Or to other people. We try not to take any notice, not to encourage them. Just play it down. I think really it's just an exercise in imagination, a sort of phantasy they like to live in. Something exciting or something sad and tragic. It doesn't matter which. But no persecution mania, thank goodness. That would never do.'

'Well, that's over,' said Tommy with a sigh, as he got into the car. 'We shan't need to come again for at least six months.'

But they didn't need to go and see her in six months, for three weeks later Aunt Ada died in her sleep.

CHAPTER 3

A Funeral

'Funerals are rather sad, aren't they?' said Tuppence.

They had just returned from attending Aunt Ada's funeral, which had entailed a long and troublesome railway journey since the burial had taken place at the country village in Lincolnshire where most of Aunt Ada's family and forebears had been buried.

'What do you expect a funeral to be?' said Tommy reasonably. 'A scene of mad gaiety?'

'Well, it could be in some places,' said Tuppence. 'I mean the Irish enjoy a wake, don't they? They have a lot of keening and wailing first and then plenty of drink and a sort of mad whoopee. *Drink*?' she added, with a look towards the sideboard.

Tommy went over to it and duly brought back what he considered appropriate. In this case a White Lady.

'Ah, that's more like it,' said Tuppence.

She took off her black hat and threw it across the room and slipped off her long black coat.

'I hate mourning,' she said. 'It always smells of moth balls because it's been laid up somewhere.'

'You don't need to go on wearing mourning. It's only to go to the funeral in,' said Tommy.

'Oh no, I know that. In a minute or two I'm going to go up and put on a scarlet jersey just to cheer things up. You can make me another White Lady.'

'Really, Tuppence, I had no idea that funerals would bring out this party feeling.'

'I said funerals were sad,' said Tuppence when she reappeared a moment or two later, wearing a brilliant cherry-red dress with a ruby and diamond lizard pinned to the shoulder of it, 'because it's funerals like Aunt Ada's that are sad. I mean elderly people and not many flowers. Not a lot of people sobbing and sniffing round. Someone old and lonely who won't be missed much.'

'I should have thought it would be much easier for you to stand that than it would if it were my funeral, for instance.'

'That's where you're entirely wrong,' said Tuppence. 'I don't particularly want to think of your funeral because I'd much prefer to die before you do. But I mean, if I were going to your funeral, at any rate it would be an orgy of grief. I should take a lot of handkerchiefs.'

'With black borders?'

'Well, I hadn't thought of black borders but it's a nice idea. And besides, the Burial service is rather lovely. Makes you feel uplifted. Real grief is real. It makes you feel awful but it *does* something to you. I mean, it works it out like perspiration.'

'Really, Tuppence, I find your remarks about my decease and the effect it will have upon you in exceedingly bad taste. I don't like it. Let's forget about funerals.'

'I agree. Let's forget.'

'The poor old bean's gone,' said Tommy, 'and she went peacefully and without suffering. So, let's leave it at that. I'd better clear up all these, I suppose.'

He went over to the writing table and ruffled through some papers.

'Now where did I put Mr Rockbury's letter?'

'Who's Mr Rockbury? Oh, you mean the lawyer who wrote to you.'

'Yes. About winding up her affairs. I seem to be the only one of the family left by now.'

'Pity she hadn't got a fortune to leave you,' said Tuppence.

'If she had had a fortune she'd have left it to that Cats' Home,' said Tommy. 'The legacy that she's left to them in her will will pretty well eat up all the spare cash. There won't be much left to come to me. Not that I need it or want it anyway.'

'Was she so fond of cats?'

'I don't know. I suppose so. I never heard her mention them. I believe,' said Tommy thoughtfully, 'she used to get rather a lot of fun out of saying to old friends of hers when they came to see her "I've left you a little something in my will, dear" or "This brooch that you're so fond of I've left you in my will." She didn't actually leave anything to anyone except the Cats' Home.'

'I bet she got rather a kick out of that,' said Tuppence. 'I can just see her saying all the things you told me to a lot of her old friends—or so-called old friends because I don't suppose they were people she really liked at all. She just enjoyed leading them up the garden path. I must say she was an old devil, wasn't she, Tommy? Only, in a funny sort of way one likes her for being an old devil. It's something to be able to get some fun out of life when you're old and stuck away in a Home. Shall we have to go to Sunny Ridge?'

'Where's the other letter, the one from Miss Packard? Oh yes, here it is. I put it with Rockbury's. Yes, she says there are certain things there, I gather, which apparently are now my property. She took some furniture with her, you know, when she went to live there. And of course there are her personal effects. Clothes and things like that. I suppose somebody will have to go through them. And letters and things. I'm her executor, so I suppose it's up to me. I don't suppose there's anything we want really, is there? Except there's a small desk there that I always liked. Belonged to old Uncle William, I believe.'

'Well, you might take that as a memento,' said Tuppence. 'Otherwise, I suppose, we just send the things to be auctioned.'

'So you don't really need to go there at all,' said Tommy.

'Oh, I think I'd like to go there,' said Tuppence.

'You'd like to? Why? Won't it be rather a bore to you?'

'What, looking through her things? No, I don't think so. I think I've got a certain amount of curiosity. Old letters and antique jewellery are always interesting and I think one ought to look at them oneself, not just send them to auction or let strangers go through them. No, we'll go and look through the things and see if there's anything we would like to keep and otherwise settle up.'

'Why do you really want to go? You've got some other reason, haven't you?'

'Oh dear,' said Tuppence, 'it is awful being married to someone who knows too much about one.'

'So you *have* got another reason?'

'Not a real one.'

'Come on, Tuppence. You're not really so fond of turning over people's belongings.'

'That, I think, is my duty,' said Tuppence firmly. 'No, the only other reason is—'

'Come on. Cough it up.'

'I'd rather like to see that—that other old pussy again.'

'What, the one who thought there was a dead child behind the fireplace?'

'Yes,' said Tuppence. 'I'd like to talk to her again. I'd like to know what was in her mind when she said all those things. Was it something she remembered or was it something that she'd just imagined? The more I think about it the more extraordinary it seems. Is it a sort of story that she wrote to herself in her mind or is there—was there once something real that happened about a fireplace or about a dead child. What made her think that the dead child might have been *my* dead child? Do I look as though I had a dead child?'

'I don't know how you expect anyone to look who has a dead child,' said Tommy. 'I shouldn't have thought so. Anyway, Tuppence, it is our duty to go and you can enjoy yourself in your *macabre* way on the side. So that's settled. We'll write to Miss Packard and fix a day.'

CHAPTER 4

Picture of a House

Tuppence drew a deep breath.

'It's just the same,' she said.

She and Tommy were standing on the front doorstep of Sunny Ridge.

'Why shouldn't it be?' asked Tommy.

'I don't know. It's just a feeling I have—something to do with time. Time goes at a different pace in different places. Some places you come back to, and you feel that time has been bustling along at a terrific rate and that all sorts of things will have happened—and changed. But here—Tommy—do you remember Ostend?'

'Ostend? We went there on our honeymoon. Of course I remember.'

'And do you remember the sign written up? TRAM-STILLSTAND—It made us laugh. It seemed so ridiculous.'

'I think it was Knock—not Ostend.'

'Never mind—you remember it. Well, this is like that word—*Tramstillstand*—a portmanteau word.

Timestillstand—nothing's happened here. Time has just stood still. Everything's going on here just the same. It's like ghosts, only the other way round.'

'I don't know what you are talking about. Are you going to stand here all day talking about time and not even ring the bell?—Aunt Ada isn't here, for one thing. That's different.' He pressed the bell.

'That's the only thing that will be different. My old lady will be drinking milk and talking about fireplaces, and Mrs Somebody-or-other will have swallowed a thimble or a teaspoon and a funny little woman will come squeaking out of a room demanding her cocoa, and Miss Packard will come down the stairs, and—'

The door opened. A young woman in a nylon overall said: 'Mr and Mrs Beresford? Miss Packard's expecting you.'

The young woman was just about to show them into the same sitting-room as before when Miss Packard came down the stairs and greeted them. Her manner was suitably not quite as brisk as usual. It was grave, and had a kind of semi-mourning about it—not too much—that might have been embarrassing. She was an expert in the exact amount of condolence which would be acceptable.

Three score years and ten was the Biblical accepted span of life, and the deaths in her establishment seldom occurred below that figure. They were to be expected and they happened.

'So good of you to come. I've got everything laid out tidily for you to look through. I'm glad you could come so soon because as a matter of fact I have already three or four people waiting for a vacancy to come here. You will understand, I'm sure, and not think that I was trying to hurry you in any way.'

'Oh no, of course, we quite understand,' said Tommy.

'It's all still in the room Miss Fanshawe occupied,' Miss Packard explained.

Miss Packard opened the door of the room in which they had last seen Aunt Ada. It had that deserted look a room has when the bed is covered with a dust sheet, with the shapes showing beneath it of folded-up blankets and neatly arranged pillows.

The wardrobe doors stood open and the clothes it had held had been laid on the top of the bed neatly folded.

'What do you usually do—I mean, what do people do mostly with clothes and things like that?' said Tuppence.

Miss Packard, as invariably, was competent and helpful.

'I can give you the name of two or three societies who are only too pleased to have things of that kind. She had quite a good fur stole and a good quality coat but I don't suppose you would have any personal use for them? But perhaps you have charities of your own where you would like to dispose of things.'

Tuppence shook her head.

'She had some jewellery,' said Miss Packard. 'I removed that for safe keeping. You will find it in the right-hand drawer of the dressing-table. I put it there just before you were due to arrive.'

'Thank you very much,' said Tommy, 'for the trouble you have taken.'

Tuppence was staring at a picture over the mantelpiece. It was a small oil painting representing a pale pink house standing adjacent to a canal spanned by a small hump-backed bridge. There was an empty boat drawn up under the bridge against the bank of the canal. In the distance were two poplar trees. It was a very pleasant little scene but nevertheless Tommy wondered why Tuppence was staring at it with such earnestness.

'How funny,' murmured Tuppence.

Tommy looked at her inquiringly. The things that Tuppence thought funny were, he knew by long experience, not really to be described by such an adjective at all.

'What do you mean, Tuppence?'

'It is funny. I never noticed that picture when I was here before. But the odd thing is that I have seen that house somewhere. Or perhaps it's a house just like that that I have seen. I remember it quite well... Funny that I can't remember when and where.'

'I expect you noticed it without really noticing you were noticing,' said Tommy, feeling his choice of words was rather clumsy and nearly as painfully repetitive as Tuppence's reiteration of the word 'funny'.

'Did *you* notice it, Tommy, when we were here last time?'

'No, but then I didn't look particularly.'

'Oh, that picture,' said Miss Packard. 'No, I don't think you would have seen it when you were here the last time because I'm almost sure it wasn't hanging over the mantelpiece then. Actually it was a picture belonging to one of our other guests, and she gave it to your aunt. Miss Fanshawe expressed admiration of it once or twice and this other old lady made her a present of it and insisted she should have it.'

'Oh I see,' said Tuppence, 'so of course I couldn't have seen it here before. But I still feel I know the house quite well. Don't you, Tommy?'

'No,' said Tommy.

'Well, I'll leave you now,' said Miss Packard briskly. 'I shall be available at any time that you want me.'

She nodded with a smile, and left the room, closing the door behind her.

'I don't think I really like that woman's teeth,' said Tuppence.

'What's wrong with them?'

'Too many of them. Or too big—"*The better to eat you with, my child*"—Like Red Riding Hood's grandmother.'

'You seem in a very odd sort of mood today, Tuppence.'

'I am rather. I've always thought of Miss Packard as very nice—but today, somehow, she seems to me rather sinister. Have you ever felt that?'

'No, I haven't. Come on, let's get on with what we came here to do—look over poor old Aunt Ada's "effects", as the lawyers call them. That's the desk I told you about—Uncle William's desk. Do you like it?'

'It's lovely. Regency, I should think. It's nice for the old people who come here to be able to bring some of their own things with them. I don't care for the horsehair chairs, but I'd like that little work-table. It's just what we need for that corner by the window where we've got that perfectly hideous whatnot.'

'All right,' said Tommy. 'I'll make a note of those two.'

'And we'll have the picture over the mantelpiece. It's an awfully attractive picture and I'm quite sure that I've seen that house somewhere. Now, let's look at the jewellery.'

They opened the dressing-table drawer. There was a set of cameos and a Florentine bracelet and ear-rings and a ring with different-coloured stones in it.

'I've seen one of these before,' said Tuppence. 'They spell a name usually. Dearest sometimes. Diamond, emerald, amethyst, no, it's not dearest. I don't think it would be really. I can't imagine anyone giving your Aunt Ada a ring that spelt dearest. Ruby, emerald—the difficulty is one never knows where to begin. I'll try again. Ruby, emerald, another ruby, no, I think it's a garnet and an amethyst and another pinky stone, it must be a ruby this time and a small diamond in the middle. Oh, of course, it's *regard*. Rather nice really. So old-fashioned and sentimental.'

She slipped it on to her finger.

'I think Deborah might like to have this,' she said, 'and the Florentine set. She's frightfully keen on Victorian things. A lot of people are nowadays. Now, I suppose we'd better do the clothes. That's always rather *macabre*, I think. Oh, this is the fur stole. Quite valuable, I should think. I wouldn't want it myself. I wonder if there's anyone here—anyone who was especially nice to Aunt Ada—or perhaps some special friend among the other inmates—visitors, I mean. They call them visitors or guests, I notice. It would be nice to offer her the stole if so. It's real sable. We'll ask Miss Packard. The rest of the things can go to the charities. So that's all settled, isn't it? We'll go and find Miss Packard now. Goodbye,

Aunt Ada,' she remarked aloud, her eyes turning to the bed. 'I'm glad we came to see you that last time. I'm sorry you didn't like me, but if it was fun to you *not* to like me and say those rude things, I don't begrudge it to you. You had to have *some* fun. And we won't forget you. We'll think of you when we look at Uncle William's desk.'

They went in search of Miss Packard. Tommy explained that they would arrange for the desk and the small work-table to be called for and despatched to their own address and that he would arrange with the local auctioneers to dispose of the rest of the furniture. He would leave the choice of any societies willing to receive clothing to Miss Packard if she wouldn't mind the trouble.

'I don't know if there's anyone here who would like her sable stole,' said Tuppence. 'It's a very nice one. One of her special friends, perhaps? Or perhaps one of the nurses who had done some special waiting on Aunt Ada?'

'That is a very kind thought of yours, Mrs Beresford. I'm afraid Miss Fanshawe hadn't any special friends among our visitors, but Miss O'Keefe, one of the nurses, did do a lot for her and was especially good and tactful, and I think she'd be pleased and honoured to have it.'

'And there's the picture over the mantelpiece,' said Tuppence. 'I'd like to have that—but perhaps the person whom it belonged to, and who gave it to her, would want to have it back. I think we ought to ask her—?'

Miss Packard interrupted. 'Oh, I'm sorry, Mrs Beresford, I'm afraid we can't do that. It was a Mrs Lancaster who gave it to Miss Fanshawe and she isn't with us any longer.'

'Isn't with you?' said Tuppence, surprised. 'A Mrs Lancaster? The one I saw last time I was here—with white hair brushed back from her face. She was drinking milk in the sitting-room downstairs. She's gone away, you say?'

'Yes. It was all rather sudden. One of her relations, a Mrs Johnson, took her away about a week ago. Mrs Johnson had returned from Africa where she's been living for the last four or five years—quite unexpectedly. She is now able to take care of Mrs Lancaster in her own home, since she and her husband are taking a house in England. I don't think,' said Miss Packard, 'that Mrs Lancaster really wanted to leave us. She had become so—set in her ways here, and she got on very well with everyone and was happy. She was very disturbed, quite tearful about it—but what can one do? She hadn't really very much say in the matter, because of course the Johnsons were paying for her stay here. I did suggest that as she had been here so long and settled down so well, it might be advisable to let her remain—'

'How long had Mrs Lancaster been with you? asked Tuppence.

'Oh, nearly six years, I think. Yes, that's about it. That's why, of course, she'd really come to feel that this was her home.'

'Yes,' said Tuppence. 'Yes, I can understand that.' She frowned and gave a nervous glance at Tommy and then stuck a resolute chin into the air.

'I'm sorry she's left. I had a feeling when I was talking to her that I'd met her before—her face seemed familiar to me. And then afterwards it came back to me that I'd met her with an old friend of mine, a Mrs Blenkinsop. I thought when I came back here again to visit Aunt Ada, that I'd find out from her if that was so. But of course if she's gone back to her own people, that's different.'

'I quite understand, Mrs Beresford. If any of our visitors can get in touch with some of their old friends or someone who knew their relations at one time, it makes a great difference to them. I can't remember a Mrs Blenkinsop ever having been mentioned by her, but then I don't suppose that would be likely to happen in any case.'

'Can you tell me a little more about her, who her relations were, and how she came to come here?'

'There's really very little to tell. As I said, it was about six years ago that we had letters from Mrs Johnson inquiring about the Home, and then Mrs Johnson herself came here and inspected it. She said she'd had mentions of Sunny Ridge from a friend and she inquired the terms and all that and—then she went away. And about a week or a fortnight later we had a letter from a firm of solicitors in London making further inquiries, and finally they wrote saying that they would like us to accept Mrs Lancaster and that Mrs Johnson would bring her here in about a week's time if we had a vacancy. As it happened, we had, and Mrs Johnson brought Mrs Lancaster here and Mrs Lancaster seemed to like the place and liked the room that we proposed to allot her. Mrs Johnson said that Mrs Lancaster would like to bring some of her own things. I quite agreed, because people usually do that and find they're much happier. So it was all arranged very satisfactorily. Mrs Johnson explained that Mrs Lancaster was a relation of her husband's, not a very near one, but that they felt worried about her because they themselves were going out to Africa—to Nigeria I think it was, her husband was taking up an appointment there and it was likely they'd be there for some years before they returned to England, so as they had no home to offer Mrs Lancaster, they wanted to make sure that she was accepted in a place where she would be really happy. They were quite sure from what they'd heard about this place that that was so. So it was all arranged very happily indeed and Mrs Lancaster settled down here very well.'

'I see.'

'Everyone here liked Mrs Lancaster very much. She was a little bit—well, you know what I mean—woolly in the head. I mean, she forgot things, confused things and couldn't remember names and addresses sometimes.'

'Did she get many letters?' said Tuppence. 'I mean letters from abroad and things?'

'Well, I think Mrs Johnson—or Mr Johnson—wrote once or twice from Africa but not after the first year. People, I'm afraid, do forget, you know. Especially when they go to a new country and a different life, and I don't think they'd been very closely in touch with her at any time. I think it was just a distant relation, and a family responsibility, and that was all it meant to them. All the financial arrangements were done through the lawyer, Mr Eccles, a very nice, reputable firm. Actually we'd had one or two dealings with that firm before so that we new about them, as they knew about us. But I think most of Mrs Lancaster's friends and relations had passed over and so she didn't hear much from anyone, and I think hardly anyone ever came to visit her. One very nice-looking man came about a year later, I think. I don't think he knew her personally at all well but he was a friend of Mr Johnson's and had also been in the Colonial service overseas. I think he just came to make sure she was well and happy.'

'And after that,' said Tuppence, 'everyone forgot about her.'

'I'm afraid so,' said Miss Packard. 'It's sad, isn't it? But it's the usual rather than the unusual thing to happen. Fortunately, most visitors to us make their own friends here. They get friendly with someone who has their own tastes or certain memories in common, and so things settle down quite happily. I think most of them forget most of their past life.'

'Some of them, I suppose,' said Tommy, 'are a little—' he hesitated for a word '—a little—' his hand went slowly to his forehead, but he drew it away. 'I don't mean—' he said.

'Oh, I know perfectly what you mean,' said Miss Packard. 'We don't take mental patients, you know, but we do take what you might call borderline cases. I mean, people who are rather senile—can't look after themselves properly, or who have certain fancies and imaginations. Sometimes they imagine themselves to be historical personages. Quite in a harmless way. We've had two Marie Antoinettes here, one of them was always talking about something called the *Petit Trianon* and drinking a lot of milk which she seemed to associate with the place. And we had one dear old soul who insisted that she was Madame Curie and that she had discovered radium. She used to read the papers with great interest, especially any news of atomic bombs or scientific discoveries. Then she always explained it was she and her husband who had first started experiments on these lines. Harmless delusions are things that manage to keep you very happy when you're elderly. They don't usually last all the time, you know. You're not Marie Antoinette every day or even Madame Curie. Usually it comes on about once a fortnight. Then I suppose presumably one gets tired of keeping the play-acting up. And of course more often it's just forgetfulness that people suffer from. They can't quite remember who they are. Or they keep saying there's something very important they've forgotten and if they could only remember it. That sort of thing.'

'I see,' said Tuppence. She hesitated, and then said, 'Mrs Lancaster—Was it always things about that particular fireplace in the sitting-room she remembered, or was it any fireplace?'

Miss Packard stared—'A fireplace? I don't understand what you mean.'

'It was something she said that I didn't understand—Perhaps she'd had some unpleasant association with a fireplace, or read some story that had frightened her.'

'Possibly.'

Tuppence said: 'I'm still rather worried about the picture she gave to Aunt Ada.'

'I really don't think you need worry, Mrs Beresford. I expect she's forgotten all about it by now. I don't think she prized it particularly. She was just pleased that Miss Fanshawe admired it and was glad for her to have it, and

I'm sure she'd be glad for you to have it because you admire it. It's a nice picture, I thought so myself. Not that I know much about pictures.'

'I tell you what I'll do. I'll write to Mrs Johnson if you'll give me her address, and just ask if it's all right to keep it.'

'The only address I've got is the hotel in London they were going to—the Cleveland, I think it was called. Yes, the Cleveland Hotel, George Street, W1. She was taking Mrs Lancaster there for about four or five days and after that I think they were going to stay with some relations in Scotland. I expect the Cleveland Hotel will have a forwarding address.'

'Well, thank you—And now, about this fur stole of Aunt Ada's.'

'I'll go and bring Miss O'Keefe to you.'

She went out of the room.

'You and your Mrs Blenkensops,' said Tommy.

Tuppence looked complacent.

'One of my best creations,' she said. 'I'm glad I was able to make use of her—I was just trying to think of a name and suddenly Mrs Blenkensop came into my mind. What fun it was, wasn't it?'

'It's a long time ago—No more spies in wartime and counter-espionage for us.'

'More's the pity. It *was* fun—living in that guest house—inventing a new personality for myself—I really began to believe I *was* Mrs Blenkensop.'

'You were lucky you got away safely with it,' said Tommy, 'and in my opinion, as I once told you, you overdid it.'

'I did not. I was perfectly in character. A nice woman, rather silly, and far too much taken up with her three sons.'

'That's what I mean,' said Tommy. 'One son would have been quite enough. Three sons were too much to burden yourself with.'

'They became quite real to me,' said Tuppence. 'Douglas, Andrew and—goodness, I've forgotten the name of the third one now. I know exactly what they looked like and their characters and just where they were stationed, and I talked most indiscreetly about the letters I got from them.'

'Well, that's over,' said Tommy. 'There's nothing to find out in this place—so forget about Mrs Blenkinsop. When I'm dead and buried and you've suitably mourned me and taken up your residence in a home for the aged, I expect you'll be thinking you are Mrs Blenkinsop half of the time.'

'It'll be rather boring to have only one role to play,' said Tuppence.

'Why do you think old people *want* to be Marie Antoinette, and Madame Curie and all the rest of it?' asked Tommy.

'I expect because they get so bored. One does get bored. I'm sure *you* would if you couldn't use your legs and walk about, or perhaps your fingers get too stiff and you can't knit. Desperately you want something to do to amuse yourself so you try on some public character and see what it feels like when you are it. I can understand that perfectly.'

'I'm sure you can,' said Tommy. 'God help the home for the aged that you go to. You'll be Cleopatra most of the time, I expect.'

'I won't be a famous person,' said Tuppence. 'I'll be someone like a kitchenmaid at Anne of Cleves' castle retailing a lot of spicy gossip that I'd heard.'

The door opened, and Miss Packard appeared in company with a tall, freckle-faced young woman in nurse's dress and a mop of red hair.

'This is Miss O'Keefe—Mr and Mrs Beresford. They have something to tell you. Excuse me, will you? One of the patients is asking for me.'

Tuppence duly made the presentation of Aunt Ada's fur stole and Nurse O'Keefe was enraptured.

'Oh! It's lovely. It's too good for me, though. You'll be wanting it yourself—'

'No, I don't really. It's on the big side for me. I'm too small. It's just right for a tall girl like you. Aunt Ada was tall.'

'Ah! she was the grand old lady—she must have been very handsome as a girl.'

'I suppose so,' said Tommy doubtfully. 'She must have been a tartar to look after, though.'

'Oh, she was that, indeed. But she had a grand spirit. Nothing got her down. And she was no fool either. You'd be surprised the way she got to know things. Sharp as a needle, she was.'

'She had a temper, though.'

'Yes, indeed. But it's the whining kind that gets you down—all complaints and moans. Miss Fanshawe was never dull. Grand stories she'd tell you of the old days—Rode a horse once up the staircase of a country house when she was a girl—or so she said—Would that be true now?'

'Well, I wouldn't put it past her,' said Tommy.

'You never know what you can believe here. The tales the old dears come and tell you. Criminals that they've recognized—We must notify the police at once—if not, we're all in danger.'

'Somebody was being poisoned last time we were here, I remember,' said Tuppence.

'Ah! that was only Mrs Lockett. It happens to her every day. But it's not the police she wants, it's a doctor to be called—she's that crazy about doctors.'

'And somebody—a little woman—calling out for cocoa—'

'That would be Mrs Moody. Poor soul, she's gone.'

'You mean left here—gone away?'

'No—it was a thrombosis took her—very sudden. She was one who was very devoted to your Aunt—not that Miss Fanshawe always had time for her—always talking nineteen to the dozen, as she did—'

'Mrs Lancaster has left, I hear.'

'Yes, her folk came for her. She didn't want to go, poor thing.'

'What was the story she told me—about the fireplace in the sitting-room?'

'Ah! she'd lots of stories, that one—about the things that happened to her—and the secrets she knew—'

'There was something about a child—a kidnapped child or a murdered child—'

'It's strange it is, the things they think up. It's the TV as often as not that gives them the ideas—'

'Do you find it a strain, working here with all these old people? It must be tiring.'

'Oh no—I like old people—That's why I took up Geriatric work—'

'You've been here long?'

'A year and a half—' She paused. '—But I'm leaving next month.'

'Oh! why?'

For the first time a certain constraint came into Nurse O'Keefe's manner.

'Well, you see, Mrs Beresford, one needs a change—'

'But you'll be doing the same kind of work?'

'Oh yes—' She picked up the fur stole. 'I'm thanking you again very much—and I'm glad, too, to have something to remember Miss Fanshawe by—She was a grand old lady—You don't find many like her nowadays.'

CHAPTER 5

Disappearance of an Old Lady

Aunt Ada's things arrived in due course. The desk was installed and admired. The little work-table dispossessed the whatnot—which was relegated to a dark corner of the hall. And the picture of the pale pink house by the canal bridge Tuppence hung over the mantelpiece in her bedroom where she could see it every morning when drinking her early morning tea.

Since her conscience still troubled her a little, Tuppence wrote a letter explaining how the picture had come into their possession but that if Mrs Lancaster would like it returned, she had only got to let them know. This she dispatched to Mrs Lancaster, c/o Mrs Johnson, at the Cleveland Hotel, George Street, London, W1.

To this there was no reply, but a week later the letter was returned with 'Not known at this address' scrawled on it.

'How tiresome,' said Tuppence.

'Perhaps they only stayed for a night or two,' suggested Tommy.

'You'd think they'd have left a forwarding address—'

'Did you put "Please forward" on it?'

'Yes, I did. I know, I'll ring them up and ask—They must have put an address in the hotel register—'

'I'd let it go if I were you,' said Tommy. 'Why make all this fuss? I expect the old pussy has forgotten all about the picture.'

'I might as well try.'

Tuppence sat down at the telephone and was presently connected to the Cleveland Hotel.

She rejoined Tommy in his study a few minutes later.

'It's rather curious, Tommy—they haven't even *been* there. No Mrs Johnson—no Mrs Lancaster—no rooms booked for them—or any trace of their having stayed there before.'

'I expect Miss Packard got the name of the hotel wrong. Wrote it down in a hurry—and then perhaps lost it—or remembered it wrong. Things like that often happen, you know.'

'I shouldn't have thought it would at Sunny Ridge. Miss Packard is so efficient always.'

'Perhaps they didn't book beforehand at the hotel and it was full, so they had to go somewhere else. You know what accommodation in London is like—*Must* you go on fussing?'

Tuppence retired.

Presently she came back.

'I know what I'm going to do. I'll ring up Miss Packard and I'll get the address of the lawyers—'

'What lawyers?'

'Don't you remember she said something about a firm of solicitors who made all the arrangements because the Johnsons were abroad?'

Tommy, who was busy over a speech he was drafting for a Conference he was shortly to attend, and murmuring under his breath—'*the proper policy if such a contingency should arise*'—said: 'How do you spell contingency, Tuppence?'

'Did you hear what I was saying?'

'Yes, very good idea—splendid—excellent—you do that—'

Tuppence went out—stuck her head in again and said: 'C-o-n-s-i-s-t-e-n-c-y.'

'Can't be—you've got the wrong word.'

'What are you writing about?'

'The Paper I'm reading next at the I.U.A.S. and I do wish you'd let me do it in peace.'

'Sorry.'

Tuppence removed herself. Tommy continued to write sentences and then scratch them out. His face was just brightening, as the pace of his writing increased—when once more the door opened.

'Here it is,' said Tuppence. 'Partingdale, Harris, Lockeridge and Partingdale, 32 Lincoln Terrace, W.C.2. Tel. Holborn 051386. The operative member of the firm is Mr Eccles.' She placed a sheet of paper by Tommy's elbow. 'Now *you* take on.'

'No!' said Tommy firmly.

'Yes! She's *your* Aunt Ada.'

'Where does Aunt Ada come in? Mrs Lancaster is no aunt of mine.'

'But it's *lawyers*,' Tuppence insisted. 'It's a man's job always to deal with lawyers. They just think women are silly and don't pay attention—'

'A very sensible point of view,' said Tommy.

'Oh! Tommy—*do* help. You go and telephone and I'll find the dictionary and look how to spell contingency.'

Tommy gave her a look, but departed.

He returned at last and spoke firmly—'This matter is now *closed*, Tuppence.'

'You got Mr Eccles?'

'Strictly speaking I got a Mr Wills who is doubtless the dogsbody of the firm of Partingford, Lockjaw and Harrison. But he was fully informed and glib. All letters and communications go via the Southern Counties Bank, Hammersmith branch, who will forward all communications. And there, Tuppence, let me tell you, the trail *stops*. Banks will forward things—but they won't yield any addresses to you or anyone else who asks. They have their code of rules and they'll stick to them—Their lips are sealed like our more pompous Prime Ministers.'

'All right, I'll send a letter care of the Bank.'

'Do that—and for goodness' sake, *leave me alone*—or I shall never get my speech done.'

'Thank you, darling,' said Tuppence. 'I don't know what I'd do without you.' She kissed the top of his head.

'It's the best butter,' said Tommy.

It was not until the following Thursday evening that Tommy asked suddenly, 'By the way, did you ever get any answer to the letter you sent care of the Bank to Mrs Johnson—'

'It's nice of you to ask,' said Tuppence sarcastically. 'No, I didn't.' She added meditatively, 'I don't think I shall, either.'

'Why not?'

'You're not really interested,' said Tuppence coldly.

'Look here, Tuppence—I know I've been rather preoccupied—It's all this I.U.A.S.—It's only once a year, thank goodness.'

'It starts on Monday, doesn't it? For five days—'

'Four days.'

'And you all go down to a Hush Hush, top secret house in the country somewhere, and make speeches and read Papers and vet young men for Super Secret assignments in Europe and beyond. I've forgotten what I.U.A.S. stands for. All these initials they have nowadays—'

'International Union of Associated Security.'

'What a mouthful! Quite ridiculous. And I expect the whole place is bugged, and everybody knows everybody else's most secret conversations.'

'Highly likely,' said Tommy with a grin.

'And I suppose you enjoy it?'

'Well, I do in a way. One sees a lot of old friends.'

'All quite ga-ga by now, I expect. Does any of it do any good?'

'Heavens, what a question! Can one ever let oneself believe that you can answer that by a plain Yes or No—'

'And are any of the people any good?'

'I'd answer Yes to that. Some of them are very good indeed.'

'Will old Josh be there?'

'Yes, he'll be there.'

'What is he like nowadays?'

'Extremely deaf, half blind, crippled with rheumatism—and you'd be surprised at the things that *don't* get past him.'

'I see,' said Tuppence. She meditated. 'I wish I were in it, too.'

Tommy looked apologetic.

'I expect you'll find something to do while I'm away.'

'I might at that,' said Tuppence meditatively.

Her husband looked at her with the vague apprehension that Tuppence could always arouse in him.

'Tuppence—what are you up to?'

'Nothing, yet—So far I'm only thinking.'

'What about?'

'Sunny Ridge. And a nice old lady sipping milk and talking in a scatty kind of way about dead children and fireplaces. It intrigued me. I thought then that I'd try and find out more from her next time we came to see Aunt Ada—But there wasn't a next time because Aunt Ada died—And when we were next in Sunny Ridge—Mrs Lancaster had—disappeared!'

'You mean her people had taken her away? That's not a disappearance—it's quite natural.'

'It's a disappearance—no traceable address—no answer to letters—it's a planned disappearance. I'm more and more sure of it.'

'But—'

Tuppence broke in upon his 'But'.

'Listen, Tommy—supposing that sometime or other a crime happened—It seemed all safe and covered up—But then suppose that someone in the family had seen something, or known something—someone elderly and garrulous—someone who chattered to people—someone whom you suddenly realized might be a danger to you—What would you do about it?'

'Arsenic in the soup?' suggested Tommy cheerfully. 'Cosh them on the head—Push them down the staircase—?'

'That's rather extreme—Sudden deaths attract attention. You'd look about for some simpler way—and you'd find one. A nice respectable Home for Elderly Ladies. You'd pay a visit to it, calling yourself Mrs Johnson or Mrs Robinson—or you would get some unsuspecting third party to make arrangements—You'd fix the financial arrangements through a firm of reliable solicitors. You've already hinted, perhaps, that your elderly relative has fancies and mild delusions sometimes—so do a good many of the other old ladies—Nobody will think it odd—if she cackles on about poisoned milk, or dead children behind a fireplace, or a sinister kidnapping; nobody will really listen. They'll just think it's old Mrs So-and-So having her fancies again—nobody will take any *notice at all.*'

'Except Mrs Thomas Beresford,' said Tommy.

'All right, *yes*,' said Tuppence. '*I've* taken notice—'

'But why did you?'

'I don't quite know,' said Tuppence slowly. 'It's like the fairy stories. *By the pricking of my thumbs—Something evil this way comes*—I felt suddenly scared. I'd always thought of Sunny Ridge as such a normal happy place—and suddenly I began to wonder—That's the only way I can put it. I wanted to find out more. And now poor old Mrs Lancaster has disappeared. Somebody's spirited her away.'

'But why should they?'

'I can only think because she was getting worse—worse from their point of view—remembering more, perhaps, talking to people more, or perhaps she recognized someone—or someone recognized her—or told her something that gave her new ideas about something that had once happened. Anyway, for some reason or other she became dangerous to someone.'

'Look here, Tuppence, this whole thing is all somethings and someones. It's just an idea you've thought up. You don't want to go mixing yourself up in things that are no business of yours—'

'There's nothing to be mixed up in according to you,' said Tuppence. 'So you needn't worry at all.'

'You leave Sunny Ridge alone.'

'I don't mean to go back to Sunny Ridge. I think they've told me all they know there. I think that that old lady was quite safe whilst she was there. I want to find out where she is *now*—I want to get to her wherever she is *in time*—before something happens to her.'

'What on earth do you think might happen to her?'

'I don't like to think. But I'm on the trail—I'm going to be Prudence Beresford, Private Investigator. Do you remember when we were Blunt's Brilliant Detectives?'

'*I* was,' said Tommy. '*You* were Miss Robinson, my private secretary.'

'Not all the time. Anyway, that's what I'm going to do while you're playing at International Espionage at Hush Hush Manor. It's the "Save Mrs Lancaster" that I'm going to be busy with.'

'You'll probably find her perfectly all right.'

'I hope I shall. Nobody would be better pleased than I should.'

'How do you propose to set about it?'

'As I told you, I've got to think first. Perhaps an advertisement of some kind? No, that would be a mistake.'

'Well, be careful,' said Tommy, rather inadequately.

Tuppence did not deign to reply.

On Monday morning, Albert, the domestic mainstay of the Beresfords' life for many long years, ever since he had been roped into anti-criminal activities by them as a carroty-haired lift-boy, deposited the tray of early morning tea on the table between the two beds, pulled back the curtains, announced that it was a fine day, and removed his now portly form from the room.

Tuppence yawned, sat up, rubbed her eyes, poured out a cup of tea, dropped a slice of lemon in it, and remarked that it seemed a nice day, but you never knew.

Tommy turned over and groaned.

'Wake up,' said Tuppence. 'Remember you're going places today.'

'Oh Lord,' said Tommy. 'So I am.'

He, too, sat up and helped himself to tea. He looked with appreciation at the picture over the mantelpiece.

'I must say, Tuppence, your picture looks very nice.'

'It's the way the sun comes in from the window sideways and lights it up.'

'Peaceful,' said Tommy.

'If only I could remember where it was I'd seen it before.'

'I can't see that it matters. You'll remember sometime or other.'

'That's no good. I want to remember *now*.'

'But why?'

'Don't you see? It's the only clue I've got. It was Mrs Lancaster's picture—'

'But the two things don't tie up together anyway,' said Tommy. 'I mean, it's true that the picture once belonged to Mrs Lancaster. But it may have been just a picture she bought at an exhibition or that somebody in her family did. It may have been a picture that somebody gave her as a present. She took it to Sunny Ridge with her because she thought it looked nice. There's no reason it should have anything to do with her *personally*. If it had, she wouldn't have given it to Aunt Ada.'

'It's the only clue I've got,' said Tuppence.

'It's a nice peaceful house,' said Tommy.

'All the same, I think it's an empty house.'

'What do you mean, empty?'

'I don't think,' said Tuppence, 'there's anybody living in it. I don't think anybody's ever going to come out of that house. Nobody's going to walk across that bridge, nobody's going to untie that boat and row away in it.'

'For goodness' sake, Tuppence.' Tommy stared at her. 'What's the matter with you?'

'I thought so the first time I saw it,' said Tuppence. 'I thought "What a nice house that would be to live in." And then I thought "But nobody does live here, I'm sure they don't." That shows you that I have seen it before. Wait a minute. Wait a minute… it's coming. It's coming.'

Tommy stared at her.

'Out of a *window*,' said Tuppence breathlessly. 'Out of a car window? No, no, that would be the wrong angle. Running alongside the canal… and a little hump-backed bridge and the pink walls of the house, the two poplar trees, more than two. There were *lots* more poplar trees. Oh dear, oh dear, if I could—'

'Oh, come off it, Tuppence.'

'It will come back to me.'

'Good Lord,' Tommy looked at his watch. 'I've got to hurry. You and your *déjà vu* picture.'

He jumped out of bed and hastened to the bathroom. Tuppence lay back on her pillows and closed her eyes, trying to force a recollection that just remained elusively out of reach.

Tommy was pouring out a second cup of coffee in the dining-room when Tuppence appeared flushed with triumph.

'I've got it—I know where I saw that house. It was out of the window of a railway train.'

'Where? When?'

'I don't know. I'll have to think. I remember saying to myself: "Someday I'll go and look at that house"—and I tried to see what the name of the next station was. But you know what railways are nowadays. They've pulled down half the stations—and the next one we went through was all torn down, and grass growing over the platforms, and no name board or anything.'

'Where the hell's my brief-case? Albert!'

A frenzied search took place.

Tommy came back to say a breathless goodbye. Tuppence was sitting looking meditatively at a fried egg.

'Goodbye,' said Tommy. 'And for God's sake, Tuppence, don't go poking into something that's none of your business.'

'I think,' said Tuppence, meditatively, 'that what I shall really do, is to take a few railway journeys.'

Tommy looked slightly relieved.

'Yes,' he said encouragingly, 'you try that. Buy yourself a season ticket. There's some scheme where you can travel a thousand miles all over the British Isles for a very reasonable fixed sum. That ought to suit you down to the ground, Tuppence. You travel by all the trains you can think of in all the likely parts. That ought to keep you happy until I come home again.'

'Give my love to Josh.'

'I will.' He added, looking at his wife in a worried manner, 'I wish you were coming with me. Don't—don't do anything stupid, will you?'

'Of course not,' said Tuppence.

CHAPTER 6

Tuppence on the Trail

'Oh dear,' sighed Tuppence, 'oh dear.' She looked round her with gloomy eyes. Never, she said to herself, had she felt more miserable. Naturally she had known she would miss Tommy, but she had no idea how much she was going to miss him.

During the long course of their married life they had hardly ever been separated for any length of time. Starting before their marriage, they had called themselves a pair of 'young adventurers'. They had been through various difficulties and dangers together, they had married, they had had two children and just as the world was seeming rather dull and middle-aged to them, the second war had come about and in what seemed an almost miraculous way they had been tangled up yet again on the outskirts of the British Intelligence. A somewhat unorthodox pair, they had been recruited by a quiet nondescript man who called himself 'Mr Carter', but to whose word everybody seemed to bow. They had had adventures, and once again they had had them together. This, by the way, had not been planned by Mr Carter. Tommy alone had been recruited. But Tuppence displaying all her natural ingenuity, had managed to eavesdrop in such a fashion that when Tommy had arrived at a guest house on the sea coast in the role of a certain Mr Meadowes, the first person he had seen there had been a middle-aged lady plying knitting needles, who had looked up at him with innocent eyes and whom he had been forced to greet as Mrs Blenkinsop. Thereafter they had worked as a pair.

'However,' thought Tuppence to herself, 'I can't do it this time.' No amount of eavesdropping, of ingenuity, or anything else would take her to the recesses of Hush Hush Manor or to participation in the intricacies of I.U.A.S. Just an Old Boys Club, she thought resentfully. Without Tommy the flat was empty, the world was lonely, and 'What on earth,' thought Tuppence, 'am I to do with myself?'

The question was really purely rhetorical for Tuppence had already started on the first steps of what she planned to do with herself. There was no question this time of intelligence work, of counter-espionage or anything of that kind. Nothing of an official nature. 'Prudence Beresford, Private Investigator, that's what I am,' said Tuppence to herself.

After a scrappy lunch had been hastily cleared away, the dining-room table was strewn with railway timetables, guide-books, maps, and a few old diaries which Tuppence had managed to disinter.

Some time in the last three years (not longer, she was sure) she had taken a railway journey, and looking out of the carriage window, had noticed a house. But, what railway journey?

Like most people at the present time, the Beresfords travelled mainly by car. The railway journeys they took were few and far between.

Scotland, of course, when they went to stay with their married daughter Deborah—but that was a night journey.

Penzance—summer holidays—but Tuppence knew that line by heart.

No, this had been a much more casual journey.

With diligence and perseverance, Tuppence had made a meticulous list of all the possible journeys she had taken which might correspond to what she was looking for. One or two race meetings, a visit to Northumberland, two possible places in Wales, a christening, two weddings, a sale they had attended, some puppies she had once delivered for a friend who bred them and who had gone down with influenza. The meeting place had been an arid-looking country junction whose name she couldn't remember.

Tuppence sighed. It seemed as though Tommy's solution was the one she might have to adopt—Buy a kind of circular ticket and actually travel over the most likely stretches of railway line.

In a small notebook she had jotted down any snatches of extra memories—vague flashes—in case they might help.

A hat, for instance—Yes, a hat that she had thrown up on the rack. She had been wearing a hat—so—a wedding or the christening—certainly not puppies.

And—another flash—kicking off her shoes—because her feet hurt. Yes—that was definite—she had been actually looking at the House—and she had kicked off her shoes because her feet hurt.

So, then, it had definitely been a social function she had either been going to, or returning from—Returning from, of course—because of the painfulness of her feet from long standing about in her best shoes. And what kind of a hat? Because that would help—a flowery hat—a summer wedding—or a velvet winter one?

Tuppence was busy jotting down details from the Railway timetables of different lines when Albert came in to ask what she wanted for supper—and what she wanted ordered in from the butcher and the grocer.

'I think I'm going to be away for the next few days,' said Tuppence. 'So you needn't order in anything. I'm going to take some railway journeys.'

'Will you be wanting some sandwiches?'

'I might. Get some ham or something.'

'Egg and cheese do you? Or there's a tin of *pâté* in the larder—it's been there a long while, time it was eaten.' It was a somewhat sinister recommendation, but Tuppence said,

'All right. That'll do.'

'Want letters forwarded?'

'I don't even know where I'm going yet,' said Tuppence.

'I see,' said Albert.

The comfortable thing about Albert was that he always accepted everything. Nothing ever had to be explained to him.

He went away and Tuppence settled down to her planning—what she wanted was: a social engagement involving a hat and party shoes. Unfortunately the ones she had listed involved different railway lines—One wedding on the Southern Railway, the other in East Anglia. The christening north of Bedford.

If she could remember a little more about the scenery... She had been sitting on the right-hand side of the train. What had she been looking at *before* the canal—Woods? Trees? Farmland? A distant village?

Straining her brain, she looked up with a frown—Albert had come back. How far she was at that moment from knowing that Albert standing there waiting for attention was neither more nor less than an answer to prayer—

'Well, what is it *now*, Albert?'

'If it's that you're going to be away all day tomorrow—'

'And the day after as well, probably—'

'Would it be all right for me to have the day off?'

'Yes, of course.'

'It's Elizabeth—come out in spots she has. Milly thinks it's measles—'

'Oh dear.' Milly was Albert's wife and Elizabeth was the youngest of his children. 'So Milly wants you at home, of course.'

Albert lived in a small neat house a street or two away.

'It's not that so much—She likes me out of the way when she's got her hands full—she doesn't want me messing things up—But it's the other kids—I could take 'em somewhere out of her way.'

'Of course. You're all in quarantine, I suppose.'

'Oh! well, best for 'em all to get it, and get it over. Charlie's had it, and so has Jean. Anyway, that'll be all right?'

Tuppence assured him that it would be all right.

Something was stirring in the depths of her subconscious—A happy anticipation—a recognition—Measles — Yes, measles. Something to do with measles.

But why should the house by the canal have anything to do with measles… ?

Of course! Anthea. Anthea was Tuppence's god-daughter—and Anthea's daughter Jane was at school—her first term—and it was Prize Giving and Anthea had rung up—her two younger children had come out in a measle rash and she had nobody in the house to help and Jane would be terribly disappointed if nobody came—Could Tuppence possibly?—

And Tuppence had said of course—She wasn't doing anything particular—she'd go down to the school and take Jane out and give her lunch and then go back to the sports and all the rest of it. There was a special school train.

Everything came back into her mind with astonishing clarity—even the dress she'd worn—a summer print of cornflowers!

She had seen the house on the return journey.

Going down there she had been absorbed in a magazine she had bought, but coming back she had had nothing to read, and she had looked out of the window until, exhausted by the activities of the day, and the pressure of her shoes, she had dropped off to sleep.

When she had woken up the train had been running beside a canal. It was partially wooded country, an occasional bridge, sometimes a twisting lane or minor road—a distant farm—no villages.

The train began to slow down, for no reason it would seem, except that a signal must be against it. It drew jerkily to a halt by a bridge, a little hump-backed bridge which spanned the canal, a disused canal presumably. On the other side of the canal, close to the water, was the house—a house that Tuppence thought at once was one of the most attractive houses she had ever seen—a quiet, peaceful house, irradiated by the golden light of the late afternoon sun.

There was no human being to be seen—no dogs, or livestock. Yet the green shutters were not fastened. The house must be lived in, but now, at this moment, it was empty.

'I must find out about that house,' Tuppence had thought. 'Someday I must come back here and look at it. It's the kind of house I'd like to live in.'

With a jerk the train lurched slowly forwards.

'I'll look out for the name of the next station—so that I'll know where it is.'

But there had been no appropriate station. It was the time when things were beginning to happen to railways—small stations were closed, even pulled down, grass sprouted on the decayed platforms. For twenty minutes—half an hour—the train ran on, but nothing identifiable was to be seen. Over fields, in the far distance, Tuppence once saw the spire of a church.

Then had come some factory complex—tall chimneys—a line of pre-fab houses, then open country again.

Tuppence had thought to herself—That house was rather like a dream! Perhaps it was a dream—I don't suppose I'll ever go and look for it—too difficult. Besides, rather a pity, perhaps—

Someday, maybe, I'll come across it by accident!

And so—she had forgotten all about it—until a picture hanging on a wall had reawakened a veiled memory.

And now, thanks to one word uttered unwittingly by Albert, the quest was ended.

Or, to speak correctly, a quest was beginning.

Tuppence sorted out three maps, a guide-book, and various other accessories.

Roughly now she knew the area she would have to search. Jane's school she marked with a large cross—the branch railway line, which ran into the main line to London—the time lapse whilst she had slept.

The final area as planned covered a considerable mileage—north of Medchester, south-east of Market Basing which was a small town, but was quite an important railway junction, west probably of Shaleborough.

She'd take the car, and start early tomorrow morning.

She got up and went into the bedroom and studied the picture over the mantelpiece.

Yes, there was no mistake. That was the house she had seen from the train three years ago. The house she had promised to look for someday—

Someday had come—Someday was tomorrow.

BOOK 2

The House on the Canal

CHAPTER 7

The Friendly Witch

Before leaving the next morning, Tuppence took a last careful look at the picture hanging in her room, not so much to fix its details firmly in her mind, but to memorize its position in the landscape. This time she would be seeing it not from the window of a train but from the road. The angle of approach would be quite different. There might be many hump-backed bridges, many similar disused canals—perhaps other houses looking like this one (but that Tuppence refused to believe).

The picture was signed, but the signature of the artist was illegible—All that could be said was that it began with B.

Turning away from the picture, Tuppence checked her paraphernalia: an A.B.C. and its attached railway map; a selection of ordnance maps; tentative names of places—Medchester, Westleigh—Market Basing—Middlesham—Inchwell—Between them, they enclosed the triangle that she had decided to examine. With her she took a small overnight bag since she would have a three hours' drive before she even arrived at the area of operations, and after that, it meant, she judged, a good deal of slow driving along country roads and lanes looking for likely canals.

After stopping in Medchester for coffee and a snack, she pushed on by a second-class road adjacent to a railway line, and leading through wooded country with plenty of streams.

As in most of the rural districts of England, signposts were plentiful, bearing names that Tuppence had never heard of, and seldom seeming to lead to the place in question. There seemed to be a certain cunning about this part of the road system of England. The road would twist off from the canal, and when you pressed on hopefully to where you thought the canal might have taken itself, you drew a blank. If you had gone in the direction of Great Michelden, the next signpost you came to offered you a choice of two roads, one to Pennington Sparrow and the other to Farlingford. You chose Farlingford and managed actually to get to such a place but almost immediately the next signpost sent you back firmly to Medchester, so that you practically retraced your steps. Actually Tuppence never did find Great Michelden, and for a long time she was quite unable to find the lost canal. If she had had any idea of which village she was looking for, things might have gone more easily. Tracking canals on maps was merely puzzling. Now and again she came to the railway which cheered her up and she would then push on hopefully for Bees Hill, South Winterton and Farrell St Edmund. Farrell St Edmund had once had a station, but it had been abolished some time ago! 'If only,' thought Tuppence, 'there was some well-behaved road that ran alongside a canal, or alongside a railway line, it would make it so much easier.'

The day wore on and Tuppence became more and more baffled. Occasionally she came upon a farm adjacent to a canal but the road having led to the farm insisted on having nothing more to do with the canal and went over a hill and arrived at something called Westpenfold which had a church with a square tower which was no use at all.

From there when disconsolately pursuing a rutted road which seemed the only way out of Westpenfold and which to Tuppence's sense of direction (which was now becoming increasingly unreliable) seemed to lead in the opposite direction to anywhere she could possibly want to go, she came abruptly to a place where two lanes forked right and left. There was the remains of a signpost between them, the arms of which had both broken off.

'Which way?' said Tuppence. 'Who knows? I don't.'

She took the left-hand one.

It meandered on, winding to left and to right. Finally it shot round a bend, widened out and climbed a hill, coming out of woods into open downlike country. Having surmounted the crest it took a steep downward course. Not very far away a plaintive cry sounded—

'Sounds like a *train*,' said Tuppence, with sudden hope.

It *was* a train—Then below her was the railway line and on it a goods train uttering cries of distress as it puffed along. And beyond it was the canal and on the other side of the canal was a house that Tuppence recognized and, leading across the canal was a small hump-backed, pink-bricked bridge. The road dipped under the railway, came up, and made for the bridge. Tuppence drove very gently over the narrow bridge. Beyond it the road went on with the house on the right-hand side of it. Tuppence drove on looking for the way in. There didn't seem to be one. A fairly high wall shielded it from the road.

The house was on her right now. She stopped the car and walked back on to the bridge and looked at what she could see of the house from there.

Most of the tall windows were shuttered with green shutters. The house had a very quiet and empty look. It looked peaceful and kindly in the setting sun. There was nothing to suggest that anyone lived in it. She went back to the car and drove a little farther. The wall, a moderately high one, ran along to her right. The left-hand side of the road was merely a hedge giving on green fields.

Presently she came to a wrought-iron gate in the wall. She parked the car by the side of the road, got out and went over to look through the ironwork of the gate. By standing on tiptoe she could look over it. What she looked into was a garden. The place was certainly not a farm now, though it might have been once. Presumably it gave on fields beyond it. The garden was tended and cultivated. It was not particularly tidy but it looked as though someone was trying rather unsuccessfully to keep it tidy.

From the iron gate a circular path curved through the garden and round to the house. This must be presumably the front door, though it didn't look like a front door. It was inconspicuous though sturdy—a back door. The house looked quite different from this side. To begin with, it was not empty. People lived there. Windows were open, curtains fluttered at them, a garbage pail stood by the door. At the far end of the garden Tuppence could see a large man digging, a big elderly man who dug slowly and with persistence. Certainly looked at from here the house held no enchantment, no artist would have wanted particularly to paint it. It was just a house and somebody lived in it. Tuppence wondered. She hesitated. Should she go on and forget the house altogether? No, she could hardly do that, not after all the trouble she had taken. What time was it? She looked at her watch but her watch had stopped. The sound of a door opening came from inside. She peered through the gate again.

The door of the house had opened and a woman came out. She put down a milk bottle and then, straightening up, glanced towards the gate. She saw Tuppence and hesitated for a moment, and then seeming to make up her mind, she came down the path towards the gate. 'Why,' said Tuppence to herself, 'why, it's a friendly witch!'

It was a woman of about fifty. She had long straggly hair which when caught by the wind, flew out behind her. It reminded Tuppence vaguely of a picture (by Nevinson?) of a young witch on a broomstick. That is perhaps why the term witch had come into her mind. But there was nothing young or beautiful about this woman. She was middle-aged, with a lined face, dressed in a rather slipshod way. She had a kind of steeple hat perched on her head and her nose and her chin came up towards each other. As a description she could have been sinister but she did not look sinister. She seemed to have a beaming and boundless good will. 'Yes,' thought Tuppence, 'you're exactly *like* a witch, but you're a *friendly* witch. I expect you're what they used to call a "white witch".'

The woman came down in a hesitating manner to the gate and spoke. Her voice was pleasant with a faint country burr in it of some kind.

'Were you looking for anything?' she said.

'I'm sorry,' said Tuppence, 'you must think it very rude of me looking into your garden in this way, but—but I wondered about this house.'

'Would you like to come in and look round the garden?' said the friendly witch.

'Well—well—thank you but I don't want to bother you.'

'Oh, it's no bother. I've nothing to do. Lovely afternoon, isn't it?'

'Yes, it is,' said Tuppence.

'I thought perhaps you'd lost your way,' said the friendly witch. 'People do sometimes.'

'I just thought,' said Tuppence, 'that this was a very attractive-looking house when I came down the hill on the other side of the bridge.'

'That's the prettiest side,' said the woman. 'Artists come and sketch it sometimes—or they used to—once.'

'Yes,' said Tuppence, 'I expect they would. I believe I—I saw a picture—at some exhibition,' she added hurriedly. 'Some house very like this. Perhaps it *was* this.'

'Oh, it may have been. Funny, you know, artists come and do a picture. And then other artists seem to come too. It's just the same when they have the local picture show every year. Artists all seem to choose the same spot. I don't know why. You know, it's either a bit of meadow and brook, or a particular oak tree, or a clump of willows, or it's the same view of the Norman church. Five or six different pictures of the same thing, most of them pretty bad, I should think. But then I don't know anything about art. Come in, do.'

'You're very kind,' said Tuppence. 'You've got a very nice garden,' she added.

'Oh, it's not too bad. We've got a few flowers and vegetables and things. But my husband can't do much work nowadays and I've got no time with one thing and another.'

'I saw this house once from the train,' said Tuppence. 'The train slowed up and I saw this house and I wondered whether I'd ever see it again. Quite some time ago.'

'And now suddenly you come down the hill in your car and there it is,' said the woman. 'Funny, things happen like that, don't they?'

'Thank goodness,' Tuppence thought, 'this woman is extraordinarily easy to talk to. One hardly has to imagine anything to explain oneself. One can almost say just what comes into one's head.'

'Like to come inside the house?' said the friendly witch. 'I can see you're interested. It's quite an old house, you know. I mean, late Georgian or something like that, they say, only it's been added on to. Of course, we've only got half the house, you know.'

'Oh I see,' said Tuppence. 'It's divided in two, is that it?'

'This is really the back of it,' said the woman. 'The front's the other side, the side you saw from the bridge. It was a funny way to partition it, I should have thought. I'd have thought it would have been easier to do it the other way. You know, right and left, so to speak. Not back and front. This is all really the back.'

'Have you lived here long?' asked Tuppence.

'Three years. After my husband retired we wanted a little place somewhere in the country where we'd be quiet. Somewhere cheap. This was going cheap because of course it's very lonely. You're not near a village or anything.'

'I saw a church steeple in the distance.'

'Ah, that's Sutton Chancellor. Two and a half miles from here. We're in the parish, of course, but there aren't any houses until you get to the village. It's a very small village too. You'll have a cup of tea?' said the friendly witch. 'I just put the kettle on not two minutes ago when I looked out and saw you.' She raised both hands to her mouth and shouted. 'Amos,' she shouted, 'Amos.'

The big man in the distance turned his head.

'Tea in ten minutes,' she called.

He acknowledged the signal by raising his hand. She turned, opened the door and motioned Tuppence to go in.

'Perry, my name is,' she said in a friendly voice. 'Alice Perry.'

'Mine's Beresford,' said Tuppence. 'Mrs Beresford.'

'Come in, Mrs Beresford, and have a look round.'

Tuppence paused for a second. She thought, 'Just for a moment I feel like Hansel and Gretel. The witch asks you into her house. Perhaps it's a gingerbread house... It ought to be.'

Then she looked at Alice Perry again and thought that it wasn't the gingerbread house of Hansel and Gretel's witch. This was just a perfectly ordinary woman. No, not quite ordinary. She had a rather strange wild friendliness about her. 'She might be able to do spells,' thought Tuppence, 'but I'm sure they'd be good spells.' She stooped her head a little and stepped over the threshold into the witch's house.

It was rather dark inside. The passages were small. Mrs Perry led her through a kitchen and into a sitting-room beyond it which was evidently the family living-room. There was nothing exciting about the house. It was, Tuppence thought, probably a late Victorian addition to the main part. Horizontally it was narrow. It seemed to consist of a horizontal passage, rather dark, which served a string of rooms. She thought to herself that it certainly was rather an odd way of dividing a house.

'Sit down and I'll bring the tea in,' said Mrs Perry.

'Let me help you.'

'Oh, don't worry, I shan't be a minute. It's all ready on the tray.'

A whistle rose from the kitchen. The kettle had evidently reached the end of its span of tranquillity. Mrs Perry went out and returned in a minute or two with the tea tray, a plate of scones, a jar of jam and three cups and saucers.

'I expect you're disappointed, now you've got inside,' said Mrs Perry.

It was a shrewd remark and very near to the truth.

'Oh no,' said Tuppence.

'Well, I should be if I was you. Because they don't match a bit, do they? I mean the front and the back side of the house don't match. But it is a comfortable house to live in. Not many rooms, not too much light but it makes a great difference in price.'

'Who divided the house and why?'

'Oh, a good many years ago, I believe. I suppose whoever had it thought it was too big or too inconvenient. Only wanted a weekend place or something of that kind. So they kept the good rooms, the dining-room and the drawing-room and made a kitchen out of a small study there was, and a couple of bedrooms and bathroom upstairs, and then walled it up and let the part that was kitchens and old-fashioned sculleries and things, and did it up a bit.'

'Who lives in the other part? Someone who just comes down for weekends?'

'Nobody lives there now,' said Mrs Perry. 'Have another scone, dear.'

'Thank you,' said Tuppence.

'At least nobody's come down here in the last two years. I don't know even who it belongs to now.'

'But when you first came here?'

'There was a young lady used to come down here—an actress they said she was. At least that's what we heard. But we never saw her really. Just caught a glimpse sometimes. She used to come down late on a Saturday night after the show, I suppose. She used to go away on the Sunday evenings.'

'Quite a mystery woman,' said Tuppence, encouragingly.

'You know that's just the way I used to think of her. I used to make up stories about her in my head. Sometimes I'd think she was like Greta Garbo. You know, the way *she* went about always in dark glasses and pulled-down hats. Goodness now, *I've* got *my* peak hat on.'

She removed the witch's headgear from her head and laughed.

'It's for a play we're having at the parish rooms in Sutton Chancellor,' she said. 'You know—a sort of fairy story play for the children mostly. I'm playing the witch,' she added.

'Oh,' said Tuppence, slightly taken aback, then added quickly, 'What fun.'

'Yes, it is fun, isn't it?' said Mrs Perry. 'Just right for the witch, aren't I?' She laughed and tapped her chin. 'You know. I've got the face for it. Hope it won't put ideas into people's heads. They'll think I've got the evil eye.'

'I don't think they'd think that of you,' said Tuppence. 'I'm sure you'd be a beneficent witch.'

'Well, I'm glad you think so,' said Mrs Perry. 'As I was saying, this actress—I can't remember her name now—Miss Marchment I think it was, but it might have been something else—you wouldn't believe the things I used to make up about her. Really, I suppose, I hardly ever saw or spoke to her. Sometimes I think she was just terribly shy and neurotic. Reporters'd come down after her and things like that, but she never would see them. At other times I used to think—well, you'll say I'm foolish—I used to think quite sinister things about her. You know, that she was afraid of being *recognized*. Perhaps she wasn't an actress at all. Perhaps the police were looking for her. Perhaps she was a criminal of some kind. It's exciting sometimes, making things up in your head. Especially when you don't—well—see many people.'

'Did nobody ever come down here with her?'

'Well, I'm not so sure about that. Of course these partition walls, you know, that they put in when they turned the house into two, well, they're pretty thin and sometimes you'd hear voices and things like that. I think she did bring down someone for weekends occasionally.' She nodded her head. 'A man of some kind. That may have been why they wanted somewhere quiet like this.'

'A married man,' said Tuppence, entering into the spirit of make-believe.

'Yes, it would be a married man, wouldn't it?' said Mrs Perry.

'Perhaps it was her husband who came down with her. He'd taken this place in the country because he wanted to murder her and perhaps he buried her in the garden.'

'My!' said Mrs Perry. 'You do have an imagination, don't you? I never thought of that one.'

'I suppose *someone* must have known all about her,' said Tuppence. 'I mean house agents. People like that.'

'Oh, I suppose so,' said Mrs Perry. 'But I rather liked *not* knowing, if you understand what I mean.'

'Oh yes,' said Tuppence, 'I do understand.'

'It's got an atmosphere, you know, this house. I mean there's a feeling in it, a feeling that anything might have happened.'

'Didn't she have any people come in to clean for her or anything like that?'

'Difficult to get anyone here. There's nobody near at hand.'

The outside door opened. The big man who had been digging in the garden came in. He went to the scullery tap and turned it, obviously washing his hands. Then he came through into the sitting-room.

'This is my husband,' said Mrs Perry. 'Amos. We've got a visitor, Amos. This is Mrs Beresford.'

'How do you do?' said Tuppence.

Amos Perry was a tall, shambling-looking man. He was bigger and more powerful than Tuppence had realized. Although he had a shambling gait and walked slowly, he was a big man of muscular build. He said,

'Pleased to meet you, Mrs Beresford.'

His voice was pleasant and he smiled, but Tuppence wondered for a brief moment whether he was really what she would have called 'all there'. There was a kind of wondering simplicity about the look in his eyes and she wondered, too, whether Mrs Perry had wanted a quiet place to live in because of some mental disability on the part of her husband.

'Ever so fond of the garden, he is,' said Mrs Perry.

At his entrance the conversation dimmed down. Mrs Perry did most of the talking but her personality seemed to have changed. She talked with rather more nervousness and with particular attention to her husband. Encouraging him, Tuppence thought, rather in a way that a mother might prompt a shy boy to talk, to display the best of himself before a visitor, and to be a little nervous that he might be inadequate. When she'd finished her tea, Tuppence got up. She said,

'I must be going. Thank you, Mrs Perry, very much for your hospitality.'

'You'll see the garden before you go.' Mr Perry rose. 'Come on, *I'll* show you.'

She went with him outdoors and he took her down to the corner beyond where he had been digging.

'Nice, them flowers, aren't they?' he said. 'Got some old-fashioned roses here—See this one, striped red and white.'

'"Commandant Beaurepaire",' said Tuppence.

'Us calls it "York and Lancaster" here,' said Perry. 'Wars of the Roses. Smells sweet, don't it?'

'Smells lovely.'

'Better than them new-fashioned Hybrid Teas.'

In a way the garden was rather pathetic. The weeds were imperfectly controlled, but the flowers themselves were carefully tied up in an amateurish fashion.

'Bright colours,' said Mr Perry. 'I like bright colours. We often get folk to see our garden,' he said. 'Glad you came.'

'Thank you very much,' said Tuppence. 'I think your garden and your house are very nice indeed.'

'You ought to see t'other side of it.'

'Is it to let or to be sold? Your wife says there's nobody living there now.'

'We don't know. We've not seen anyone and there's no board up and nobody's ever come to see over it.'

'It would be a nice house, I think, to live in.'

'You wanting a house?'

'Yes,' said Tuppence, making up her mind quickly. 'Yes, as a matter of fact, we are looking round for some small place in the country, for when my husband retires. That'll be next year probably, but we like to look about in plenty of time.'

'It's quiet here if you like quiet.'

'I suppose,' said Tuppence, 'I could ask the local house agents. Is that how you got your house?'

'Saw an advertisement first we did in the paper. Then we went to the house agents, yes.'

'Where was that—in Sutton Chancellor? That's your village, isn't it?'

'Sutton Chancellor? No. Agents' place is in Market Basing. Russell & Thompson, that's the name. You could go to them and ask.'

'Yes,' said Tuppence, 'so I could. How far is Market Basing from here?'

'It's two miles to Sutton Chancellor and it's seven miles to Market Basing from there. There's a proper road from Sutton Chancellor, but it's all lanes hereabouts.'

'I see,' said Tuppence. 'Well, goodbye, Mr Perry, and thank you very much for showing me your garden.'

'Wait a bit.' He stooped, cut off an enormous paeony and taking Tuppence by the lapel of her coat, he inserted this through the buttonhole in it. 'There,' he said, 'there you are. Looks pretty, it does.'

For a moment Tuppence felt a sudden feeling of panic. This large, shambling, good-natured man suddenly frightened her. He was looking down at her, smiling. Smiling rather wildly, almost leering. 'Pretty it looks on you,' he said again. 'Pretty.'

Tuppence thought 'I'm glad I'm not a young girl... I don't think I'd like him putting a flower on me then.' She said goodbye again and hurried away.

The house door was open and Tuppence went in to say goodbye to Mrs Perry. Mrs Perry was in the kitchen, washing up the tea things and Tuppence almost automatically pulled a teacloth off the rack and started drying.

'Thank you so much,' she said, 'both you and your husband. You've been so kind and hospitable to me—*What's that*?'

From the wall of the kitchen, or rather behind the wall where an old-fashioned range had once stood, there came a loud screaming and squawking and a scratching noise too.

'That'll be a jackdaw,' said Mrs Perry, 'dropped down the chimney in the other house. They do this time of the year. One came down our chimney last week. They make nests in the chimneys, you know.'

'What—in the other house?'

'Yes, there it is again.'

Again the squawking and crying of a distressed bird came to their ears. Mrs Perry said, 'There's no one to bother, you see, in the empty house. The chimneys ought to be swept and all that.'

The squawking scratching noises went on.

'Poor bird,' said Tuppence.

'I know. It won't be able to get up again.'

'You mean it'll just die there?'

'Oh yes. One came down our chimney as I say. Two of them, actually. One was a young bird. It was all right, we put it out and it flew away. The other one was dead.'

The frenzied scuffling and squeaking went on.

'Oh,' said Tuppence, 'I wish we could get at it.'

Mr Perry came in through the door. 'Anything the matter?' he said, looking from one to the other.

'There's a bird, Amos. It must be in the drawing-room chimney next door. Hear it?'

'Eh, it's come down from the jackdaws' nest.'

'I wish we could get in there,' said Mrs Perry.

'Ah, you can't do anything. They'll die from the fright, if nothing else.'

'Then it'll smell,' said Mrs Perry.

'You won't smell anything in here. You're soft-hearted,' he went on, looking from one to the other, 'like all females. We'll get it if you like.'

'Why, is one of the windows open?'

'We can get in through the door.'

'What door?'

'Outside here in the yard. The key's hanging up among those.'

He went outside and along to the end, opening a small door there. It was a kind of potting shed really, but a door from it led into the other house and near the door of the potting shed were six or seven rusty keys hanging on a nail.

'This one fits,' said Mr Perry.

He took down the key and put it in the door, and after exerting a good deal of cajolery and force, the key turned rustily in the lock.

'I went in once before,' he said, 'when I heard water running. Somebody'd forgotten to turn the water off properly.'

He went in and the two women followed him. The door led into a small room which still contained various flower vases on a shelf and a sink with a tap.

'A flower room, I shouldn't wonder,' he said. 'Where people used to do the flowers. See? A lot of the vases left here.'

There was a door out of the flower room. This was not even locked. He opened it and they went through. It was like, Tuppence thought, going through into another world. The passageway outside was covered with a pile carpet. A little way along there was a door half-open and from there the sounds of a bird in distress were coming. Perry pushed the door open and his wife and Tuppence went in.

The windows were shuttered but one side of a shutter was hanging loose and light came in. Although it was dim, there was a faded but beautiful carpet on the floor, a deep sage-green in colour. There was a bookshelf against the wall but no chairs or tables. The furniture had been removed no doubt, the curtains and carpets had been left as fittings to be passed on to the next tenant.

Mrs Perry went towards the fireplace. A bird lay in the grate scuffling and uttering loud squawking sounds of distress. She stooped, picked it up, and said,

'Open the window if you can, Amos.'

Amos went over, pulled the shutter aside, unfastened the other side of it and then pushed at the latch of the window. He raised the lower sash which came gratingly. As soon as it was open Mrs Perry leaned out and released the jackdaw. It flopped on to the lawn, hopped a few paces.

'Better kill it,' said Perry. 'It's damaged.'

'Leave it a bit,' said his wife. 'You never know. They recover very quickly, birds. It's fright that makes them so paralysed looking.'

Sure enough, a few moments later the jackdaw, with a final struggle, a squawk, a flapping of wings, flew off.

'I only hope,' said Alice Perry, 'that it doesn't come down that chimney again. Contrary things, birds. Don't know what's good for them. Get into a room, they can never get out of it by themselves. Oh,' she added, 'what a mess.'

She, Tuppence and Mr Perry all stared at the grate. From the chimney had come down a mass of soot, of odd rubble and of broken bricks. Evidently it had been in a bad state of repair for some time.

'Somebody ought to come and live here,' said Mrs Perry, looking round her.

'Somebody ought to look after it,' Tuppence agreed with her. 'Some builder ought to look at it or do something about it or the whole house will come down soon.'

'Probably water has been coming through the roof in the top rooms. Yes, look at the ceiling up there, it's come through there.'

'Oh, what a shame,' said Tuppence, 'to ruin a beautiful house—it really is a beautiful room, isn't it.'

She and Mrs Perry looked together round it appreciatively. Built in 1790 it had all the graciousness of a house of that period. It had had originally a pattern of willow leaves on the discoloured paper.

'It's a ruin now,' said Mr Perry.

Tuppence poked the debris in the grate.

'One ought to sweep it up,' said Mrs Perry.

'Now what do you want to bother yourself with a house that doesn't belong to you?' said her husband. 'Leave it alone, woman. It'll be in just as bad a state tomorrow morning.'

Tuppence stirred the bricks aside with a toe.

'Ooh,' she said with an exclamation of disgust.

There were two dead birds lying in the fireplace. By the look of them they had been dead for some time.

'That's the nest that came down a good few weeks ago. It's a wonder it doesn't smell more than it does,' said Perry.

'What's this thing?' said Tuppence.

She poked with her toe at something lying half hidden in the rubble. Then she bent and picked it up.

'Don't you touch a dead bird,' said Mrs Perry.

'It's not a bird,' said Tuppence. 'Something else must have come down the chimney. Well I never,' she added, staring at it. 'It's a doll. It's a child's doll.'

They looked down at it. Ragged, torn, its clothes in rags, its head lolling from the shoulders, it had originally been a child's doll. One glass eye dropped out. Tuppence stood holding it.

'I wonder,' she said, 'I wonder how a child's doll ever got up a chimney. Extraordinary.'

CHAPTER 8

Sutton Chancellor

After leaving the canal house, Tuppence drove slowly on along the narrow winding road which she had been assured would lead her to the village of Sutton Chancellor. It was an isolated road. There were no houses to be seen from it—only field gates from which muddy tracks led inwards. There was little traffic—one tractor came along, and one lorry proudly announcing that it carried Mother's Delight and the picture of an enormous and unnatural-looking loaf. The church steeple she had noticed in the distance seemed to have disappeared entirely—but it finally reappeared quite near at hand after the lane had bent suddenly and sharply round a belt of trees. Tuppence glanced at the speedometer and saw she had come two miles since the canal house.

It was an attractive old church standing in a sizeable churchyard with a lone yew tree standing by the church door.

Tuppence left the car outside the lych-gate, passed through it, and stood for a few moments surveying the church and the churchyard round it. Then she went to the church door with its rounded Norman arch and lifted the heavy handle. It was unlocked and she went inside.

The inside was unattractive. The church was an old one, undoubtedly, but it had had a zealous wash and brush up in Victorian times. Its pitch pine pews and its flaring red and blue glass windows had ruined any antique charm it had once possessed. A middle-aged woman in a tweed coat and skirt was arranging flowers in brass vases round the pulpit—she had already finished the altar. She looked round at Tuppence with a sharply inquiring glance. Tuppence wandered up an aisle looking at memorial tablets on the walls. A family called Warrender seemed to be most fully represented in early years. All of The Priory, Sutton Chancellor. Captain Warrender, Major Warrender, Sarah Elisabeth Warrender, dearly beloved wife of George Warrender. A newer tablet recorded the death of Julia Starke (another beloved wife) of Philip Starke, also of The Priory, Sutton Chancellor—so it would seem the Warrenders had died out. None of them were particularly suggestive or interesting. Tuppence passed out of the church again and walked round it on the outside. The outside, Tuppence thought, was much more attractive than the inside. 'Early Perp. and Dec.,' said Tuppence to herself, having been brought up on familiar terms with ecclesiastical architecture. She was not particularly fond of early Perp. herself.

It was a fair-sized church and she thought that the village of Sutton Chancellor must once have been a rather more important centre of rural life than it was now. She left the car where it was and walked on to the village. It had a village shop and a post office and about a dozen small houses or cottages. One or two of them were thatched but the others were rather plain and unattractive. There were six council houses at the end of the village street looking slightly self-conscious. A brass plate on a door announced 'Arthur Thomas, Chimney Sweep'.

Tuppence wondered if any responsible house agents were likely to engage his services for the house by the canal which certainly needed them. How silly she had been, she thought, not to have asked the name of the house.

She walked back slowly towards the church, and her car, pausing to examine the churchyard more closely. She liked the churchyard. There were very few new burials in it. Most of the stones commemorated Victorian burials, and earlier ones—half defaced by lichen and time. The old stones were attractive. Some of them were upright slabs with cherubs on the tops, with wreaths round them. She wandered about, looking at the inscriptions. Warrenders again. Mary Warrender, aged 47, Alice Warrender, aged 33, Colonel John Warrender killed in Afghanistan. Various infant Warrenders—deeply regretted—and eloquent verses of pious hopes. She wondered if any Warrenders lived here still. They'd left off being buried here apparently. She couldn't find any tombstones later than 1843. Rounding the big yew tree she came upon an elderly clergyman who was stooping over a row of old tombstones near a wall behind the church. He straightened up and turned round as Tuppence approached.

'Good afternoon,' he said pleasantly.

'Good afternoon,' said Tuppence, and added, 'I've been looking at the church.'

'Ruined by Victorian renovation,' said the clergyman.

He had a pleasant voice and a nice smile. He looked about seventy, but Tuppence presumed he was not quite as far advanced in age as that, though he was certainly rheumatic and rather unsteady on his legs.

'Too much money about in Victorian times,' he said sadly. 'Too many ironmasters. They were pious, but had, unfortunately, no sense of the artistic. No taste. Did you see the east window?' he shuddered.

'Yes,' said Tuppence. 'Dreadful,' she said.

'I couldn't agree with you more. I'm the vicar,' he added, rather unnecessarily.

'I thought you must be,' said Tuppence politely. 'Have you been here long?' she added.

'Ten years, my dear,' he said. 'It's a nice parish. Nice people, what there are of them. I've been very happy here. They don't like my sermons very much,' he added sadly. 'I do the best I can, but of course I can't pretend to be really modern. Sit down,' he added hospitably, waving to a nearby tombstone.

Tuppence sat down gratefully and the vicar took a seat on another one nearby.

'I can't stand very long,' he said, apologetically. He added, 'Can I do anything for you or are you just passing by?'

'Well, I'm really just passing by,' said Tuppence. 'I thought I'd just look at the church. I'd rather lost myself in a car wandering around the lanes.'

'Yes, yes. Very difficult to find one's way about round here. A lot of signposts are broken, you know, and the council don't repair them as they should.' He added, 'I don't know that it matters very much. People who drive down these lanes aren't usually trying to get anywhere in particular. People who *are* keep to the main roads. Dreadful,' he added again. 'Especially the new Motorway. At least, *I* think so. The noise and the speed and the reckless driving. Oh well! pay no attention to me. I'm a crusty old fellow. You'd never guess what I'm doing here,' he went on.

'I saw you were examining some of the gravestones,' said Tuppence. 'Has there been any vandalism? Have teenagers been breaking bits off them?'

'No. One's mind *does* turn that way nowadays what with so many telephone boxes wrecked and all those other things that these young vandals do. Poor children, they don't know any better, I suppose. Can't think of anything more amusing to do than to smash things. Sad, isn't it? Very sad. No,' he said, 'there's been no damage of that kind here. The boys round here are a nice lot on the whole. No, I'm just looking for a child's grave.'

Tuppence stirred on her tombstone. 'A child's grave?' she said.

'Yes. Somebody wrote to me. A Major Waters, he asked if by any possibility a child had been buried here. I looked it up in the parish register, of course, but there was no record of any such name. All the same, I came out here and looked round the stones. I thought, you know, that perhaps whoever wrote might have got hold of some wrong name, or that there had been a mistake.'

'What was the Christian name?' asked Tuppence.

'He didn't know. Perhaps Julia after the mother.'

'How old was the child?'

'Again he wasn't sure—Rather vague, the whole thing. I think myself that the man must have got hold of the wrong village altogether. I never remember a Waters living here or having heard of one.'

'What about the Warrenders?' asked Tuppence, her mind going back to the names in the church. 'The church seems full of tablets to them and their names are on lots of gravestones out here.'

'Ah, that family's died out by now. They had a fine property, an old fourteenth-century Priory. It was burnt down—oh, nearly a hundred years ago now, so I suppose any Warrenders there were left, went away and didn't come back. A new house was built on the site, by a rich Victorian called Starke. A very ugly house but comfortable, they say. Very comfortable. Bathrooms, you know, and all that. I suppose that sort of thing *is* important.'

'It seems a very odd thing,' said Tuppence, 'that someone should write and ask you about a child's grave. Somebody—a relation?'

'The father of the child,' said the vicar. 'One of these war tragedies, I imagine. A marriage that broke up when the husband was on service abroad. The young wife ran away with another man while the husband was serving abroad. There was a child, a child he'd never seen. She'd be grown up by now, I suppose, if she were alive. It must be twenty years ago or more.'

'Isn't it a long time after to be looking for her?'

'Apparently he only heard there *was* a child quite recently. The information came to him by pure chance. Curious story, the whole thing.'

'What made him think that the child had been buried here?'

'I gather somebody who had come across his wife in wartime had told him that his wife had said she was living at Sutton Chancellor. It happens, you know. You meet someone, a friend or acquaintance you haven't seen for years, and they sometimes can give you news from the past that you wouldn't get in any other way. But she's certainly not living here now. Nobody of that name has lived here—not since I've been here. Or in the neighbourhood as far as I know. Of course, the mother *might* have been going by another name. However, I gather the father is employing solicitors and inquiry agents and all that sort of thing, and they will probably be able to get results in the end. It will take time—'

'*Was it your poor child*?' murmured Tuppence.

'I beg your pardon, my dear?'

'Nothing,' said Tuppence. 'Something somebody said to me the other day. "*Was it your poor child*?" It's rather a startling thing to hear suddenly. But I don't really think the old lady who said it knew what she was talking about.'

'I know. I know. I'm often the same. I say things and I don't really know what I mean by them. Most vexing.'

'I expect you know everything about the people who live here *now*?' said Tuppence.

'Well, there certainly aren't very many to know. Yes. Why? Is there someone you wanted to know about?'

'I wondered if there had ever been a Mrs Lancaster living here.'

'Lancaster? No, I don't think I recollect that name.'

'And there's a house—I was driving today rather aimlessly—not minding particularly where I went, just following lanes—'

'I know. Very nice, the lanes round here. And you can find quite rare specimens. Botanical, I mean. In the hedges here. Nobody ever picks flowers in these hedges. We never get any tourists round here or that sort of thing. Yes, I've found some very rare specimens sometimes. Dusty Cranesbell, for instance—'

'There was a house by a canal,' said Tuppence, refusing to be side-tracked into botany. 'Near a little hump-backed bridge. It was about two miles from here. I wondered what its name was.'

'Let me see. Canal—hump-backed bridge. Well... there are several houses like that. There's Merricot Farm.'

'It wasn't a farm.'

'Ah, now, I expect it was the Perrys' house—Amos and Alice Perry.'

'That's right,' said Tuppence. 'A Mr and Mrs Perry.'

'She's a striking-looking woman, isn't she? Interesting, I always think. Very interesting. Medieval face, didn't you think so? She's going to play the witch in our play we're getting up. The school children, you know. She looks rather like a witch, doesn't she?'

'Yes,' said Tuppence. 'A friendly witch.'

'As you say, my dear, absolutely rightly. Yes, a friendly witch.'

'But he—'

'Yes, poor fellow,' said the vicar. 'Not completely *compos mentis*—but no harm in him.'

'They were very nice. They asked me in for a cup of tea,' said Tuppence. 'But what I wanted to know was the *name* of the house. I forgot to ask them. They're only living in half of it, aren't they?'

'Yes, yes. In what used to be the old kitchen quarters. *They* call it "Waterside", I think, though I believe the ancient name for it was "Watermead". A pleasanter name, I think.'

'Who does the other part of the house belong to?'

'Well, the whole house used to belong originally to the Bradleys. That was a good many years ago. Yes, thirty or forty at least, I should think. And then it was sold, and then sold again and then it remained empty for a long time. When I came here it was just being used as a kind of weekend place. By some actress—Miss Margrave, I believe. She was not here very much. Just used to come down from time to time. I never knew her. She never came to church. I saw her in the distance sometimes. A beautiful creature. A very beautiful creature.'

'Who does it actually belong to *now*?' Tuppence persisted.

'I've no idea. Possibly it still belongs to her. The part the Perrys live in is only rented to them.'

'I recognized it, you know,' said Tuppence, 'as soon as I saw it, because I've got a picture of it.'

'Oh really? That must have been one of Boscombe's, or was his name Boscobel—I can't remember now. Some name like that. He was a Cornishman, fairly well-known artist,

I believe. I rather imagine he's dead now. Yes, he used to come down here fairly often. He used to sketch all round this part of the world. He did some oils here, too. Very attractive landscapes, some of them.'

'This particular picture,' said Tuppence, 'was given to an old aunt of mine who died about a month ago. It was given to her by a Mrs Lancaster. That's why I asked if you knew the name.'

But the vicar shook his head once more.

'Lancaster? Lancaster. No, I don't seem to remember the name. Ah! but here's the person you must ask. Our dear Miss Bligh. Very active, Miss Bligh is. She knows all about the parish. She runs everything. The Women's Institute, the Boy Scouts and the Guides—everything. You ask *her*. She's very active, very active indeed.'

The vicar sighed. The activity of Miss Bligh seemed to worry him. 'Nellie Bligh, they call her in the village. The boys sing it after her sometimes. *Nellie Bligh, Nellie Bligh*. It's not her proper name. That's something more like Gertrude or Geraldine.'

Miss Bligh, who was the tweed-clad woman Tuppence had seen in the church, was approaching them at a rapid trot, still holding a small watering can. She eyed Tuppence with deep curiosity as she approached, increasing her pace and starting a conversation before she reached them.

'Finished my job,' she exclaimed merrily. 'Had a bit of a rush today. Oh yes, had a bit of a rush. Of course, as you know, Vicar, I usually do the church in the morning. But today we had the emergency meeting in the parish rooms and really you wouldn't believe the time it took! So much *argument*, you know. I really think sometimes people object to things just for the fun of doing so. Mrs Partington was particularly irritating. Wanting everything fully discussed, you know, and wondering whether we'd got enough different prices from different firms. I mean, the whole thing is such a small cost anyway, that really a few shillings here or there can't make much difference. And Burkenheads have always been most reliable. I don't think really, Vicar, you know, that you ought to sit on that tombstone.'

'Irreverent, perhaps?' suggested the vicar.

'Oh no, no, of course I didn't mean that *at all*, Vicar. I meant the *stone*, you know, the damp does come through and with your rheumatism—' Her eyes slid sideways to Tuppence questioningly.

'Let me introduce you to Miss Bligh,' said the vicar. 'This is—this is—' he hesitated.

'Mrs Beresford,' said Tuppence.

'Ah yes,' said Miss Bligh. 'I saw you in the church, didn't I, just now, looking round it. I would have come and spoken to you, called your attention to one or two interesting points, but I was in such a hurry to finish my job.'

'I ought to have come and helped you,' said Tuppence, in her sweetest voice. 'But it wouldn't have been much use, would it, because I could see you knew so exactly where every flower ought to go.'

'Well now, it's very nice of you to say so, but it's quite true. I've done the flowers in the church for—oh, I don't know *how* many years it is. We let the school children arrange their own particular pots of wild flowers for festivals, though of course they haven't the least idea, poor little things. I do think a *little* instruction, but Mrs Peake will never have any instruction. She's so particular. She says it spoils their initiative. Are you staying down here?' she asked Tuppence.

'I was going on to Market Basing,' said Tuppence. 'Perhaps you can tell me a nice quiet hotel to stay there?'

'Well, I expect you'll find it a little disappointing. It's just a market town, you know. It doesn't cater at all for the motoring trade. The Blue Dragon is a two-star but really I don't think these stars mean anything *at all* sometimes. I think you'd find The Lamb better. Quieter, you know. Are you staying there for long?'

'Oh no,' said Tuppence, 'just a day or two while I'm looking round the neighbourhood.'

'Not very much to see, I'm afraid. No interesting antiquities or anything like that. We're purely a rural and agricultural district,' said the vicar. 'But peaceful, you know, very peaceful. As I told you, some interesting wild flowers.'

'Ah yes,' said Tuppence, 'I've heard that and I'm anxious to collect a few specimens in the intervals of doing a little mild house hunting,' she added.

'Oh dear, how interesting,' said Miss Bligh. 'Are you thinking of settling in this neighbourhood?'

'Well, my husband and I haven't decided very definitely on any one neighbourhood in particular,' said Tuppence. 'And we're in no hurry. He won't be retiring for another eighteen months. But it's always as well, I think, to look about. Personally, what *I* prefer to do is to stay in one neighbourhood for four or five days, get a list of likely small properties and drive about to see them. Coming down for one day from London to see one particular house is very tiring, I find.'

'Oh yes, you've got your car here, have you?'

'Yes,' said Tuppence. 'I shall have to go to a house agent in Market Basing tomorrow morning. There's nowhere, I suppose, to stay in the village here, is there?'

'Of course, there's Mrs Copleigh,' said Miss Bligh. 'She takes people in the summer, you know. Summer visitors. She's beautifully clean. All her rooms are. Of course, she only does bed and breakfast and perhaps a light meal in the evening. But I don't think she takes anyone in much before August or July at the earliest.'

'Perhaps I could go and see her and find out,' said Tuppence.

'She's a very worthy woman,' said the vicar. 'Her tongue wags a good deal,' he added. 'She never stops talking, not for one single minute.'

'A lot of gossip and chattering is always going on in these small villages,' said Miss Bligh. 'I think it would be a very good idea if I helped Mrs Beresford. I could take her along to Mrs Copleigh and just see what chances there are.'

'That would be very kind of you,' said Tuppence.

'Then we'll be off,' said Miss Bligh briskly. 'Goodbye, Vicar. Still on your quest? A sad task and so unlikely to meet with success. I really think it was a *most* unreasonable request to make.'

Tuppence said goodbye to the vicar and said she would be glad to help him if she could.

'I could easily spend an hour or two looking at the various gravestones. I've got very good eyesight for my age. It's just the name Waters you are looking for?'

'Not really,' said the vicar. 'It's the age that matters, I think. A child of perhaps seven, it would be. A girl. Major Waters thinks that his wife might have changed her name and that probably the child might be known by the name she had taken. And as he doesn't know what that name is, it makes it all very difficult.'

'The whole thing's impossible, so far as I can see,' said Miss Bligh. 'You ought never to have said you would do such a thing, Vicar. It's monstrous, suggesting anything of the kind.'

'The poor fellow seems very upset,' said the vicar. 'A sad history altogether, so far as I can make out. But I mustn't keep you.'

Tuppence thought to herself as she was shepherded by Miss Bligh that no matter what the reputation of Mrs Copleigh for talking, she could hardly talk more than Miss Bligh did. A stream of pronouncements both rapid and dictatorial poured from her lips.

Mrs Copleigh's cottage proved to be a pleasant and roomy one set back from the village street with a neat garden of flowers in front, a whitened doorstep and a brass handle well polished. Mrs Copleigh herself seemed to Tuppence like a character straight out of the pages of Dickens. She was very small and very round, so that she came rolling towards you rather like a rubber ball. She had bright twinkling eyes, blonde hair rolled up in sausage curls on her head and an air of tremendous vigour. After displaying a little doubt to begin with—'Well, I don't usually, you know. No. My husband and I say "summer visitors, that's different". Everyone does that if they can nowadays. And have to, I'm sure. But not this time of year so much, we don't. Not until July. However, if it's just for a few days and the lady wouldn't mind things being a bit rough, perhaps—'

Tuppence said she didn't mind things being rough and Mrs Copleigh, having surveyed her with close attention, whilst not stopping her flow of conversation, said perhaps the lady would like to come up and see the room, and then things might be arranged.

At that point Miss Bligh tore herself away with some regret because she had not so far been able to extract all the information she wanted from Tuppence, as to where she came from, what her husband did, how old she was, if she had any children and other matters of interest. But it appeared that she had a meeting at her house over which she was going to preside and was terrified at the risk that someone else might seize that coveted post.

'You'll be quite all right with Mrs Copleigh,' she assured Tuppence, 'she'll look after you, I'm sure. Now what about your car?'

'Oh, I'll fetch it presently,' said Tuppence. 'Mrs Copleigh will tell me where I had better put it. I can leave it outside here really because it isn't a very narrow street, is it?'

'Oh, my husband can do better than that for you,' said Mrs Copleigh. 'He'll put it in the field for you. Just round the side lane here, and it'll be quite all right, there. There's a shed he can drive it into.'

Things were arranged amicably on that basis and Miss Bligh hurried away to her appointment. The question of an evening meal was next raised. Tuppence asked if there was a pub in the village.

'Oh, we have nothing as a lady could go to,' said Mrs Copleigh, 'but if you'd be satisfied with a couple of eggs and a slice of ham and maybe some bread and homemade jam—'

Tuppence said that would be splendid. Her room was small but cheerful and pleasant with a rosebud wallpaper and a comfortable-looking bed and a general air of spotless cleanliness.

'Yes, it's a nice wallpaper, miss,' said Mrs Copleigh, who seemed determined to accord Tuppence single status. 'Chose it we did so that any newly married couple should come here on honeymoon. Romantic, if you know what I mean.'

Tuppence agreed that romance was a very desirable thing.

'They haven't got so much to spend nowadays, newly marrieds. Not what they used to. Most of them you see are saving for a house or are making down payments already. Or they've got to buy some furniture on the hire purchase and it doesn't leave anything over for having a posh honeymoon or anything of that kind. They're careful, you know, most of the young folk. They don't go bashing all their money.'

She clattered downstairs again talking briskly as she went. Tuppence lay down on the bed to have half an hour's sleep after a somewhat tiring day. She had, however, great hopes of Mrs Copleigh, and felt that once thoroughly rested herself, she would be able to lead the conversation to the most fruitful subjects possible. She would hear, she was sure, all about the house by the bridge, who had lived there, who had been of evil or good repute in the neighbourhood, what scandals there were and other such likely topics. She was more convinced of this than ever when she had been introduced to Mr Copleigh, a man who barely opened his mouth. His conversation was mostly made up of amiable grunts, usually signifying an affirmative. Sometimes, in more muted tones, a disagreement.

He was content so far as Tuppence could see, to let his wife talk. He himself more or less abstracted his attention, part of the time busy with his plans for the next day which appeared to be market day.

As far as Tuppence was concerned nothing could have turned out better. It could have been distinguished by a slogan—'You want information, we have it'. Mrs Copleigh was as good as a wireless set or a television. You had only to turn the button and words poured out accompanied by gestures and lots of facial expression. Not only was her figure like a child's rubber ball, her face might also have been made of indiarubber. The various people she was talking about almost came alive in caricature before Tuppence's eyes.

Tuppence ate bacon and eggs and had slices of thick bread and butter and praised the blackberry jelly, home-made, her favourite kind, she truthfully announced, and did her best to absorb the flood of information so that she could write notes down in her notebook later. A whole panorama of the past in this country district seemed to be spread out before her.

There was no chronological sequence which occasionally made things difficult. Mrs Copleigh jumped from fifteen years ago to two years ago to last month, and then back to somewhere in the twenties. All this would want a lot of sorting out. And Tuppence wondered whether in the end she would get anything.

The first button she had pressed had not given her any result. That was a mention of Mrs Lancaster.

'I think she came from hereabouts,' said Tuppence, allowing a good deal of vagueness to appear in her voice. 'She had a picture—a very nice picture done by an artist who I believe was known down here.'

'Who did you say now?'

'A Mrs Lancaster.'

'No, I don't remember any Lancasters in these parts. Lancaster. Lancaster. A gentleman had a car accident, I remember. No, it's the car I'm thinking of. A Lancaster that was. No Mrs Lancaster. It wouldn't be Miss Bolton, would it? She'd be about seventy now I think. She might have married a Mr Lancaster. She went away and travelled abroad and I do hear she married someone.'

'The picture she gave my aunt was by a Mr Boscobel—I think the name was,' said Tuppence. 'What a lovely jelly.'

'I don't put no apple in it either, like most people do. Makes it jell better, they say, but it takes all the flavour out.'

'Yes,' said Tuppence. 'I quite agree with you. It does.'

'Who did you say now? It began with a B but I didn't quite catch it.'

'Boscobel, I think.'

'Oh, I remember Mr Boscowan well. Let's see now. That must have been—fifteen years ago it was at least that he came down here. He came several years running, he did. He liked the place. Actually rented a cottage. One of Farmer Hart's cottages it was, that he kept for his labourer. But they built a new one, they did, the Council. Four new cottages specially for labourers.

'Regular artist, Mr B was,' said Mrs Copleigh. 'Funny kind of coat he used to wear. Sort of velvet or corduroy. It used to have holes in the elbows and he wore green and yellow shirts, he did. Oh, very colourful, he was. I liked his pictures, I did. He had a showing of them one year. Round about Christmas time it was, I think. No, of course not, it must have been in the summer. He wasn't here in the winter. Yes, very nice. Nothing exciting, if you know what I mean. Just a house with a couple of trees or two cows looking over a fence. But all nice and quiet and pretty colours. Not like some of these young chaps nowadays.'

'Do you have a lot of artists down here?'

'Not really. Oh no, not to speak of. One or two ladies comes down in the summer and does sketching sometimes, but I don't think much of them. We had a young fellow a year ago, called himself an artist. Didn't shave properly. I can't say I liked any of his pictures much. Funny colours all swirled round anyhow. Nothing you could recognize a bit. Sold a lot of his pictures, he did at that. And they weren't cheap, mind you.'

'Ought to have been five pounds,' said Mr Copleigh entering the conversation for the first time so suddenly that Tuppence jumped.

'What my husband thinks is,' said Mrs Copleigh, resuming her place as interpreter to him. 'He thinks no picture ought to cost more than five pounds. Paints wouldn't cost as much as that. That's what he says, don't you, George?'

'Ah,' said George.

'Mr Boscowan painted a picture of that house by the bridge and the canal—Waterside or Watermead, isn't it called? I came that way today.'

'Oh, you came along that road, did you? It's not much of a road, is it? Very narrow. Lonely that house is, I always think. *I* wouldn't like to live in that house. Too lonely. Don't you agree, George?'

George made the noise that expressed faint disagreement and possibly contempt at the cowardice of women.

'That's where Alice Perry lives, that is,' said Mrs Copleigh.

Tuppence abandoned her researches on Mr Boscowan to go along with an opinion on the Perrys. It was, she perceived, always better to go along with Mrs Copleigh who was a jumper from subject to subject.

'Queer couple *they* are,' said Mrs Copleigh.

George made his agreeing sound.

'Keep themselves to themselves, they do. Don't mingle much, as you'd say. And she goes about looking like nothing on earth, Alice Perry does.'

'Mad,' said Mr Copleigh.

'Well, I don't know as I'd say *that*. She *looks* mad all right. All that scatty hair flying about. And she wears men's coats and great rubber boots most of the time. And she says odd things and doesn't sometimes answer you right when you ask her a question. But I wouldn't say she was *mad*. Peculiar, that's all.'

'Do people like her?'

'Nobody knows her hardly, although they've been there several years. There's all sorts of *tales* about her but then, there's always tales.'

'What sort of tales?'

Direct questions were never resented by Mrs Copleigh, who welcomed them as one who was only too eager to answer.

'Calls up spirits, they say, at night. Sitting round a table. And there's stories of lights moving about the house at night. And she reads a lot of clever books, they say. With things drawn in them—circles and stars. If you ask me, it's Amos Perry as is the one that's not quite all right.'

'He's just simple,' said Mr Copleigh indulgently.

'Well, you may be right about that. But there were tales said of him once. Fond of his garden, but doesn't know much.'

'It's only half a house though, isn't it?' said Tuppence. 'Mrs Perry asked me in very kindly.'

'Did she now? Did she really? I don't know as I'd have liked to go into that house,' said Mrs Copleigh.

'Their part of it's all right,' said Mr Copleigh.

'Isn't the other part all right?' said Tuppence. 'The front part that gives on the canal.'

'Well, there used to be a lot of stories about it. Of course, nobody's lived in it for years. They say there's something queer about it. Lot of stories told. But when you come down to it, it's not stories in anybody's memory here. It's all long ago. It was built over a hundred years ago, you know. They say as there was a pretty lady kept there first, built for her, it was, by one of the gentlemen at Court.'

'Queen Victoria's Court?' asked Tuppence with interest.

'I don't think it would be her. *She* was particular, the old Queen was. No, I'd say it was before that. Time of one of them Georges. This gentleman, he used to come down and see her and the story goes that they had a quarrel and he cut her throat one night.'

'How terrible!' said Tuppence. 'Did they hang him for it?'

'No. Oh no, there was nothing of that sort. The story is, you see, that he had to get rid of the body and he walled her up in the fireplace.'

'Walled her up in the fireplace!'

'Some ways they tell it, they say she was a nun, and she had run away from a convent and that's why she had to be walled up. That's what they do at convents.'

'But it wasn't nuns who walled her up.'

'No, no. He did it. Her lover, what had done her in. And he bricked up all the fireplace, they say, and nailed a big sheet of iron over it. Anyway, she was never seen again, poor soul, walking about in her fine dresses. Some said, of course, she'd gone away with him. Gone away to live in town or back to some other place. People used to hear noises and see lights in the house, and a lot of people don't go near it after dark.'

'But what happened later?' said Tuppence, feeling that to go back beyond the reign of Queen Victoria seemed a little too far into the past for what she was looking for.

'Well, I don't rightly know as there was very much. A farmer called Blodgick took it over when it came up for sale, I believe. He weren't there long either. What they called a gentleman farmer. That's why he liked the house, I suppose, but the farming land wasn't much use to him, and he didn't know how to deal with it. So he sold it again. Changed hands ever so many times it has—Always builders coming along and making alterations—new bathrooms—that sort of thing—A couple had it who were doing chicken farming, I believe, at one time. But it got a name, you know, for being unlucky. But all that's a bit before my time. I believe Mr Boscowan himself thought of buying it at one time. That was when he painted the picture of it.'

'What sort of age was Mr Boscowan when he was down here?'

'Forty, I would say, or maybe a bit more than that. He was a good-looking man in his way. Run into fat a bit, though. Great one for the girls, he was.'

'Ah,' said Mr Copleigh. It was a warning grunt this time.

'Ah well, we all know what artists are like,' said Mrs Copleigh, including Tuppence in this knowledge. 'Go over to France a lot, you know, and get French ways, they do.'

'He wasn't married?'

'Not then he wasn't. Not when he was first down here. Bit keen he was on Mrs Charrington's daughter, but nothing came of it. She was a lovely girl, though, but too young for him. She wasn't more than twenty-five.'

'Who was Mrs Charrington?' Tuppence felt bewildered at this introduction of new characters.

'What the hell am I doing here, anyway?' she thought suddenly as waves of fatigue swept over her—'I'm just listening to a lot of gossip about people, and imagining things like murder which aren't true at all. *I can see now*—It started when a nice but addle-headed old pussy got a bit mixed up in her head and began reminiscing about stories this Mr Boscowan, or someone like him who may have given the picture to her, told about the house and the legends about it, of someone being walled up alive in a fireplace and she thought it was a child for some reason. And here I am going round investigating mares' nests. Tommy told me I was a fool, and he was quite right—I *am* a fool.'

She waited for a break to occur in Mrs Copleigh's even flow of conversation, so that she could rise, say good night politely and go upstairs to bed.

Mrs Copleigh was still in full and happy spate.

'Mrs Charrington? Oh, she lived in Watermead for a bit,' said Mrs Copleigh. 'Mrs Charrington, and her daughter. She was a nice lady, she was, Mrs Charrington. Widow of an army officer, I believe. Badly off, but the house was being rented cheap. Did a lot of gardening. She was very fond of gardening. Not much good at keeping the house clean, she wasn't. I went and obliged for her, once or twice, but I couldn't keep it up. I had to go on my bicycle, you see, and it's over two miles. Weren't any buses along that road.'

'Did she live there long?'

'Not more than two or three years, I think. Got scared, I expect, after the troubles came. And then she had her own troubles about her daughter, too. Lilian, I think her name was.'

Tuppence took a draught of the strong tea with which the meal was fortified, and resolved to get finished with Mrs Charrington before seeking repose.

'What was the trouble about the daughter? Mr Boscowan?'

'No, it wasn't Mr Boscowan as got her into trouble. I'll never believe that. It was the other one.'

'Who was the other one?' asked Tuppence. 'Someone else who lived down here?'

'I don't think he lived down in these parts. Someone she'd met up in London. She went up there to study ballet dancing, would it be? Or art? Mr Boscowan arranged for her to join some school there. Slate I think its name was.'

'Slade?' suggested Tuppence.

'May have been. That sort of name. Anyway, she used to go up there and that's how she got to know this fellow, whoever he was. Her mother didn't like it. She forbade her to meet him. Fat lot of good that was likely to do. She was a silly woman in some ways. Like a lot of those army officers' wives were, you know. She thought girls would do as they were told. Behind the times, she was. Been out in India and those parts, but when it's a question of a good-looking young fellow and you take your eye off a girl, you won't find she's doing what you told her. Not her. He used to come down here now and then and they used to meet outside.'

'And then she got into trouble, did she?' Tuppence said, using the well-known euphemism, hoping that under that form it would not offend Mr Copleigh's sense of propriety.

'Must have been him, I suppose. Anyway, there it was plain as plain. I saw how it was long before her own mother did. Beautiful creature, she was. Big and tall and handsome. But I don't think, you know, that she was one that could stand up to things. She'd break up, you know. She used to walk about rather wild-like, muttering to herself. If you ask me he treated her bad, that fellow did. Went away and left her when he found out what was happening. Of course, a mother as was a mother would have gone and talked to him and made him see where his duty lay, but Mrs Charrington, she wouldn't have had the spirit to do that. Anyway, her mother got wise, and she took the girl away. Shut up the house, she did and afterwards it was put up for sale. They came back to pack up, I believe, but they never came to the village or said anything to anyone. They never come back here, neither of them. There was some story got around. I never knew if there was any truth in it.'

'Some folk'll make up anything,' said Mr Copleigh unexpectedly.

'Well, you're right there, George. Still they may have been true. Such things happen. And as you say, that girl didn't look quite right in the head to me.'

'What was the story?' demanded Tuppence.

'Well, really, I don't like to say. It's a long time since and I wouldn't like to say anything as I wasn't sure of it. It was Mrs Badcock's Louise who put it about. Awful liar that girl was. The things she'd say. Anything to make up a good story.'

'But what was it?' said Tuppence.

'Said this Charrington girl had killed the baby and after that killed herself. Said her mother went half mad with grief and her relations had to put her in a nursing home.'

Again Tuppence felt confusion mounting in her head. She felt almost as though she was swaying in her chair. Could Mrs Charrington be Mrs Lancaster? Changed her name, gone slightly batty, obsessed about her daughter's fate. Mrs Copleigh's voice was going on remorselessly.

'I never believed a word of that myself. That Badcock girl would say anything. We weren't listening much to hearsay and stories just then—we'd had other things to worry about. Scared stiff we'd been, all over the countryside on account of the things that had been going on—REAL things—'

'Why? What had been happening?' asked Tuppence, marvelling at the things that seemed to happen, and to centre round the peaceful-looking village of Sutton Chancellor.

'I daresay as you'll have read about it all in the papers at the time. Let's see, near as possible it would have been twenty years ago. You'll have read about it for sure. Child murders. Little girl of nine years old first. Didn't come home from school one day. Whole neighbourhood was out searching for her. Dingley Copse she was found in. Strangled, she'd been. It makes me shiver still to think of it. Well, that was the first, then about three weeks later another. The other side of Market Basing, that was. But within the district, as you might say. A man with a car could have done it easy enough.

'And then there were others. Not for a month or two sometimes. And then there'd be another one. Not more than a couple of miles from here, one was; almost in the village, though.'

'Didn't the police—didn't anyone know who'd done it?'

'They tried hard enough,' said Mrs Copleigh. 'Detained a man quite soon, they did. Someone from t'other side of Market Basing. Said he was helping them in their inquiries. You know what that always means. They think they've got him. They pulled in first one and then another but always after twenty-four hours or so they had to let him go again. Found out he couldn't have done it or wasn't in these parts or somebody gave him an alibi.'

'You don't know, Liz,' said Mr Copleigh. 'They may have known quite well who done it. I'd say they *did*. That's often the way of it, or so I've heard. The police know who it is but they can't get the evidence.'

'That's wives, that is,' said Mrs Copleigh, 'wives or mothers or fathers even. Even the police can't do much no matter what they may think. A mother says "my boy was here that night at dinner" or his young lady says she went to the pictures with him that night, and he was with her the whole time, or a father says that he and his son were out in the far field together doing something—well, you can't do anything against it. They may think the father or the mother or his sweetheart's lying, but unless someone else come along and say they saw the boy or the man or whatever it is in some other place, there's not much they can do. It was a terrible time. Right het up we all were round here. When we heard another child was missing we'd make parties up.'

'Aye, that's right,' said Mr Copleigh.

'When they'd got together they'd go out and they'd search. Sometimes they found her at once and sometimes they wouldn't find her for weeks. Sometimes she was quite near her home in a place you'd have thought we must have looked at already. Maniac, I suppose it must have been. It's awful,' said Mrs Copleigh in a righteous tone, 'it's awful, that there should be men like that. They ought to be shot. They ought to be strangled themselves. And I'd do it to them for one, if anyone would let me. Any man who kills children and assaults them. What's the good putting them in loony bins and treating them with all the home comforts and living soft. And then sooner or later they let 'em out again, say they're cured and send them home. That happened somewhere in Norfolk. My sister lives there and she told me about it. He went back home and two days later he'd done in someone else. Crazy they are, these doctors, some of them, saying these men are cured when they are not.'

'And you've no idea down here who it might have been?' said Tuppence. 'Do you think really it was a stranger?'

'Might have been a stranger to us. But it must have been someone living within—oh! I'd say a range of twenty miles around. It mightn't have been here in this village.'

'You always thought it was, Liz.'

'You get het up,' said Mrs Copleigh. 'You think it's sure to be here in your own neighbourhood because you're afraid, I suppose. I used to look at people. So did you, George. You'd say to yourself I wonder if it could be *that* chap, he's seemed a bit queer lately. That sort of thing.'

'I don't suppose really he looked queer at all,' said Tuppence. 'He probably looked just like everyone else.'

'Yes, it could be you've got something there. I've heard it said that you wouldn't know, and whoever it was had never seemed mad at all, but other people say there's always a terrible glare in their eyes.'

'Jeffreys, he was the sergeant of police here then,' said Mr Copleigh, 'he always used to say he had a good idea but there was nothing doing.'

'They never caught the man?'

'No. Over six months it was, nearly a year. Then the whole thing stopped. And there's never been anything of that kind round here since. No, I think he must have gone away. Gone away altogether. That's what makes people think they might know who it was.'

'You mean because of people who *did* leave the district?'

'Well, of course it made people talk, you know. They'd say it might be so-and-so.'

Tuppence hesitated to ask the next question, but she felt that with Mrs Copleigh's passion for talking it wouldn't matter if she did.

'Who did *you* think it was?' she asked.

'Well, it's that long ago I'd hardly like to say. But there *was* names mentioned. Talked of, you know, and looked at. Some as thought it might be Mr Boscowan.'

'Did they?'

'Yes, being an artist and all, artists are queer. They say that. But I didn't think it was him!'

'There was more as said it was Amos Perry,' said Mr Copleigh.

'Mrs Perry's husband?'

'Yes. He's a bit queer, you know, simple-minded. He's the sort of chap that might have done it.'

'Were the Perrys living here then?'

'Yes. Not at Watermead. They had a cottage about four or five miles away. Police had an eye on him, I'm sure of that.'

'Couldn't get anything on him, though,' said Mrs Copleigh. 'His wife spoke for him always. Stayed at home with her in the evenings, he did. Always, she said. Just went along sometimes to the pub on a Saturday night, but none of these murders took place on a Saturday night, so there wasn't anything in that. Besides, Alice Perry was the kind you'd believe when she gave evidence. She'd never let up or back down. You couldn't frighten her out of it. Anyway, *he's* not the one. I never thought so. I know I've nothing to go on but I've a sort of feeling if I'd had to put my finger on anyone I'd have put it on Sir Philip.'

'Sir Philip?' Again Tuppence's head reeled. Yet another character was being introduced. Sir Philip. 'Who's Sir Philip?' she asked.

'Sir Philip Starke—Lives up in the Warrender House. Used to be called the Old Priory when the Warrenders lived in it—before it burnt down. You can see the Warrender graves in the churchyard and tablets in the church, too. Always been Warrenders here practically since the time of King James.'

'Was Sir Philip a relation of the Warrenders?'

'No. Made his money in a big way, I believe, or his father did. Steelworks or something of that kind. Odd sort of man was Sir Philip. The works were somewhere up north, but he lived here. Kept to himself he did. What they call a rec—rec—rec-something.'

'Recluse,' suggested Tuppence.

'That's the word I'm looking for. Pale he was, you know, and thin and bony and fond of flowers. He was a botanist. Used to collect all sorts of silly little wild flowers, the kind you wouldn't look at twice. He even wrote a book on them, I believe. Oh yes, he was clever, very clever. His wife was a nice lady, and very handsome, but sad looking, I always thought.'

Mr Copleigh uttered one of his grunts. 'You're daft,' he said. 'Thinking it might have been Sir Philip. He was fond of children, Sir Philip was. He was always giving parties for them.'

'Yes I know. Always giving fêtes, having lovely prizes for the children. Egg and spoon races—all those strawberry and cream teas he'd give. He'd no children of his own, you see. Often he'd stop children in a lane and give them a sweet or give them a sixpence to buy sweets. But I don't know. *I* think he overdid it. He was an odd man. I thought there was something wrong when his wife suddenly up and left him.'

'When did his wife leave him?'

'It'd be about six months after all this trouble began. Three children had been killed by then. Lady Starke went away suddenly to the south of France and she never came back. She wasn't the kind, you'd say, to do that. She was a quiet lady, respectable. It's not as though she left him for any other man. No, she wasn't the kind to do that. So *why* did she go and leave him? I always say it's because she knew something—found out about something—'

'Is he still living here?'

'Not regular, he isn't. He comes down once or twice a year but the house is kept shut up most of the time with a caretaker there. Miss Bligh in the village—she used to be his secretary—she sees to things for him.'

'And his wife?'

'She's dead, poor lady. Died soon after she went abroad. There's a tablet put up to her in the church. Awful for her it would be. Perhaps she wasn't sure at first, then perhaps she began to suspect her husband, and then perhaps she got to be quite sure. She couldn't bear it and she went away.'

'The things you women imagine,' said Mr Copleigh.

'All I say is there was *something* that wasn't right about Sir Philip. He was too fond of children, I think, and it wasn't in a natural kind of way.'

'Women's fancies,' said Mr Copleigh.

Mrs Copleigh got up and started to move things off the table.

'About time,' said her husband. 'You'll give this lady here bad dreams if you go on about things as were over years ago and have nothing to do with anyone here any more.'

'It's been very interesting hearing,' said Tuppence. 'But I am very sleepy. I think I'd better go to bed now.'

'Well, we usually goes early to bed,' said Mrs Copleigh, 'and you'll be tired after the long day you've had.'

'I am. I'm frightfully sleepy.' Tuppence gave a large yawn. 'Well, good night and thank you very much.'

'Would you like a call and a cup of tea in the morning? Eight o'clock too early for you?'

'No, that would be fine,' said Tuppence. 'But don't bother if it's a lot of trouble.'

'No trouble at all,' said Mrs Copleigh.

Tuppence pulled herself wearily up to bed. She opened her suitcase, took out the few things she needed, undressed, washed and dropped into bed. It was true what she had told Mrs Copleigh. She was dead tired. The things she had heard passed through her head in a kind of kaleidoscope of moving figures and of all sorts of horrific imaginings. Dead children—too many dead children. Tuppence wanted just one dead child behind a fireplace. The fireplace had to do perhaps with Waterside. The child's doll. A child that had been killed by a demented young girl driven off her rather weak brains by the fact that her lover had deserted her. Oh dear me, what melodramatic language I'm using, thought Tuppence. All such a muddle—the chronology all mixed up—one can't be sure what happened when.

She went to sleep and dreamt. There was a kind of Lady of Shalott looking out of the window of the house. There was a scratching noise coming from the chimney. Blows were coming from behind a great iron plate nailed up there. The clanging sounds of the hammer. Clang, clang, clang. Tuppence woke up. It was Mrs Copleigh knocking on the door. She came in brightly, put the tea down by Tuppence's bed, pulled the curtains, hoped Tuppence had slept well. No one had ever, Tuppence thought, looked more cheerful than Mrs Copleigh did. *She* had had no bad dreams!

CHAPTER 9

A Morning in Market Basing

'Ah well,' said Mrs Copleigh, as she bustled out of the room. 'Another day. That's what I always say when I wake up.'

'Another day?' thought Tuppence, sipping strong black tea. 'I wonder if I'm making an idiot of myself… ? Could be… Wish I had Tommy here to talk to. Last night muddled me.'

Before she left her room, Tuppence made entries in her notebook on the various facts and names that she had heard the night before, which she had been far too tired to do when she went up to bed. Melodramatic stories, of the past, containing perhaps grains of truth here and there but mostly hearsay, malice, gossip, romantic imagination.

'Really,' thought Tuppence. 'I'm beginning to know the love lives of a quantity of people right back to the eighteenth century, I think. But what does it all amount to? And what am I looking for? I don't even *know* any longer. The awful thing is that I've got involved and I can't leave off.'

Having a shrewd suspicion that the first thing she might be getting involved with was Miss Bligh, whom Tuppence recognized as the overall menace of Sutton Chancellor, she circumvented all kind offers of help by driving off to Market Basing post haste, only pausing, when the car was accosted by Miss Bligh with shrill cries, to explain to that lady that she had an urgent appointment... When would she be back? Tuppence was vague—Would she care to lunch?—Very kind of Miss Bligh, but Tuppence was afraid—

'Tea, then. Four-thirty I'll expect you.' It was almost a Royal Command. Tuppence smiled, nodded, let in the clutch and drove on.

Possibly, Tuppence thought—if she got anything interesting out of the house agents in Market Basing—Nellie Bligh might provide additional useful information. She was the kind of woman who prided herself on knowing all about everyone. The snag was that she would be determined to know all about Tuppence. Possibly by this afternoon Tuppence would have recovered sufficiently to be once more her own inventive self!

'Remember, Mrs Blenkinsop,' said Tuppence, edging round a sharp corner and squeezing into a hedge to avoid being annihilated by a frolicsome tractor of immense bulk.

Arrived in Market Basing she put the car in a parking lot in the main square, and went into the post office and entered a vacant telephone box.

The voice of Albert answered—using his usual response—a single 'Hallo' uttered in a suspicious voice.

'Listen, Albert—I'll be home tomorrow. In time for dinner, anyway—perhaps earlier. Mr Beresford will be back, too, unless he rings up. Get us something—chicken, I think.'

'Right, Madam. Where are you—'

But Tuppence had rung off.

The life of Market Basing seemed centred in its important main square—Tuppence had consulted a classified directory before leaving the post office and three out of the four house and estate agents were situated in the square—the fourth in something called George Street.

Tuppence scribbled down the names and went out to look for them.

She started with Messrs Lovebody & Slicker which appeared to be the most imposing.

A girl with spots received her.

'I want to make some inquiries about a house.'

The girl received this news without interest. Tuppence might have been inquiring about some rare animal.

'I don't know, I'm sure,' said the girl, looking round to ascertain if there was one of her colleagues to whom she could pass Tuppence on—

'A *house*,' said Tuppence. 'You *are* house agents, aren't you?'

'House agents and auctioneers. The Cranberry Court auction's on Wednesday if it's that you're interested in, catalogues two shillings.'

'I'm not interested in auctions. I want to ask about a house.'

'Furnished?'

'Unfurnished—To buy—or rent.'

Spots brightened a little.

'I think you'd better see Mr Slicker.'

Tuppence was all for seeing Mr Slicker and was presently seated in a small office opposite a tweed-suited young man in horsy checks, who began turning over a large number of particulars of desirable residences—murmuring comments to himself…'8 Mandeville Road—architect built, three bed, American kitchen—Oh, no, that's gone—Amabel Lodge—picturesque residence, four acres—reduced price for quick sale—'

Tuppence interrupted him forcefully: 'I have seen a house I like the look of—In Sutton Chancellor—or rather, near Sutton Chancellor—by a canal—'

'Sutton Chancellor,' Mr Slicker looked doubtful—'I don't think we have any property there on our books at present. What name?'

'It doesn't seem to have any written up—Possibly Waterside. Rivermead—once called Bridge House. I gather,' said Tuppence, 'the house is in two parts. One half is let but the tenant there could not tell me anything about the other half, which fronts on the canal and which is the one in which I am interested. It appears to be unoccupied.'

Mr Slicker said distantly that he was afraid he couldn't help her, but condescended to supply the information that perhaps Messrs Blodget & Burgess might do so. By the tone in his voice the clerk seemed to imply this Messrs Blodget & Burgess were a very inferior firm.

Tuppence transferred herself to Messrs Blodget & Burgess who were on the opposite side of the square—and whose premises closely resembled those of Messrs Lovebody & Slicker—the same kind of sale bills and forthcoming auctions in their rather grimy windows. Their front door had recently been repainted a rather bilious shade of green, if that was accounted to be a merit.

The reception arrangements were equally discouraging, and Tuppence was given over to a Mr Sprig, an elderly man of apparently despondent disposition. Once more Tuppence retailed her wants and requirements.

Mr Sprig admitted to being aware of the existence of the residence in question, but was not helpful, or as far as it seemed, much interested.

'It's not in the market, I'm afraid. The owner doesn't want to sell.'

'Who is the owner?'

'Really I doubt if I know. It has changed hands rather frequently—there was a rumour at one moment of a compulsory purchase order.'

'What did any local government want it for?'

'Really, Mrs—er—(he glanced down at Tuppence's name jotted down on his blotter)—Mrs Beresford, if you could tell me the answer to that question you would be wiser than most victims are these days. The ways of local councils and planning societies are always shrouded in mystery. The rear portion of the house had a few necessary repairs done to it and was let at an exceedingly low rent to a—er—ah yes, a Mr and Mrs Perry. As to the actual owners of the property, the gentleman in question lives abroad and seems to have lost interest in the place. I imagine there was some question of a minor inheriting, and it was administered by executors. Some small legal difficulties arose—the law tends to be expensive, Mrs Beresford—I fancy the owner is quite content for the house to fall down—no repairs are done except to the portion the Perrys inhabit. The actual land, of course, might always prove valuable in the future—the repair of derelict houses is seldom profitable. If you are interested in a property of that kind, I am sure we could offer you something far more worth your while. What, if I may ask, is there which especially appealed to you in this property?'

'I liked the look of it,' said Tuppence. 'It's a very *pretty* house—I saw it first from the train—'

'Oh, I see—' Mr Sprig masked as best he could an expression of 'the foolishness of women is incredible'—and said soothingly, 'I should really forget all about it if I were you.'

'I suppose you could write and ask the owners if they would be prepared to sell—or if you would give me their—or his address—'

'We will get into communication with the owners' solicitors if you insist—but I can't hold out much hope.'

'I suppose one always has to go through solicitors for everything nowadays.' Tuppence sounded both foolish and fretful...'And lawyers are always so *slow* over everything.'

'Ah yes—the law is prolific of delays—'

'And so are *banks*—just as bad!'

'Banks—' Mr Sprig sounded a little startled.

'So many people give you a *bank* as an address. That's tiresome too.'

'Yes—yes—as you say—But people are so restless these days and move about so much—living abroad and all that.' He opened a desk drawer. 'Now I have a property here, Crossgates—two miles from Market Basing—very good condition—nice garden—'

Tuppence rose to her feet.

'No thank you.'

She bade Mr Sprig a firm goodbye and went out into the square.

She paid a brief visit to the third establishment which seemed to be mainly preoccupied with sales of cattle, chicken farms and general farms in a derelict condition.

She paid a final visit to Messrs Roberts & Wiley in George Street—which seemed to be a small but pushing business, anxious to oblige—but generally uninterested and ignorant of Sutton Chancellor and anxious to sell residences as yet only half built at what seemed ridiculously exorbitant sums—an illustration of one made Tuppence shudder. The eager young man seeing his possible client firm in departure, admitted unwillingly that such a place as Sutton Chancellor did exist.

'Sutton Chancellor you mentioned. Better try Blodget & Burgess in the square. They handle some property thereabouts—but it's all in very poor condition—run down—'

'There's a pretty house near there, by a canal bridge —I saw it from the train. Why does nobody want to live there?'

'Oh! I know the place, this—Riverbank—You wouldn't get anyone to live in it—Got a reputation as haunted.'

'You mean—ghosts?'

'So they say—Lots of tales about it. Noises at nights. And groans. If you ask me, it's death-watch beetle.'

'Oh dear,' said Tuppence. 'It looked to me so nice and isolated.'

'Much too isolated most people would say. Floods in winter—think of that.'

'I see that there's a lot to think about,' said Tuppence bitterly.

She murmured to herself as she sent her steps towards The Lamb and Flag at which she proposed to fortify herself with lunch.

'A lot to think about—floods, death-watch beetle, ghosts, clanking chains, absentee owners and landlords, solicitors, banks—a house that nobody wants or loves—except perhaps *me*... Oh well, what I want now is FOOD.'

The food at The Lamb and Flag was good and plentiful—hearty food for farmers rather than phony French menus for tourists passing through—Thick savoury soup, leg of pork and apple sauce, Stilton cheese—or plums and custard if you preferred it—which Tuppence didn't—

After a desultory stroll round, Tuppence retrieved her car and started back to Sutton Chancellor—unable to feel that her morning had been fruitful.

As she turned the last corner and Sutton Chancellor church came into view, Tuppence saw the vicar emerging from the churchyard. He walked rather wearily. Tuppence drew up by him.

'Are you still looking for that grave?' she asked.

The vicar had one hand at the small of his back.

'Oh dear,' he said, 'my eyesight is not very good. So many of the inscriptions are nearly erased. My back troubles me, too. So many of these stones lie flat on the ground. Really, when I bend over sometimes I fear that I shall never get up again.'

'I shouldn't do it any more,' said Tuppence. 'If you've looked in the parish register and all that, you've done all you can.'

'I know, but the poor fellow seemed so keen, so earnest. I'm quite sure that it's all wasted labour. However, I really felt it was my duty. I have still got a short stretch I haven't done, over there from beyond the yew tree to the far wall—although most of the stones are eighteenth century. But I should like to feel I had finished my task properly. Then I could not reproach myself. However, I shall leave it till tomorrow.'

'Quite right,' said Tuppence. 'You mustn't do too much in one day. I tell you what,' she added. 'After I've had a cup of tea with Miss Bligh, I'll go and have a look myself. From the yew tree to the wall, do you say?'

'Oh, but I couldn't possibly ask you—'

'That's all right. I shall quite like to do it. I think it's very interesting prowling round in a churchyard. You know, the older inscriptions give you a sort of picture of the people who lived here and all that sort of thing. I shall quite enjoy it, I shall really. Do go back home and rest.'

'Well, of course, I really have to do something about my sermon this evening, it's quite true. You are a very kind friend, I'm sure. A *very* kind friend.'

He beamed at her and departed into the vicarage. Tuppence glanced at her watch. She stopped at Miss Bligh's house. 'Might as well get it over,' thought Tuppence. The front door was open and Miss Bligh was just carrying a plate of fresh-baked scones across the hall into the sitting-room.

'Oh! so there you are, dear Mrs Beresford. I'm *so* pleased to see you. Tea's quite ready. The kettle is on. I've only got to fill up the teapot. I hope you did all the shopping you wanted,' she added, looking in a rather marked manner at the painfully evident empty shopping bag hanging on Tuppence's arm.

'Well, I didn't have much luck really,' said Tuppence, putting as good a face on it as she could. 'You know how it is sometimes—just one of those days when people just haven't got the particular colour or the particular kind of thing you want. But I always enjoy looking round a new place even if it isn't a very interesting one.'

A whistling kettle let forth a strident shriek for attention and Miss Bligh shot back into the kitchen to attend to it, scattering a batch of letters waiting for the post on the hall table.

Tuppence stooped and retrieved them, noticing as she put them back on the table that the topmost one was addressed to a Mrs Yorke, Rosetrellis Court for Elderly Ladies—at an address in Cumberland.

'Really,' thought Tuppence. 'I am beginning to feel as if the whole of the country is full of nothing but Homes for the Elderly! I suppose in next to no time Tommy and I will be living in one!'

Only the other day, some would-be kind and helpful friend had written to recommend a very nice address in Devon—married couples—mostly retired Service people. Quite good cooking—You brought your own furniture and personal belongings.

Miss Bligh reappeared with the teapot and the two ladies sat down to tea.

Miss Bligh's conversation was of a less melodramatic and juicy nature than that of Mrs Copleigh, and was concerned more with the procuring of information, than of giving it.

Tuppence murmured vaguely of past years of Service abroad—the domestic difficulties of life in England, gave details of a married son and a married daughter both with children and gently steered the conversation to the activities of Miss Bligh in Sutton Chancellor which were numerous—The Women's Institute, Guides, Scouts, the Conservative Ladies Union, Lectures, Greek Art, Jam Making, Flower Arrangement, the Sketching Club, the Friends of Archaeology—The vicar's health, the necessity of making him take care of himself, his absentmindedness—Unfortunate differences of opinion between churchwardens—

Tuppence praised the scones, thanked her hostess for her hospitality and rose to go.

'You are so wonderfully energetic, Miss Bligh,' she said. 'How you manage to do all you do, I cannot imagine. I must confess that after a day's excursion and shopping, I like just a nice little rest on my bed—just half an hour or so of shut-eye—A very comfortable bed, too. I must thank you very much for recommending me to Mrs Copleigh—'

'A most reliable woman, though of course she talks too much—'

'Oh! I found all her local tales most entertaining.'

'Half the time she doesn't know what she's talking about! Are you staying here for long?'

'Oh no—I'm going home tomorrow. I'm disappointed at not having heard of any suitable little property—I had hopes of that very picturesque house by the canal—'

'You're well out of that. It's in a very poor state of repair—Absentee landlords—it's a disgrace—'

'I couldn't even find out who it belongs to. I expect *you* know. You seem to know everything here—'

'I've never taken much interest in that house. It's always changing hands—One can't keep pace. The Perrys live in half of it—and the other half just goes to rack and ruin.'

Tuppence said goodbye again and drove back to Mrs Copleigh's. The house was quiet and apparently empty. Tuppence went up to her bedroom, deposited her empty shopping bag, washed her face and powdered her nose, tiptoed out of the house again, looking up and down the street, then leaving her car where it was, she walked swiftly round the corner, and took a footpath through the field behind the village which eventually led to a stile into the churchyard.

Tuppence went over the stile into the churchyard, peaceful in the evening sun, and began to examine the tombstones as she had promised. She had not really had any ulterior motive in doing so. There was nothing here she hoped to discover. It was really just kindliness on her part. The elderly vicar was rather a dear, and she would like him to feel that his conscience was entirely satisfied. She had brought a notebook and pencil with her in case there was anything of interest to note down for him. She presumed she was merely to look for a gravestone that might have been put up commemorating the death of some child of the required age. Most of the graves here were of an older date. They were not very interesting, not old enough to be quaint or to have touching or tender inscriptions. They were mostly of fairly elderly people. Yet she lingered a little as she went along, making mental pictures in her mind. Jane Elwood, departed this life January the 6th, aged 45. William Marl, departed this life January the 5th, deeply regretted. Mary Treves, five years old. March 14th 1835. That was too far back. 'In thy presence is the fulness of joy.' Lucky little Mary Treves.

She had almost reached the far wall now. The graves here were neglected and overgrown, nobody seemed to care about this bit of the cemetery. Many of the stones were no longer upright but lay about on the ground. The wall here was damaged and crumbling. In places it had been broken down.

Being right behind the church, it could not be seen from the road—and no doubt children came here to do what damage they could. Tuppence bent over one of the stone slabs—The original lettering was worn away and unreadable—But heaving it up sideways, Tuppence saw some coarsely scrawled letters and words, also by now partly overgrown.

She stopped to trace them with a forefinger, and got a word here and there—

Whoever... offend... one of these little ones...

Millstone... Millstone... Millstone... and below—in uneven cutting by an amateur hand:

Here lies Lily Waters.

Tuppence drew a deep breath—She was conscious of a shadow behind her, but before she could turn her head—something hit her on the back of her head and she fell forwards on to the tombstone into pain and darkness.

BOOK 3

Missing—A Wife

CHAPTER 10

A Conference—and After

'Well, Beresford,' said Major-General Sir Josiah Penn, K.M.G., C.B., D.S.O., speaking with the weight appropriate to the impressive stream of letters after his name. 'Well, what do you think of all that yackety-yack?'

Tommy gathered by that remark that Old Josh, as he was irreverently spoken of behind his back, was not impressed with the result of the course of the conferences in which they had been taking part.

'Softly, softly catchee monkey,' said Sir Josiah, going on with his remarks. 'A lot of talk and nothing said. If anybody does say anything sensible now and then, about four beanstalks immediately get up and howl it down. *I* don't know why we come to these things. At least, I *do* know. I know why I do. Nothing else to do. If I didn't come to these shows, I'd have to stay at home. Do you know what happens to me there? I get bullied, Beresford. Bullied by my housekeeper, bullied by my gardener. He's an elderly Scot and he won't so much as let me touch my own peaches. So

I come along here, throw my weight about and pretend to myself that I'm performing a useful function, ensuring the security of this country! Stuff and nonsense.

'What about you? You're a relatively young man. What do you come and waste your time for? Nobody'll listen to you, even if you do say something worth hearing.'

Tommy, faintly amused that despite his own, as he considered, advanced age, he could be regarded as a youngster by Major-General Sir Josiah Penn, shook his head. The General must be, Tommy thought, considerably past eighty, he was rather deaf, heavily bronchial, but he was nobody's fool.

'Nothing would ever get done at all if you weren't here, sir,' said Tommy.

'I like to think so,' said the General. 'I'm a toothless bulldog—but I can still bark. How's Mrs Tommy? Haven't seen her for a long time.'

Tommy replied that Tuppence was well and active.

'She was always active. Used to make me think of a dragonfly sometimes. Always darting off after some apparently absurd idea of her own and then we'd find it wasn't absurd. Good fun!' said the General, with approval. 'Don't like these earnest middle-aged women you meet nowadays, all got a Cause with a capital C. And as for the girls nowadays—' he shook his head. 'Not what they used to be when I was a young man. Pretty as a picture, they used to be then. Their muslin frocks! *Cloche* hats, they used to wear at one time. Do you remember? No, I suppose you'd have been at school. Had to look right down underneath the brim before you could see the girl's face. Tantalizing it was, *and* they knew it! I remember now—let me see—she was a relative of yours—an aunt wasn't she?—Ada. Ada Fanshawe—'

'Aunt Ada?'

'Prettiest girl I ever knew.'

Tommy managed to contain the surprise he felt. That his Aunt Ada could ever have been considered pretty seemed beyond belief. Old Josh was dithering on.

'Yes, pretty as a picture. Sprightly, too! Gay! Regular tease. Ah, I remember last time I saw her. I was a subaltern just off to India. We were at a moonlight picnic on the beach... She and I wandered away together and sat on a rock looking at the sea.'

Tommy looked at him with great interest. At his double chins, his bald head, his bushy eyebrows and his enormous paunch. He thought of Aunt Ada, of her incipient moustache, her grim smile, her iron-grey hair, her malicious glance. Time, he thought. What Time does to one! He tried to visualize a handsome young subaltern and a pretty girl in the moonlight. He failed.

'Romantic,' said Sir Josiah Penn with a deep sigh. 'Ah yes, romantic. I would have liked to propose to her that night, but you couldn't propose if you were a subaltern. Not on your pay. We'd have had to wait five years before we could be married. That was too long an engagement to ask any girl to agree to. Ah well! you know how things happen. I went out to India and it was a long time before I came home on leave. We wrote to one another for a bit, then things slacked off. As it usually happens. I never saw her again. And yet, you know, I never quite forgot her.

Often thought of her. I remember I nearly wrote to her once, years later. I'd heard she was in the neighbourhood where I was staying with some people. I thought I'd go and see her, ask if I could call. Then I thought to myself "Don't be a damn' fool. She probably looks quite different by now."

'I heard a chap mention her some years later. Said she was one of the ugliest women he'd ever seen. I could hardly believe it when I heard him say that, but I think now perhaps I was lucky I never *did* see her again. What's she doing now? Alive still?'

'No. She died about two or three weeks ago, as a matter of fact,' said Tommy.

'Did she really, did she really? Yes, I suppose she'd be—what now, she'd be seventy-five or seventy-six? Bit older than that perhaps.'

'She was eighty,' said Tommy.

'Fancy now. Dark-haired lively Ada. Where did she die? Was she in a nursing home or did she live with a companion or—she never married, did she?'

'No,' said Tommy, 'she never married. She was in an old ladies' home. Rather a nice one, as a matter of fact. Sunny Ridge, it's called.'

'Yes, I've heard of that. Sunny Ridge. Someone my sister knew was there, I believe. A Mrs—now what was the name—a Mrs Carstairs? D'you ever come across her?'

'No. I didn't come across anyone much there. One just used to go and visit one's own particular relative.'

'Difficult business, too, I think. I mean, one never knows what to say to them.'

'Aunt Ada was particularly difficult,' said Tommy. 'She was a tartar, you know.'

'She would be.' The General chuckled. 'She could be a regular little devil when she liked when she was a girl.'

He sighed.

'Devilish business, getting old. One of my sister's friends used to get fancies, poor old thing. Used to say she'd killed somebody.'

'Good Lord,' said Tommy. 'Had she?'

'Oh, I don't suppose so. Nobody seems to think she had. I suppose,' said the General, considering the idea thoughtfully, 'I suppose she *might* have, you know. If you go about saying things like that quite cheerfully, nobody *would* believe you, would they? Entertaining thought that, isn't it?'

'Who did she think she'd killed?'

'Blessed if I know. Husband perhaps? Don't know who he was or what he was like. She was a widow when we first came to know her. Well,' he added with a sigh, 'sorry to hear about Ada. Didn't see it in the paper. If I had I'd have sent flowers or something. Bunch of rosebuds or something of that kind. That's what girls used to wear on their evening dresses. A bunch of rosebuds on the shoulder of an evening dress. Very pretty it was. I remember Ada had an evening dress—sort of hydrangea colour, mauvy. Mauvy-blue and she had pink rosebuds on it. She gave me one once. They weren't real, of course. Artificial. I kept it for a long time—years. I know,' he added, catching Tommy's eye, 'makes you laugh to think of it, doesn't it. I tell you, my boy, when you get really old and *gaga* like I am, you get sentimental again. Well, I suppose I'd better toddle off and go back to the last act of this ridiculous show. Best regards to Mrs T. when you get home.'

In the train the next day, Tommy thought back over this conversation, smiling to himself and trying again to picture his redoubtable aunt and the fierce Major-General in their young days.

'I must tell Tuppence this. It'll make her laugh,' said Tommy. 'I wonder what Tuppence has been doing while I've been away?'

He smiled to himself.

The faithful Albert opened the front door with a beaming smile of welcome.

'Glad to see you back, sir.'

'I'm glad to be back—' Tommy surrendered his suitcase—'Where's Mrs Beresford?'

'Not back yet, sir.'

'Do you mean she's away?'

'Been away three or four days. But she'll be back for dinner. She rang up yesterday and said so.'

'What's she up to, Albert?'

'I couldn't say, sir. She took the car, but she took a lot of railway guides as well. She might be anywhere, as you might say.'

'You might indeed,' said Tommy with feeling. 'John o' Groat's—or Land's End—and probably missed the connection at Little Dither on the Marsh on the way back. God bless British Railways. She rang up yesterday, you say. Did she say where she was ringing from?'

'She didn't say.'

'What time yesterday was this?'

'Yesterday morning. Before lunch. Just said everything was all right. She wasn't quite sure of what time she'd get home, but she thought she'd be back well before dinner and suggested a chicken. That do you all right, sir?'

'Yes,' said Tommy, regarding his watch, 'but she'll have to make it pretty quickly now.'

'I'll hold the chicken back,' said Albert.

Tommy grinned. 'That's right,' he said. 'Catch it by the tail. How've you been, Albert? All well at home?'

'Had a scare of measles—But it's all right. Doctor says it's only strawberry rash.'

'Good,' said Tommy. He went upstairs, whistling a tune to himself. He went into the bathroom, shaved and washed, strode from there into the bedroom and looked around him. It had that curious look of disoccupancy some bedrooms put on when their owner is away. Its atmosphere was cold and unfriendly. Everything was scrupulously tidy and scrupulously clean. Tommy had the depressed feeling that a faithful dog might have had. Looking round him, he thought it was as though Tuppence had never been. No spilled powder, no book cast down open with its back splayed out.

'Sir.'

It was Albert, standing in the doorway.

'Well?'

'I'm getting worried about the chicken.'

'Oh damn the chicken,' said Tommy. 'You seem to have that chicken on your nerves.'

'Well, I took it as you and she wouldn't be later than eight. Not later than eight, sitting down, I mean.'

'I should have thought so, too,' said Tommy, glancing at his wrist watch. 'Good Lord, is it nearly five and twenty to nine?'

'Yes it is, sir. And the chicken—'

'Oh, come on,' said Tommy, 'you get that chicken out of the oven and you and I'll eat it between us. Serve Tuppence right. Getting back well before dinner indeed!'

'Of course some people do eat dinner late,' said Albert. 'I went to Spain once and believe me, you couldn't get a meal before ten o'clock. Ten p.m. I ask you! Heathens!'

'All right,' said Tommy, absentmindedly. 'By the way, have you no idea where she has been all this time?'

'You mean the missus? I dunno, sir. Rushing around, I'd say. Her first idea was going to places by train, as far as I can make out. She was always looking in A.B.C.s and timetables and things.'

'Well,' said Tommy, 'we all have our ways of amusing ourselves, I suppose. Hers seems to have been railway travel. I wonder where she is all the same. Sitting in the Ladies' Waiting Room at Little Dither on the Marsh, as likely as not.'

'She knew as you was coming home today though, didn't she, sir?' said Albert. 'She'll get here somehow. Sure to.'

Tommy perceived that he was being offered loyal allegiance. He and Albert were linked together in expressing disapprobation of a Tuppence who in the course of her flirtations with British Railways was neglecting to come home in time to give a returning husband his proper welcome.

Albert went away to release the chicken from its possible fate of cremation in the oven.

Tommy, who had been about to follow him, stopped and looked towards the mantelpiece. He walked slowly to it and looked at the picture that hung there. Funny, her being so sure that she had seen that particular house before. Tommy felt quite certain that *he* hadn't seen it. Anyway, it was quite an ordinary house. There must be plenty of houses like that.

He stretched up as far as he could towards it and then, still not able to get a good view, unhooked it and took it close to the electric lamp. A quiet, gentle house. There was the artist's signature. The name began with a B though he couldn't make out exactly what the name was. Bosworth—Bouchier—He'd get a magnifying glass and look at it more closely. A merry chime of cowbells came from the hall. Albert had highly approved of the Swiss cowbells that Tommy and Tuppence had brought back some time or other from Grindelwald. He was something of a virtuoso on them. Dinner was served. Tommy went to the dining-room. It was odd, he thought, that Tuppence hadn't turned up by now. Even if she had had a puncture, which seemed probable, he rather wondered that she hadn't rung up to explain or excuse her delay.

'She might know that I'd worry,' said Tommy to himself. Not, of course, that he ever *did* worry—not about Tuppence. Tuppence was always all right. Albert contradicted this mood.

'Hope she hasn't had an accident,' he remarked, presenting Tommy with a dish of cabbage, and shaking his head gloomily.

'Take that away. You know I hate cabbage,' said Tommy. 'Why should she have had an accident? It's only half past nine now.'

'Being on the road is plain murder nowadays,' said Albert. 'Anyone might have an accident.'

The telephone bell rang. 'That's her,' said Albert. Hastily reposing the dish of cabbage on the sideboard, he hurried out of the room. Tommy rose, abandoning his plate of chicken, and followed Albert. He was just saying 'Here, I'll take it,' when Albert spoke.

'Yes, sir? Yes, Mr Beresford is at home. Here he is now.' He turned his head to Tommy. 'It's a Dr Murray for you, sir.'

'Dr Murray?' Tommy thought for a moment. The name seemed familiar but for the moment he couldn't remember who Dr Murray was. If Tuppence had had an accident—and then with a sigh of relief he remembered that Dr Murray had been the doctor who attended the old ladies at Sunny Ridge. Something, perhaps, to do with Aunt Ada's funeral forms. True child of his time, Tommy immediately assumed that it must be a question of some form or other—something he ought to have signed, or Dr Murray ought to have signed.

'Hullo,' he said, 'Beresford here.'

'Oh, I'm glad to catch you. You remember me, I hope. I attended your aunt, Miss Fanshawe.'

'Yes, of course I remember. What can I do?'

'I really wanted to have a word or two with you sometime. I don't know if we can arrange a meeting, perhaps in town one day?'

'Oh I expect so, yes. Quite easily. But—er—is it something you can't say over the phone?'

'I'd rather not say it over the telephone. There's no immediate hurry. I won't pretend there is but—but I should like to have a chat with you.'

'Nothing wrong?' said Tommy, and wondered why he put it that way. Why should there be anything wrong?

'Not really. I may be making a mountain out of a molehill. Probably am. But there have been some rather curious developments at Sunny Ridge.'

'Nothing to do with Mrs Lancaster, is it?' asked Tommy.

'Mrs Lancaster?' The doctor seemed surprised. 'Oh no. She left some time ago. In fact—before your aunt died. This is something quite different.'

'I've been away—only just got back. May I ring you up tomorrow morning—we could fix something then.'

'Right. I'll give you my telephone number. I shall be at my surgery until ten a.m.'

'Bad news?' asked Albert as Tommy returned to the dining-room.

'For God's sake, don't croak, Albert,' said Tommy irritably. 'No—of course it isn't bad news.'

'I thought perhaps the missus—'

'She's all right,' said Tommy. 'She always is. Probably gone haring off after some wild-cat clue or other—You know what she's like. I'm not going to worry any more. Take away this plate of chicken—You've been keeping it hot in the oven and it's inedible. Bring me some coffee. And then I'm going to bed.

'There will probably be a letter tomorrow. Delayed in the post—you know what our posts are like—or there will be a wire from her—or she'll ring up.'

But there was no letter next day—no telephone call—no wire.

Albert eyed Tommy, opened his mouth and shut it again several times, judging quite rightly that gloomy predictions on his part would not be welcomed.

At last Tommy had pity on him. He swallowed a last mouthful of toast and marmalade, washed it down with coffee, and spoke—

'All right, Albert, I'll say it first—*Where is she?* What's happened to her? And what are we going to do about it?'

'Get on to the police, sir?'

'I'm not sure. You see—' Tommy paused.

'If she's had an accident—'

'She's got her driving licence on her—and plenty of identifying papers—Hospitals are very prompt at reporting these things—and getting in touch with relatives—all that. I don't want to be precipitate—she—she mightn't want it. You've no idea—no idea at all, Albert, where she was going—Nothing she said? No particular place—or county. Not a mention of some name?'

Albert shook his head.

'What was she feeling like? Pleased?—Excited? Unhappy? Worried?'

Albert's response was immediate.

'Pleased as Punch—Bursting with it.'

'Like a terrier off on the trail,' said Tommy.

'That's right, sir—you know how she gets—'

'On to something—Now I wonder—' Tommy paused in consideration.

Something had turned up, and, as he had just said to Albert, Tuppence had rushed off like a terrier on the scent. The day before yesterday she had rung up to announce her return. Why, then, hadn't she returned? Perhaps, at this moment, thought Tommy, she's sitting somewhere telling lies to people so hard that she can't think of anything else!

If she were engrossed in pursuit, she would be extremely annoyed if he, Tommy, were to rush off to the police bleating like a sheep that his wife had disappeared—He could hear Tuppence saying 'How you could be so fatuous as to do such a thing! I can look after myself *perfectly*. You ought to know that by this time!' (But could she look after herself?)

One was never quite sure where Tuppence's imagination could take her.

Into *danger*? There hadn't, so far, been any evidence of danger in this business—Except, as aforesaid, in Tuppence's imagination.

If he were to go to the police, saying his wife had not returned home as she announced she was going to do—The police would sit there, looking tactful though possibly grinning inwardly, and would then presumably, still in a tactful way, ask what men friends his wife had got!

'I'll find her myself,' declared Tommy. 'She's *somewhere*. Whether it's north, south, east or west I've no idea—and she was a silly cuckoo not to leave word when she rang up, where she was.'

'A gang's got her, perhaps—' said Albert.

'Oh! be your age, Albert, you've outgrown that sort of stuff years ago!'

'What are you going to do, sir?'

'I'm going to London,' said Tommy, glancing at the clock. 'First I'm going to have lunch at my club with Dr Murray who rang me up last night, and who's got something to say to me about my late deceased aunt's affairs—I might possibly get a useful hint from him—After all, this business started at Sunny Ridge. I am also taking that picture that's hanging over our bedroom mantelpiece up with me—'

'You mean you're taking it to Scotland Yard?'

'No,' said Tommy. 'I'm taking it to Bond Street.'

CHAPTER 11

Bond Street and Dr Murray

Tommy jumped out of a taxi, paid the driver and leaned back into the cab to take out a rather clumsily done up parcel which was clearly a picture. Tucking as much of it as he could under his arm, he entered the New Athenian Galleries, one of the longest established and most important picture galleries in London.

Tommy was not a great patron of the arts but he had come to the New Athenian because he had a friend who officiated there.

'Officiated' was the only word to use because the air of sympathetic interest, the hushed voice, the pleasurable smile, all seemed highly ecclesiastical.

A fair-haired young man detached himself and came forward, his face lighting up with a smile of recognition.

'Hullo, Tommy,' he said. 'Haven't seen you for a long time. What's that you've got under your arm? Don't tell me you've been taking to painting pictures in your old age? A lot of people do—results usually deplorable.'

'I doubt if creative art was ever my long suit,' said Tommy. 'Though I must admit I found myself strongly attracted the other day by a small book telling in the simplest terms how a child of five can learn to paint in water colours.'

'God help us if you're going to take to that. Grandma Moses in reverse.'

'To tell you the truth, Robert, I merely want to appeal to your expert knowledge of pictures. I want your opinion on this.'

Deftly Robert took the picture from Tommy and skilfully removed its clumsy wrappings with the expertise of a man accustomed to handle the parcelling up and deparcelling of all different-sized works of art. He took the picture and set it on a chair, peered into it to look at it, and then withdrew five or six steps away. He turned his gaze towards Tommy.

'Well,' he said, 'what about it? What do you want to know? Do you want to sell it, is that it?'

'No,' said Tommy, 'I don't want to sell it, Robert. I want to know about it. To begin with, I want to know who painted it.'

'Actually,' said Robert, 'if you *had* wanted to sell it, it would be quite saleable nowadays. It wouldn't have been, ten years ago. But Boscowan's just coming into fashion again.'

'Boscowan?' Tommy looked at him inquiringly. 'Is that the name of the artist? I saw it was signed with something beginning with B but I couldn't read the name.'

'Oh, it's Boscowan all right. Very popular painter about twenty-five years ago. Sold well, had plenty of shows. People bought him all right. Technically a very good painter.

Then, in the usual cycle of events, he went out of fashion. Finally, hardly any demand at all for his works but lately he's had a revival. He, Stitchwort, and Fondella. They're all coming up.'

'Boscowan,' repeated Tommy.

'B-o-s-c-o-w-a-n,' said Robert obligingly.

'Is he still painting?'

'No. He's dead. Died some years ago. Quite an old chap by then. Sixty-five, I think, when he died. Quite a prolific painter, you know. A lot of his canvases about. Actually we're thinking of having a show of him here in about four or five months' time. We ought to do well over it, I think. Why are you so interested in him?'

'It'd be too long a story to tell you,' said Tommy. 'One of these days I'll ask you out to lunch and give you the doings from the beginning. It's a long, complicated and really rather an idiotic story. All I wanted to know is all about this Boscowan and if you happen to know by any chance where this house is that's represented here.'

'I couldn't tell you the last for a moment. It's the sort of thing he did paint, you know. Small country houses in rather isolated spots usually, sometimes a farmhouse, sometimes just a cow or two around. Sometimes a farm cart, but if so, in the far distance. Quiet rural scenes. Nothing sketchy or messy. Sometimes the surface looks almost like enamel. It was a peculiar technique and people liked it. A good many of the things he painted were in France, Normandy mostly. Churches. I've got one picture of his here now. Wait a minute and I'll get it for you.'

He went to the head of the staircase and shouted down to someone below. Presently he came back holding a small canvas which he propped on another chair.

'There you are,' he said. 'Church in Normandy.'

'Yes,' said Tommy, 'I see. The same sort of thing. My wife says nobody ever lived in that house—the one I brought in. I see now what she meant. I don't see that anybody was attending service in that church or ever will.'

'Well, perhaps your wife's got something. Quiet, peaceful dwellings with no human occupancy. He didn't often paint people, you know. Sometimes there's a figure or two in the landscape, but more often not. In a way I think that gives them their special charm. A sort of isolationist feeling. It was as though he removed all the human beings, and the peace of the countryside was all the better without them. Come to think of it, that's maybe why the general taste has swung round to him. Too many people nowadays, too many cars, too many noises on the road, too much noise and bustle. Peace, perfect peace. Leave it all to Nature.'

'Yes, I shouldn't wonder. What sort of a man was he?'

'I didn't know him personally. Before my time. Pleased with himself by all accounts. Thought he was a better painter than he was, probably. Put on a bit of side. Kindly, quite likeable. Eye for the girls.'

'And you've no idea where this particular piece of countryside exists? It *is* England, I suppose.'

'I should think so, yes. Do you want me to find out for you?'

'Could you?'

'Probably the best thing to do would be to ask his wife, his widow rather. He married Emma Wing, the sculptor. Well known. Not very productive. Does quite powerful work. You could go and ask her. She lives in Hampstead. I can give you the address. We've been corresponding with her a good deal lately over the question of this show of her husband's work we're doing. We're having a few of her smaller pieces of sculpture as well. I'll get the address for you.'

He went to the desk, turned over a ledger, scrawled something on a card and brought it back.

'There you are, Tommy,' he said. 'I don't know what the deep dark mystery is. Always been a man of mystery, haven't you? It's a nice representation of Boscowan's work you've got there. We might like to use it for the show. I'll send you a line to remind you nearer the time.'

'You don't know a Mrs Lancaster, do you?'

'Well, I can't think of one off-hand. Is she an artist or something of the kind?'

'No, I don't think so. She's just an old lady living for the last few years in an old ladies' home. She comes into it because this picture belonged to her until she gave it away to an aunt of mine.'

'Well I can't say the name means anything to me. Better go and talk to Mrs Boscowan.'

'What's she like?'

'She was a good bit younger than he was, I should say. Quite a personality.' He nodded his head once or twice. 'Yes, quite a personality. You'll find that out, I expect.'

He took the picture, handed it down the staircase with instructions to someone below to do it up again.

'Nice for you having so many myrmidons at your beck and call,' said Tommy.

He looked round him, noticing his surroundings for the first time.

'What's this you've got here now?' he said with distaste.

'Paul Jaggerowski—Interesting young Slav. Said to produce all his works under the influence of drugs—Don't you like him?'

Tommy concentrated his gaze on a big string bag which seemed to have enmeshed itself in a metallic green field full of distorted cows.

'Frankly, no.'

'Philistine,' said Robert. 'Come out and have a bite of lunch.'

'Can't. I've got a meeting with a doctor at my club.'

'Not ill, are you?'

'I'm in the best of health. My blood pressure is so good that it disappoints every doctor to whom I submit it.'

'Then what do you want to see a doctor for?'

'Oh,' said Tommy cheerfully—'I've just got to see a doctor about a body. Thanks for your help. Goodbye.'

Tommy greeted Dr Murray with some curiosity—He presumed it was some formal matter to do with Aunt Ada's decease, but why on earth Dr Murray would not at least mention the subject of his visit over the telephone, Tommy couldn't imagine.

'I'm afraid I'm a little late,' said Dr Murray, shaking hands, 'but the traffic was pretty bad and I wasn't exactly sure of the locality. I don't know this part of London very well.'

'Well, too bad you had to come all the way here,' said Tommy. 'I could have met you somewhere more convenient, you know.'

'You've time on your hands then just now?'

'Just at the moment, yes. I've been away for the last week.'

'Yes, I believe someone told me so when I rang up.'

Tommy indicated a chair, suggested refreshment, placed cigarettes and matches by Dr Murray's side. When the two men had established themselves comfortably Dr Murray opened the conversation.

'I'm sure I've aroused your curiosity,' he said, 'but as a matter of fact we're in a spot of trouble at Sunny Ridge. It's a difficult and perplexing matter and in one way it's nothing to do with you. I've no earthly right to trouble you with it but there's just an off chance that you might know something which would help me.'

'Well, of course, I'll do anything I can. Something to do with my aunt, Miss Fanshawe?'

'Not directly, no. But in a way she does come into it. I can speak to you in confidence, can't I, Mr Beresford?'

'Yes, certainly.'

'As a matter of fact I was talking the other day to a mutual friend of ours. He was telling me a few things about you. I gather that in the last war you had rather a delicate assignment.'

'Oh, I wouldn't put it quite as seriously as that,' said Tommy, in his most non-committal manner.

'Oh no, I quite realize that it's not a thing to be talked about.'

'I don't really think that matters nowadays. It's a good long time since the war. My wife and I were younger then.'

'Anyway, it's nothing to do with that, that I want to talk to you about, but at least I feel that I can speak frankly to you, that I can trust you not to repeat what I am now saying, though it's possible that it all may have to come out later.'

'A spot of trouble at Sunny Ridge, you say?'

'Yes. Not very long ago one of our patients died. A Mrs Moody. I don't know if you ever met her or if your aunt ever talked about her.'

'Mrs Moody?' Tommy reflected. 'No, I don't think so. Anyway, not so far as I remember.'

'She was not one of our older patients. She was still on the right side of seventy and she was not seriously ill in any way. It was just a case of a woman with no near relatives and no one to look after her in the domestic line. She fell into the category of what I often call to myself a flutterer. Women who more and more resemble hens as they grow older. They cluck. They forget things. They run themselves into difficulties and they worry. They get themselves wrought up about nothing at all. There is very little the matter with them. They are not strictly speaking mentally disturbed.'

'But they just cluck,' Tommy suggested.

'As you say. Mrs Moody clucked. She caused the nurses a fair amount of trouble although they were quite fond of her. She had a habit of forgetting when she'd had her meals, making a fuss because no dinner had been served to her when as a matter of fact she had actually just eaten a very good dinner.'

'Oh,' said Tommy, enlightened, 'Mrs Cocoa.'

'I beg your pardon?'

'I'm sorry,' said Tommy, 'it's a name my wife and I had for her. She was yelling for Nurse Jane one day when we passed along the passage and saying she hadn't had her cocoa. Rather a nice-looking scatty little woman. But it made us both laugh, and we fell into the habit of calling her Mrs Cocoa. And so she's died.'

'I wasn't particularly surprised when the death happened,' said Dr Murray. 'To be able to prophesy with any exactitude when elderly women will die is practically impossible. Women whose health is seriously affected, who, one feels as a result of physical examination, will hardly last the year out, sometimes are good for another ten years. They have a tenacious hold on life which mere physical disability will not quench. There are other people whose health is reasonably good and who may, one thinks, make old bones. They on the other hand, catch bronchitis, or 'flu, seem unable to have the stamina to recuperate from it, and die with surprising ease. So, as I say, as a medical attendant to an elderly ladies' home, I am not surprised when what might be called a fairly unexpected death occurs. This case of Mrs Moody, however, was somewhat different. She died in her sleep without having exhibited any sign of illness and I could not help feeling that in my opinion her death was unexpected. I will use the phrase that has always intrigued me in Shakespeare's play, *Macbeth*. I have always wondered what Macbeth meant when he said of his wife, "She should have died hereafter."'

'Yes, I remember wondering once myself what Shakespeare was getting at,' said Tommy. 'I forget whose production it was and who was playing Macbeth, but there was a strong suggestion in that particular production, and Macbeth certainly played it in a way to suggest that he was hinting to the medical attendant that Lady Macbeth would be better out of the way. Presumably the medical attendant took the hint. It was then that Macbeth, feeling safe after his wife's death, feeling that she could no longer damage him by her indiscretions or her rapidly failing mind, expresses his genuine affection and grief for her. "She should have died hereafter."'

'Exactly,' said Dr Murray. 'It is what I felt about Mrs Moody. I felt that she should have died hereafter. Not just three weeks ago of no apparent cause—'

Tommy did not reply. He merely looked at the doctor inquiringly.

'Medical men have certain problems. If you are puzzled over the cause of a patient's death there is only one sure way to tell. By a post mortem. Post mortems are not appreciated by relatives of the deceased, but if a doctor demands a post mortem and the result is, as it perfectly well may be, a case of natural causes, or some disease or malady which does not always give outward signs or symptoms, then the doctor's career can be quite seriously affected by his having made a questionable diagnosis—'

'I can see that it must have been difficult.'

'The relatives in question are distant cousins. So I took it upon myself to get their consent as it was a matter of medical interest to know the cause of death. When a patient dies in her sleep it is advisable to add to one's medical knowledge. I wrapped it up a good bit, mind you, didn't make it too formal. Luckily they couldn't care less. I felt very relieved in mind. Once the autopsy had been performed and if all was well, I could give a death certificate without a qualm. Anyone can die of what is amateurishly called heart failure, from one of several different causes. Actually Mrs Moody's heart was in really very good shape for her age. She suffered from arthritis and rheumatism and occasional trouble with her liver, but none of these things seemed to accord with her passing away in her sleep.'

Dr Murray came to a stop. Tommy opened his lips and then shut them again. The doctor nodded.

'Yes, Mr Beresford. You can see where I am tending. Death has resulted from an overdose of morphine.'

'Good Lord!' Tommy stared and the ejaculation escaped him.

'Yes. It seemed quite incredible, but there was no getting away from the analysis. The question was: How was that morphia administered? She was not on morphia. She was not a patient who suffered pain. There were three possibilities, of course. She might have taken it by accident. Unlikely. She might have got hold of some other patient's medicine by mistake but that again is not particularly likely. Patients are not entrusted with supplies of morphia, and we do not accept drug addicts who might have a supply of such things in their possession. It could have been deliberate suicide but I should be very slow to accept that. Mrs Moody, though a worrier, was of a perfectly cheerful disposition and I am quite sure had never thought of ending her life. The third possibility is that a fatal overdose was deliberately administered to her. But by whom, and why? Naturally, there are supplies of morphia and other drugs which Miss Packard as a registered hospital nurse and matron, is perfectly entitled to have in her possession and which she keeps in a locked cupboard. In such cases as sciatica or rheumatoid arthritis there can be such severe and desperate pain that morphia is occasionally administered. We have hoped that we may come across some circumstance in which Mrs Moody had a dangerous amount of morphia administered to her by mistake or which she herself took under the delusion that it was a cure for indigestion or insomnia. We have not been able to find any such circumstances possible. The next thing we have done, at Miss Packard's suggestion and I agreed with her, is to look carefully into the records of such deaths as have taken place at Sunny Ridge in the last two years. There have not been many of them, I am glad to say. I think seven in all, which is a pretty fair average for people of that age group. Two deaths of bronchitis, perfectly straightforward, two of 'flu, always a possible killer during the winter months owing to the slight resistance offered by frail, elderly women. And three others.'

He paused and said, 'Mr Beresford, I am not satisfied about those three others, certainly not about two of them. They were perfectly probable, they were not unexpected, but I will go as far as saying that they were *unlikely*. They are not cases that on reflection and research I am entirely satisfied about. One has to accept the possibility that, unlikely as it seems, there is someone at Sunny Ridge who is, possibly for mental reasons, a killer. An entirely unsuspected killer.'

There was silence for some moments. Tommy gave a sigh.

'I don't doubt what you've told me,' he said, 'but all the same, frankly, it seems unbelievable. These things—surely, they can't happen.'

'Oh yes,' said Dr Murray grimly, 'they happen all right. You go over some of the pathological cases. A woman who took on domestic service. She worked as a cook in various households. She was a nice, kind, pleasant-seeming woman, gave her employers faithful service, cooked well, enjoyed being with them. Yet, sooner or later, things happened. Usually a plate of sandwiches. Sometimes picnic food. For no apparent motive arsenic was added. Two or three poisoned sandwiches among the rest. Apparently sheer chance dictated who took and ate them. There seemed no personal venom. Sometimes no tragedy happened. The same woman was three or four months in a situation and there was no trace of illness. Nothing. Then she left to go to another job, and in that next job, within three weeks, two of the family died after eating bacon for breakfast. The fact that all these things happened in different parts of England and at irregular intervals made it some time before the police got on her track. She used a different name, of course, each time. But there are so many pleasant, capable, middle-aged women who can cook, it was hard to find out which particular woman it was.'

'Why did she do it?'

'I don't think anybody has ever really known. There have been several different theories, especially of course by psychologists. She was a somewhat religious woman and it seems possible that some form of religious insanity made her feel that she had a divine command to rid the world of certain people, but it does not seem that she herself had borne them any personal animus.

'Then there was the French woman, Jeanne Gebron, who was called The Angel of Mercy. She was so upset when her neighbours had ill children, she hurried to nurse those children. Sat devotedly at their bedside. There again it was some time before people discovered that the children she nursed *never recovered. Instead they all died*. And *why*? It is true that when she was young her own child died. She appeared to be prostrated with grief. Perhaps that was the cause of her career of crime. If *her* child died so should the children of other women. Or it may be, as some thought, that her own child was also one of the victims.'

'You're giving me chills down my spine,' said Tommy.

'I'm taking the most melodramatic examples,' said the doctor. 'It may be something much simpler than that. You remember in the case of Armstrong, anyone who had in any way offended him or insulted him, or indeed, if he even thought anyone had insulted him, that person was quickly asked to tea and given arsenic sandwiches. A sort of intensified touchiness. His first crimes were obviously mere crimes for personal advantage. Inheriting of money. The removal of a wife so that he could marry another woman.

'Then there was Nurse Warriner who kept a Home for elderly people. They made over what means they had to her, and were guaranteed a comfortable old age until death came—But death did not delay very long. There, too, it was morphia that was administered—a very kindly woman, but with no scruples—she regarded herself, I believe, as a benefactor.'

'You've no idea, if your surmise about these deaths is true, who it could be?'

'No. There seems no pointer of any kind. Taking the view that the killer is probably insane, insanity is a very difficult thing to recognize in some of its manifestations. Is it somebody, shall we say, who dislikes elderly people, who had been injured or has had her life ruined or so she thinks, by somebody elderly? Or is it possibly someone who has her own ideas of mercy killing and thinks that everyone over sixty years of age should be kindly exterminated. It could be anyone, of course. A patient? Or a member of the staff—a nurse or a domestic worker?

'I have discussed this at great length with Millicent Packard who runs the place. She is a highly competent woman, shrewd, businesslike, with keen supervision both of the guests there and of her own staff. She insists that she has no suspicion and no clue whatever and I am sure that is perfectly true.'

'But why come to me? What can I do?'

'Your aunt, Miss Fanshawe, was a resident there for some years—she was a woman of very considerable mental capacity, though she often pretended otherwise. She had unconventional ways of amusing herself by putting on an appearance of senility. But she was actually very much all there—What I want you to try and do, Mr Beresford, is to think hard—you and your wife, too—Is there anything you can remember that Miss Fanshawe ever said or hinted, that might give us a clue—Something she had seen or noticed, something that someone had told her, something that she herself had thought peculiar. Old ladies see and notice a lot, and a really shrewd one like Miss Fanshawe would know a surprising amount of what went on in a place like Sunny Ridge. These old ladies are not busy, you see, they have all the time in the world to look around them and make deductions—and even jump to conclusions—that may seem fantastic, but are sometimes, surprisingly, entirely correct.'

Tommy shook his head.

'I know what you mean—But I can't remember anything of that kind.'

'Your wife's away from home, I gather. You don't think she might remember something that hadn't struck you?'

'I'll ask her—but I doubt it.' He hesitated, then made up his mind. 'Look here, there was something that worried my wife—about one of the old ladies, a Mrs Lancaster.'

'Mrs Lancaster? Yes?'

'My wife's got it into her head that Mrs Lancaster has been taken away by some so-called relations very suddenly. As a matter of fact, Mrs Lancaster gave a picture to my aunt as a present, and my wife felt that she ought to offer to return the picture to Mrs Lancaster, so she tried to get in touch with her to know if Mrs Lancaster would like the picture returned to her.'

'Well, that was very thoughtful of Mrs Beresford, I'm sure.'

'Only she found it very hard to get in touch with her. She got the address of the hotel where they were supposed to be staying—Mrs Lancaster and her relations—but nobody of that name had been staying there or had booked rooms there.'

'Oh? That was rather odd.'

'Yes. Tuppence thought it was rather odd, too. They had left no other forwarding address at Sunny Ridge. In fact, we have made several attempts to get in touch with Mrs Lancaster, or with this Mrs—Johnson I think the name was—but have been quite unable to get in touch with them. There was a solicitor who I believe paid all the bills—and made all the arrangements with Miss Packard and we got into communication with him. But he could only give me the address of a bank. Banks,' said Tommy drily, 'don't give you any information.'

'Not if they've been told not to by their clients, I agree.'

'My wife wrote to Mrs Lancaster care of the bank, and also to Mrs Johnson, but she's never had any reply.'

'That seems a little unusual. Still, people don't always answer letters. They may have gone abroad.'

'Quite so—it didn't worry me. But it has worried my wife. She seems convinced that something has happened to Mrs Lancaster. In fact, during the time I was away from home, she said she was going to investigate further—I don't know what exactly she meant to do, perhaps see the hotel personally, or the bank, or try the solicitor. Anyway, she was going to try and get a little more information.'

Dr Murray looked at him politely, but with a trace of patient boredom in his manner.

'What did she think exactly—?'

'She thinks that Mrs Lancaster is in danger of some kind—even that something may have happened to her.'

The doctor raised his eyebrows.

'Oh! really, I should hardly think—'

'This may seem quite idiotic to you,' said Tommy, 'but you see, my wife rang up saying she would be back yesterday evening—and—*she didn't arrive*.'

'She said definitely that she *was* coming back?'

'Yes. She knew I was coming home, you see, from this conference business. So she rang up to let our man, Albert, know that she'd be back to dinner.'

'And that seems to you an unlikely thing for her to do?' said Murray. He was now looking at Tommy with some interest.

'Yes,' said Tommy. 'It's *very* unlike Tuppence. If she'd been delayed or changed her plans she would have rung up again or sent a telegram.'

'And you're worried about her?'

'Yes, I am,' said Tommy.

'H'm! Have you consulted the police?'

'No,' said Tommy. 'What'd the police think? It's not as though I had any reason to believe that she is in trouble or danger or anything of that kind. I mean, if she'd had an accident or was in a hospital, anything like that, somebody would communicate with me soon enough, wouldn't they?'

'I should say so—yes—if she had some means of identification on her.'

'She'd have her driving licence on her. Probably letters and various other things.'

Dr Murray frowned.

Tommy went on in a rush:

'And now you come along—And bring up all this business of Sunny Ridge—People who've died when they oughtn't to have died. Supposing this old bean got on to something—saw something, or suspected something—and began chattering about it—She'd have to be silenced in some way, so she was whisked out of it quickly, and taken off to some place or other where she wouldn't be traced. I can't help feeling that the whole thing ties up somehow—'

'It's odd—it's certainly odd—What do you propose to do next?'

'I'm going to do a bit of searching myself—Try these solicitors first—They may be quite all right, but I'd like to have a look at them, and draw my own conclusions.'

CHAPTER 12

Tommy Meets an Old Friend

From the opposite side of the road, Tommy surveyed the premises of Messrs. Partingdale, Harris, Lockeridge and Partingdale.

They looked eminently respectable and old-fashioned. The brass plate was well worn but nicely polished. He crossed the street and passed through swing doors to be greeted by the muted note of typewriters at full speed.

He addressed himself to an open mahogany window on his right which bore the legend INQUIRIES—

Inside was a small room where three women were typing and two male clerks were bending over desks copying documents.

There was a faint, musty atmosphere with a decidedly legal flavour.

A woman of thirty-five odd, with a severe air, faded blonde hair, and *pince-nez* rose from her typewriter and came to the window.

'Can I help you?'

'I would like to see Mr Eccles.'

The woman's air of severity redoubled.

'Have you an appointment?'

'I'm afraid not. I'm just passing through London today.'

'I'm afraid Mr Eccles is rather busy this morning. Perhaps another member of the firm—'

'It was Mr Eccles I particularly wanted to see. I have already had some correspondence with him.'

'Oh I see. Perhaps you'll give me your name.'

Tommy gave his name and address and the blonde woman retired to confer with the telephone on her desk. After a murmured conversation she returned.

'The clerk will show you into the waiting-room. Mr Eccles will be able to see you in about ten minutes' time.'

Tommy was ushered into a waiting-room which had a bookcase of rather ancient and ponderous-looking law tomes and a round table covered with various financial papers. Tommy sat there and went over in his own mind his planned methods of approach. He wondered what Mr Eccles would be like. When he was shown in at last and Mr Eccles rose from a desk to receive him, he decided for no particular reason that he could name to himself that he did not like Mr Eccles. He also wondered why he did not like Mr Eccles. There seemed no valid reason for dislike. Mr Eccles was a man of between forty and fifty with greyish hair thinning a little at the temples. He had a long rather sad-looking face with a particularly wooden expression, shrewd eyes, and quite a pleasant smile which from time to time rather unexpectedly broke up the natural melancholy of his countenance.

'Mr Beresford?'

'Yes. It is really rather a trifling matter, but my wife has been worried about it. She wrote to you, I believe, or possibly she may have rung you up, to know if you could give her the address of a Mrs Lancaster.'

'Mrs Lancaster,' said Mr Eccles, retaining a perfect poker face. It was not even a question. He just left the name hanging in the air.

'A cautious man,' thought Tommy, 'but then it's second nature for lawyers to be cautious. In fact, if they were one's own lawyers one would prefer them to be cautious.'

He went on:

'Until lately living at a place called Sunny Ridge, an establishment—and a very good one—for elderly ladies. In fact, an aunt of my own was there and was extremely happy and comfortable.'

'Oh yes, of course, of course. I remember now. Mrs Lancaster. She is, I think, no longer living there? That is right, is it not?'

'Yes,' said Tommy.

'At the moment I do not exactly recall—' he stretched out a hand towards the telephone—'I will just refresh my memory—'

'I can tell you quite simply,' said Tommy. 'My wife wanted Mrs Lancaster's address because she happens to be in possession of a piece of property which originally belonged to Mrs Lancaster. A picture, in fact. It was given by Mrs Lancaster as a present to my aunt, Miss Fanshawe. My aunt died recently, and her few possessions have come into our keeping. This included the picture which was given her by Mrs Lancaster. My wife likes it very much but she feels rather guilty about it. She thinks that it may be a picture Mrs Lancaster values and in that case she feels she ought to offer to return it to Mrs Lancaster.'

'Ah, I see,' said Mr Eccles. 'It is very conscientious of your wife, I am sure.'

'One never knows,' said Tommy, smiling pleasantly, 'what elderly people may feel about their possessions. She may have been glad for my aunt to have it since my aunt admired it, but as my aunt died very soon after having received this gift, it seems, perhaps, a little unfair that it should pass into the possession of strangers. There is no particular title on the picture. It represents a house somewhere in the country. For all I know it may be some family house associated with Mrs Lancaster.'

'Quite, quite,' said Mr Eccles, 'but I don't think—'

There was a knock and the door opened and a clerk entered and produced a sheet of paper which he placed before Mr Eccles. Mr Eccles looked down.

'Ah yes, ah yes, I remember now. Yes, I believe Mrs—' he glanced down at Tommy's card lying on his desk—'Beresford rang up and had a few words with me. I advised her to get into touch with the Southern Counties Bank, Hammersmith branch. This is the only address I myself know. Letters addressed to the bank's address, care of Mrs Richard Johnson would be forwarded. Mrs Johnson is, I believe, a niece or distant cousin of Mrs Lancaster's and it was Mrs Johnson who made all the arrangements with me for Mrs Lancaster's reception at Sunny Ridge. She asked me to make full inquiries about the establishment, since she had only heard about it casually from a friend. We did so, I can assure you, most carefully. It was said to be an excellent establishment and I believe Mrs Johnson's relative, Mrs Lancaster, spent several years there quite happily.'

'She left there, though, rather suddenly,' Tommy suggested.

'Yes. Yes, I believe she did. Mrs Johnson, it seems, returned rather unexpectedly recently from East Africa—so many people have done so! She and her husband had, I believe, resided in Kenya for many years. They were making various new arrangements and felt able to assume personal care of their elderly relative. I am afraid I have no knowledge of Mrs Johnson's present whereabouts. I had a letter from her thanking me and settling accounts she owed, and directing that if there was any necessity for communicating with her I should address my letters care of the bank as she was undecided as yet where she and her husband would actually be residing. I am afraid, Mr Beresford, that that is all I know.'

His manner was gentle but firm. It displayed no embarrassment of any kind nor disturbance. But the finality of his voice was very definite. Then he unbent and his manner softened a little.

'I shouldn't really worry, you know, Mr Beresford,' he said reassuringly. 'Or rather, I shouldn't let your wife worry. Mrs Lancaster, I believe, is quite an old lady and inclined to be forgetful. She's probably forgotten all about this picture that she gave away. She is, I believe, seventy-five or seventy-six years of age. One forgets very easily at that age, you know.'

'Did you know her personally?'

'No, I never actually met her.'

'But you knew Mrs Johnson?'

'I met her when she came here occasionally to consult me as to arrangements. She seemed a pleasant, business-like woman. Quite competent in the arrangements she was making.' He rose and said, 'I am so sorry I can't help you, Mr Beresford.'

It was a gentle but firm dismissal.

Tommy came out on to the Bloomsbury street and looked about him for a taxi. The parcel he was carrying, though not heavy, was of a fairly awkward size. He looked up for a moment at the building he had just left. Eminently respectable, long established. Nothing you could fault there, nothing apparently wrong with Messrs Partingdale, Harris, Lockeridge and Partingdale, nothing wrong with Mr Eccles, no signs of alarm or despondency, no shiftiness or uneasiness. In books, Tommy thought gloomily, a mention of Mrs Lancaster or Mrs Johnson should have brought a guilty start or a shifty glance. Something to show that the names registered, that all was not well. Things didn't seem to happen like that in real life. All Mr Eccles had looked like was a man who was too polite to resent having his time wasted by such an inquiry as Tommy had just made.

But all the same, thought Tommy to himself, *I don't like Mr Eccles*. He recalled to himself vague memories of the past, of other people that he had for some reason not liked. Very often those hunches—for hunches is all they were—had been right. But perhaps it was simpler than that.

If you had had a good many dealings in your time with personalities, you had a sort of feeling about them, just as an expert antique dealer knows instinctively the taste and look and feel of a forgery before getting down to expert tests and examinations. The thing just is *wrong*. The same with pictures. The same presumably with a cashier in a bank who is offered a first-class spurious banknote.

'He sounds all right,' thought Tommy. 'He looks all right, he speaks all right, but all the same—' He waved frantically at a taxi which gave him a direct and cold look, increased its speed and drove on. 'Swine,' thought Tommy.

His eyes roved up and down the street, seeking for a more obliging vehicle. A fair amount of people were walking on the pavement. A few hurrying, some strolling, one man gazing at a brass plate just across the road from him. After a close scrutiny, he turned round and Tommy's eyes opened a little wider. He knew that face. He watched the man walk to the end of the street, pause, turn and walk back again. Somebody came out of the building behind Tommy and at that moment the man opposite increased his pace a little, still walking on the other side of the road but keeping pace with the man who had come out of the door. The man who had come out of Messrs Partingdale, Harris, Lockeridge and Partingdale's doorway was, Tommy thought, looking after his retreating figure, almost certainly Mr Eccles. At the same moment a taxi lingering in a pleasant tempting manner, came along. Tommy raised his hand, the taxi drew up, he opened the door and got in.

'Where to?'

Tommy hesitated for a moment, looking at his parcel. About to give an address he changed his mind and said, '14 Lyon Street.'

A quarter of an hour later he had reached his destination. He rang the bell after paying off the taxi and asked for Mr Ivor Smith. When he entered a second-floor room, a man sitting at a table facing the window, swung round and said with faint surprise,

'Hullo, Tommy, fancy seeing you. It's a long time. What are you doing here? Just tooling round looking up your old friends?'

'Not quite as good as that, Ivor.'

'I suppose you're on your way home after the Conference?'

'Yes.'

'All a lot of the usual talky-talky, I suppose? No conclusions drawn and nothing helpful said.'

'Quite right. All a sheer waste of time.'

'Mostly listening to old Bogie Waddock shooting his mouth off, I expect. Crashing bore. Gets worse every year.'

'Oh! well—'

Tommy sat down in the chair that was pushed towards him, accepted a cigarette, and said,

'I just wondered—it's a very long shot—whether you know anything of a derogatory nature about one Eccles, solicitor, of the firm of Messrs Partingdale, Harris, Lockeridge and Partingdale.'

'Well, well, well,' said the man called Ivor Smith. He raised his eyebrows. They were very convenient eyebrows for raising. The end of them near the nose went up and the opposite end of the cheek went down for an almost astonishing extent. They made him on very little provocation look like a man who had had a severe shock, but actually it was quite a common gesture with him. 'Run up against Eccles somewhere, have you?'

'The trouble is,' said Tommy, 'that I know nothing about him.'

'And you want to know something about him?'

'Yes.'

'Hm. What made you come to see me?'

'I saw Anderson outside. It was a long time since I'd seen him but I recognized him. He was keeping someone or other under observation. Whoever it was, it was someone in the building from which I had just emerged. Two firms of lawyers practise there and one firm of chartered accountants. Of course it may be any one of them or any member of any one of them. But a man walking away down the street looked to me like Eccles. And I just wondered if by a lucky chance it could have been my Mr Eccles that Anderson was giving his attention to?'

'Hm,' said Ivor Smith. 'Well, Tommy, you always were a pretty good guesser.'

'Who *is* Eccles?'

'Don't you know? Haven't you any idea?'

'I've no idea whatever,' said Tommy. 'Without going into a long history, I went to him for some information about an old lady who has recently left an old ladies' home. The solicitor employed to make arrangements for her was Mr Eccles. He appears to have done it with perfect decorum and efficiency. I wanted her present address. He says he hasn't got it. Quite possibly he hasn't...but I wondered. He's the only clue to her whereabouts I've got.'

'And you want to find her?'

'Yes.'

'I don't think it sounds as though I'm going to be much good to you. Eccles is a very respectable, sound solicitor who makes a large income, has a good many highly respectable clients, works for the landed gentry, professional classes and retired soldiers and sailors, generals and admirals and all that sort of thing. He's the acme of respectability. I should imagine from what you're talking about, that he was strictly within his lawful activities.'

'But you're—interested in him,' suggested Tommy.

'Yes, we're very interested in Mr James Eccles.' He sighed. 'We've been interested in him for at least six years. We haven't progressed very far.'

'Very interesting,' said Tommy. 'I'll ask you again. Who exactly *is* Mr Eccles?'

'You mean what do we suspect Eccles of? Well, to put it in a sentence, we suspect him of being one of the best organizing brains in criminal activity in this country.'

'Criminal activity?' Tommy looked surprised.

'Oh yes, yes. No cloak and dagger. No espionage, no counter-espionage. No, plain criminal activity. He is a man who has so far as we can discover never performed a criminal act in his life. He has never stolen anything, he's never forged anything, he's never converted funds, we can't get any kind of evidence against him. But all the same whenever there's a big planned organized robbery, there we find, somewhere in the background, Mr Eccles leading a blameless life.'

'Six years,' said Tommy thoughtfully.

'Possibly even longer than that. It took a little time, to get on to the pattern of things. Bank holdups, robberies of private jewels, all sorts of things where the big money was. They're all jobs that followed a certain pattern. You couldn't help feeling that the same mind had planned them. The people who directed them and who carried them out never had to do any planning at all. They went where they were told, they did what they were ordered, they never had to think. Somebody else was doing the thinking.'

'And what made you hit on Eccles?'

Ivor Smith shook his head thoughtfully. 'It would take too long to tell you. He's a man who has a lot of acquaintances, a lot of friends. There are people he plays golf with, there are people who service his car, there are firms of stockbrokers who act for him. There are companies doing a blameless business in which he is interested. The plan is getting clearer but his part in it hasn't got much clearer, except that he is very conspicuously absent on certain occasions. A big bank robbery cleverly planned (and no expense spared, mind you), consolidating the get-away and all the rest of it, and where's Mr Eccles when it happens? Monte Carlo or Zurich or possibly even fishing for salmon in Norway. You can be quite sure Mr Eccles is never within a hundred miles of where criminal activities are happening.'

'Yet you suspect him?'

'Oh yes. I'm quite sure in my own mind. But whether we'll ever catch him I don't know. The man who tunnelled through the floor of a bank, the man who knocked out the night watchman, the cashier who was in it from the beginning, the bank manager who supplied the information, none of them know Eccles, probably they've never even seen him. There's a long chain leading away—and no one seems to know more than just one link beyond themselves.'

'The good old plan of the cell?'

'More or less, yes, but there's some original thinking. Some day we'll get a chance. Somebody who oughtn't to know *anything*, will know *something*. Something silly and trivial, perhaps, but something that strangely enough may be evidence at last.'

'Is he married—got a family?'

'No, he has never taken risks like that. He lives alone with a housekeeper and a gardener and a butler-valet. He entertains in a mild and pleasant way, and I dare swear that every single person who's entered his house as his guest is beyond suspicion.'

'And nobody's getting rich?'

'That's a good point you've put your finger on, Thomas. Somebody *ought* to be getting rich. Somebody ought to be *seen* to be getting rich. But that part of it's very cleverly arranged. Big wins on race courses, investments in stocks and shares, all things which are natural, just chancy enough to make big money at, and all apparently genuine transactions. There's a lot of money stacked up abroad in different countries and different places. It's a great big, vast, money-making concern—and the money's always on the move—going from place to place.'

'Well,' said Tommy, 'good luck to you. I hope you get your man.'

'I think I shall, you know, some day. There might be a hope if one could jolt him out of his routine.'

'Jolt him with what?'

'Danger,' said Ivor. 'Make him feel he's in danger. Make him feel someone's on to him. Get him uneasy. If you once get a man uneasy, he may do something foolish. He may make a mistake. That's the way you get chaps, you know. Take the cleverest man there is, who can plan brilliantly and never put a foot wrong. Let some little thing rattle him and he'll make a mistake. So I'm hoping. Now let's hear your story. You might know something that would be useful.'

'Nothing to do with crime, I'm afraid—very small beer.'

'Well, let's hear about it.'

Tommy told his story without undue apologies for the triviality of it. Ivor, he knew, was not a man to despise triviality. Ivor, indeed, went straight to the point which had brought Tommy on his errand.

'And your wife's disappeared, you say?'

'It's not like her.'

'That's serious.'

'Serious to me all right.'

'So I can imagine. I only met your missus once. She's sharp.'

'If she goes after things she's like a terrier on a trail,' said Thomas.

'You've not been to the police?'

'No.'

'Why not?'

'Well, first because I can't believe that she's anything but all right. Tuppence is always all right. She just goes all out after any hare that shows itself. She mayn't have had time to communicate.'

'Mmm. I don't like it very much. She's looking for a house, you say? That just *might* be interesting because among various odds and ends that we followed, which incidentally have not led to much, are a kind of trail of house agents.'

'House agents?' Tommy looked surprised.

'Yes. Nice, ordinary, rather mediocre house agents in small provincial towns in different parts of England, but none of them so very far from London. Mr Eccles's firm does a lot of business with and for house agents. Sometimes he's the solicitor for the buyers and sometimes for the sellers, and he employs various house agencies, on behalf of clients. Sometimes we rather wondered why. None of it seems very profitable, you see—'

'But you think it might mean something or lead to something?'

'Well, if you remember the big London Southern Bank robbery some years ago, there was a house in the country—a lonely house. That was the thieves' rendezvous. They weren't very noticeable there, but that's where the stuff was brought and cached away. People in the neighbourhood began to have a few stories about them, and wonder who these people were who came and went at rather unusual hours. Different kinds of cars arriving in the middle of the night and going away again. People are curious about their neighbours in the country. Sure enough, the police raided the place, they got some of the loot, and they got three men, including one who was recognized and identified.'

'Well, didn't that lead you somewhere?'

'Not really. The men wouldn't talk, they were well defended and represented, they got long sentences in gaol and within a year and a half they were all out of the jug again. Very clever rescues.'

'I seem to remember reading about it. One man disappeared from a criminal court where he was brought up by two warders.'

'That's right. All very cleverly arranged and an enormous amount of money spent on the escape.

'But we think that whoever was responsible for the staff work realized he made a mistake in having one house for too long a time, so that the local people got interested. Somebody, perhaps, thought it would be a better idea to get subsidiaries living in, say, as many as *thirty* houses in *different places*. People come and take a house, mother and daughter, say, a widow, or a retired army man and his wife. Nice quiet people. They have a few repairs done to the house, get a local builder in and improve the plumbing, and perhaps some other firm down from London to decorate, and then after a year or a year and a half circumstances arise, and the occupiers sell the house and go off abroad to live. Something like that. All very natural and pleasant. During their tenancy that house has been used perhaps for rather unusual purposes! But no one suspects such a thing. Friends come to see them, not very often. Just occasionally. One night, perhaps, a kind of anniversary party for a middle-aged, or elderly couple; or a coming of age party. A lot of cars coming and going. Say there are five major robberies done within six months but each time the loot passes through, or is cached in, not just one of these houses, but five different houses in five different parts of the countryside. It's only a supposition as yet, my dear Tommy, but we're working on it. Let's say your old lady lets a picture of a certain house go out of her possession and supposing that's a *significant* house. And supposing that that's the house that your missus has recognized somewhere, and has gone dashing off to investigate. And supposing someone doesn't want that particular house investigated—It might tie up, you know.'

'It's very far-fetched.'

'Oh yes—I agree. But these times we live in are far-fetched times—In our particular world incredible things happen.'

Somewhat wearily Tommy alighted from his fourth taxi of the day and looked appraisingly at his surroundings. The taxi had deposited him in a small *cul-de-sac* which tucked itself coyly under one of the protuberances of Hampstead Heath. The *cul-de-sac* seemed to have been some artistic 'development'. Each house was wildly different from the house next to it. This particular one seemed to consist of a large studio with skylights in it, and attached to it (rather like a gumboil), on one side was what seemed to be a little cluster of three rooms. A ladder staircase painted bright green ran up the outside of the house. Tommy opened the small gate, went up a path and not seeing a bell applied himself to the knocker. Getting no response, he paused for a few moments and then started again with the knocker, a little louder this time.

The door opened so suddenly that he nearly fell backwards. A woman stood on the doorstep. At first sight Tommy's first impression was that this was one of the plainest women he had ever seen. She had a large expanse of flat, pancake-like face, two enormous eyes which seemed of impossibly different colours, one green and one brown, a noble forehead with a quantity of wild hair rising up from it in a kind of thicket. She wore a purple overall with blotches of clay on it, and Tommy noticed that the hand that held the door open was one of exceeding beauty of structure.

'Oh,' she said. Her voice was deep and rather attractive. 'What is it? I'm busy.'

'Mrs Boscowan?'

'Yes. What do you want?'

'My name's Beresford. I wondered if I might speak to you for a few moments.'

'I don't know. Really, must you? What is it—something about a picture?' Her eye had gone to what he held under his arm.

'Yes. It's something to do with one of your husband's pictures.'

'Do you want to sell it? I've got plenty of his pictures. I don't want to buy any more of them. Take it to one of these galleries or something. They're beginning to buy him now. You don't look as though you needed to sell pictures.'

'Oh no, I don't want to sell anything.'

Tommy felt extraordinary difficulty in talking to this particular woman. Her eyes, unmatching though they were, were very fine eyes and they were looking now over his shoulder down the street with an air of some peculiar interest at something in the far distance.

'Please,' said Tommy. 'I wish you would let me come in. It's so difficult to explain.'

'If you're a painter I don't want to talk to you,' said Mrs Boscowan. 'I find painters very boring always.'

'I'm not a painter.'

'Well, you don't look like one, certainly.' Her eyes raked him up and down. 'You look more like a civil servant,' she said disapprovingly.

'Can I come in, Mrs Boscowan?'

'I'm not sure. Wait.'

She shut the door rather abruptly. Tommy waited. After about four minutes had passed the door opened again.

'All right,' she said. 'You can come in.'

She led him through the doorway, up a narrow staircase and into the large studio. In a corner of it there was a figure and various implements standing by it. Hammers and chisels. There was also a clay head. The whole place looked as though it had recently been savaged by a gang of hooligans.

'There's never any room to sit up here,' said Mrs Boscowan.

She threw various things off a wooden stool and pushed it towards him.

'There. Sit down here and speak to me.'

'It's very kind of you to let me come in.'

'It is rather, but you looked so worried. You are worried, aren't you, about something?'

'Yes I am.'

'I thought so. What are you worried about?'

'My wife,' said Tommy, surprising himself by his answer.

'Oh, worried about your wife? Well, there's nothing unusual in that. Men are always worrying about their wives. What's the matter—has she gone off with someone or playing up?'

'No. Nothing like that.'

'Dying? Cancer?'

'No,' said Tommy. 'It's just that I don't know where she is.'

'And you think I might? Well, you'd better tell me her name and something about her if you think I can find her for you. I'm not sure, mind you,' said Mrs Boscowan, 'that I shall want to. I'm warning you.'

'Thank God,' said Tommy, 'you're more easy to talk to than I thought you were going to be.'

'What's the picture got to do with it? It is a picture, isn't it—must be, that shape.'

Tommy undid the wrappings.

'It's a picture signed by your husband,' said Tommy. 'I want you to tell me what you can about it.'

'I see. What exactly do you want to know?'

'When it was painted and where it is.'

Mrs Boscowan looked at him and for the first time there was a slight look of interest in her eyes.

'Well, that's not difficult,' she said. 'Yes, I can tell you all about it. It was painted about fifteen years ago—no, a good deal longer than that I should think. It's one of his fairly early ones. Twenty years ago, I should say.'

'You know where it is—the place I mean?'

'Oh yes, I can remember quite well. Nice picture. I always liked it. That's the little hump-backed bridge and the house and the name of the place is Sutton Chancellor. About seven or eight miles from Market Basing. The house itself is about a couple of miles from Sutton Chancellor. Pretty place. Secluded.'

She came up to the picture, bent down and peered at it closely.

'That's funny,' she said. 'Yes, that's very odd. I wonder now.'

Tommy did not pay much attention.

'What's the name of the house?' he asked.

'I can't really remember. It got renamed, you know. Several times. I don't know what there was about it. A couple of rather tragic things happened there, I think, then the next people who came along renamed it. Called the Canal House once, or Canal Side. Once it was called Bridge House then Meadowside—or Riverside was another name.'

'Who lived there—or who lives there now? Do you know?'

'Nobody I know. Man and a girl lived there when first I saw it. Used to come down for weekends. Not married, I think. The girl was a dancer. May have been an actress—no, I think she was a dancer. Ballet dancer. Rather beautiful but dumb. Simple, almost wanting. William was quite soft about her, I remember.'

'Did he paint her?'

'No. He didn't often paint people. He used to say sometimes he wanted to do a sketch of them, but he never did much about it. He was always silly over girls.'

'They were the people who were there when your husband was painting the house?'

'Yes, I think so. Part of the time anyway. They only came down weekends. Then there was some kind of a bust up. They had a row, I think, or he went away and left her or she went away and left him. I wasn't down there myself. I was working in Coventry then doing a group. After that I think there was just a governess in the house and the child. I don't know who the child was or where she came from but I suppose the governess was looking after her. Then I think something happened to the child. Either the governess took her away somewhere or perhaps she died. What do you want to know about the people who lived in the house twenty years ago? Seems to me idiotic.'

'I want to hear anything I can about that house,' said Tommy. 'You see, my wife went away to look for that house. She said she'd seen it out of a train somewhere.'

'Quite right,' said Mrs Boscowan, 'the railway line runs just the other side of the bridge. You can see the house very well from it, I expect.' Then she said, 'Why did she want to find that house?'

Tommy gave a much abridged explanation—she looked at him doubtfully.

'You haven't come out of a mental home or anything, have you?' said Mrs Boscowan. 'On parole or something, whatever they call it.'

'I suppose I must sound a little like that,' said Tommy, 'but it's quite simple really. My wife wanted to find out about this house and so she tried to take various train journeys to find out where it was she'd seen it. Well, I think she did find out. I think she went there to this place—something Chancellor?'

'Sutton Chancellor, yes. Very one-horse place it used to be. Of course it may be a big development or even one of these new dormitory towns by now.'

'It might be anything, I expect,' said Tommy. 'She telephoned she was coming back but she didn't come back. And I want to know what's happened to her. I think she went and started investigating that house and perhaps—perhaps she ran into danger.'

'What's dangerous about it?'

'I don't know,' said Tommy. 'Neither of us knew. I didn't even think there could be any danger about it, but my wife did.'

'E.S.P.?'

'Possibly. She's a little like that. She has hunches. You never heard of or knew a Mrs Lancaster twenty years ago or any time up to a month ago?'

'Mrs Lancaster? No, I don't think so. Sort of name one might remember, mightn't it be. No. What about Mrs Lancaster?'

'She was the woman who owned this picture. She gave it as a friendly gesture to an aunt of mine. Then she left an old people's home rather suddenly. Her relatives took her away. I've tried to trace her but it isn't easy.'

'Who's the one who's got the imagination, you or your wife? You seem to have thought up a lot of things and to be rather in a state, if I may say so.'

'Oh yes, you can say so,' said Tommy. 'Rather in a state and all about nothing at all. That's what you mean, isn't it? I suppose you're right too.'

'No,' said Mrs Boscowan. Her voice had altered slightly. 'I wouldn't say about nothing at all.'

Tommy looked at her inquiringly.

'There's one thing that's odd about that picture,' said Mrs Boscowan. 'Very odd. I remember it quite well, you know. I remember most of William's pictures although he painted such a lot of them.'

'Do you remember who it was sold to, if it was sold?'

'No, I don't remember that. Yes, I think it was sold. There was a whole batch of his paintings sold from one of his exhibitions. They ran back for about three or four years before this and a couple of years later than this. Quite a lot of them were sold. Nearly all of them. But I can't remember by now who it was sold to. That's asking too much.'

'I'm very grateful to you for all you have remembered.'

'You haven't asked me yet why I said there was something odd about the picture. This picture that you brought here.'

'You mean it isn't your husband's—somebody else painted it?'

'Oh no. That's the picture that William painted. "House by a Canal", I think he called it in the catalogue. But it isn't as it was. You see, there's something wrong with it.'

'What's wrong with it?'

Mrs Boscowan stretched out a clay-smeared finger and jabbed at a spot just below the bridge spanning the canal.

'There,' she said. 'You see? There's a boat tied up under the bridge, isn't there?'

'Yes,' said Tommy puzzled.

'Well, that boat wasn't there, not when I saw it last. William never painted that boat. When it was exhibited *there was no boat of any kind.*'

'You mean that somebody not your husband painted the boat in here afterwards?'

'Yes. Odd, isn't it? I wonder why. First of all I was surprised to see the boat there, a place where there wasn't any boat, then I can see quite well that it wasn't painted by William. *He* didn't put it in at any time. Somebody else did. I wonder who?'

She looked at Tommy.

'And I wonder why?'

Tommy had no solution to offer. He looked at Mrs Boscowan. His Aunt Ada would have called her a scatty woman but Tommy did not think of her in that light. She was vague, with an abrupt way of jumping from one subject to another. The things she said seemed to have very little relation to the last thing she had said a minute before. She was the sort of person, Tommy thought, who might know a great deal more than she chose to reveal. Had she loved her husband or been jealous of her husband or despised her husband? There was really no clue whatever in her manner, or indeed her words. But he had the feeling that that small painted boat tied up under the bridge had caused her uneasiness. She hadn't liked the boat being there. Suddenly he wondered if the statement she had made was true. Could she really remember from long years back whether Boscowan had painted a boat at the bridge or had not? It seemed really a very small and insignificant item. If it had been only a year ago when she had seen the picture last—but apparently it was a much longer time than that. And it had made Mrs Boscowan uneasy. He looked at her again and saw that she was looking at him. Her curious eyes resting on him not defiantly, but only thoughtfully. Very, very thoughtfully.

'What are you going to do now?' she said.

That at least was easy. Tommy had no difficulty in knowing what he was going to do now.

'I shall go home tonight—see if there is any news of my wife—any word from her. If not, tomorrow I shall go to this place,' he said. 'Sutton Chancellor. I hope that I may find my wife there.'

'It would depend,' said Mrs Boscowan.

'Depend on what?' said Tommy sharply.

Mrs Boscowan frowned. Then she murmured, seemingly to herself, 'I wonder where she is?'

'You wonder where who is?'

Mrs Boscowan had turned her glance away from him. Now her eyes swept back.

'Oh,' she said. 'I meant your wife.' Then she said, 'I hope she is all right.'

'Why shouldn't she be all right? Tell me, Mrs Boscowan, is there something wrong with that place—with Sutton Chancellor?'

'With Sutton Chancellor? With the place?' She reflected. 'No, I don't think so. Not with the *place*.'

'I suppose I meant the house,' said Tommy. 'This house by the canal. Not Sutton Chancellor village.'

'Oh, the house,' said Mrs Boscowan. 'It was a good house really. Meant for lovers, you know.'

'Did lovers live there?'

'Sometimes. Not often enough really. If a house is built for lovers, it ought to be lived in by lovers.'

'Not put to some other use by someone.'

'You're pretty quick,' said Mrs Boscowan. 'You saw what I meant, didn't you? You mustn't put a house that was meant for one thing to the wrong use. It won't like it if you do.'

'Do you know anything about the people who have lived there of late years?'

She shook her head. 'No. No. I don't know anything about the house at all. It was never important to me, you see.'

'But you're thinking of something—no, someone?'

'Yes,' said Mrs Boscowan. 'I suppose you're right about that. I was thinking of—someone.'

'Can't you tell me about the person you were thinking of?'

'There's really nothing to say,' said Mrs Boscowan. 'Sometimes, you know, one just wonders where a person is. What's happened to them or how they might have—developed. There's a sort of feeling—' She waved her hands— 'Would you like a kipper?' she said unexpectedly.

'A kipper?' Tommy was startled.

'Well, I happen to have two or three kippers here. I thought perhaps you ought to have something to eat before you catch a train. Waterloo is the station,' she said. 'For Sutton Chancellor, I mean. You used to have to change at Market Basing. I expect you still do.'

It was a dismissal. He accepted it.

CHAPTER 13

Albert on Clues

Tuppence blinked her eyes. Vision seemed rather dim. She tried to lift her head from the pillow but winced as a sharp pain ran through it, and let it drop again on to the pillow. She closed her eyes. Presently she opened them again and blinked once more.

With a feeling of achievement she recognized her surroundings. 'I'm in a hospital ward,' thought Tuppence. Satisfied with her mental progress so far, she attempted no more brainy deduction. She was in a hospital ward and her head ached. Why it ached, why she was in a hospital ward, she was not quite sure. 'Accident?' thought Tuppence.

There were nurses moving around beds. That seemed natural enough. She closed her eyes and tried a little cautious thought. A faint vision of an elderly figure in clerical dress, passed across a mental screen. 'Father?' said Tuppence doubtfully. 'Is it Father?' She couldn't really remember. She supposed so.

'But what am I doing being ill in a hospital?' thought Tuppence. 'I mean, I nurse in a hospital, so I ought to be in uniform. V.A.D. uniform. Oh dear,' said Tuppence.

Presently a nurse materialized near her bed.

'Feeling better now, dear?' said the nurse with a kind of false cheerfulness. 'That's nice, isn't it?'

Tuppence wasn't quite sure whether it *was* nice. The nurse said something about a nice cup of tea.

'I seem to be a patient,' said Tuppence rather disapprovingly to herself. She lay still, resurrecting in her own mind various detached thoughts and words.

'Soldiers,' said Tuppence. 'V.A.D.s. That's it, of course. I'm a V.A.D.'

The nurse brought her some tea in a kind of feeding cup and supported her whilst she sipped it. The pain went through her head again. 'A V.A.D., that's what I am,' said Tuppence aloud.

The nurse looked at her in an uncomprehending fashion.

'My head hurts,' said Tuppence, adding a statement of fact.

'It'll be better soon,' said the nurse.

She removed the feeding cup, reporting to a sister as she passed along. 'Number 14's awake. She's a bit wonky, though, I think.'

'Did she say anything?'

'Said she was a V.I.P.,' said the nurse.

The ward sister gave a small snort indicating that that was how she felt towards unimportant patients who reported themselves to be V.I.P.s.

'We shall see about that,' said the sister. 'Hurry up, Nurse, don't be all day with that feeding cup.'

Tuppence remained half drowsy on her pillows. She had not yet got beyond the stage of allowing thoughts to flit through her mind in a rather disorganized procession.

There was somebody who ought to be here, she felt, somebody she knew quite well. There was something very strange about this hospital. It wasn't the hospital she remembered. It wasn't the one she had nursed in. 'All soldiers, that was,' said Tuppence to herself. 'The surgical ward, I was on A and B rows.' She opened her eyelids and took another look round. She decided it was a hospital she had never seen before and that it had nothing to do with the nursing of surgical cases, military or otherwise.

'I wonder where this is,' said Tuppence. 'What place?' She tried to think of the name of some place. The only places she could think of were London and Southampton.

The ward sister now made her appearance at the bedside.

'Feeling a little better, I hope,' she said.

'I'm all right,' said Tuppence. 'What's the matter with me?'

'You hurt your head. I expect you find it rather painful, don't you?'

'It aches,' said Tuppence. 'Where am I?'

'Market Basing Royal Hospital.'

Tuppence considered this information. It meant nothing to her at all.

'An old clergyman,' she said.

'I beg your pardon?'

'Nothing particular. I—'

'We haven't been able to write your name on your diet sheet yet,' said the ward sister.

She held her Biro pen at the ready and looked inquiringly at Tuppence.

'My name?'

'Yes,' said the sister. 'For the records,' she added helpfully.

Tuppence was silent, considering. Her name. What was her name? 'How silly,' said Tuppence to herself, 'I seem to have forgotten it. And yet I must have a name.' Suddenly a faint feeling of relief came to her. The elderly clergyman's face flashed suddenly across her mind and she said with decision,

'Of course. Prudence.'

'P-r-u-d-e-n-c-e?'

'That's right,' said Tuppence.

'That's your Christian name. The surname?'

'Cowley. C-o-w-l-e-y.'

'Glad to get that straight,' said the sister, and moved away again with the air of one whose records were no longer worrying her.

Tuppence felt faintly pleased with herself. Prudence Cowley. Prudence Cowley in the V.A.D. and her father was a clergyman at—at something vicarage and it was wartime and... 'Funny,' said Tuppence to herself, 'I seem to be getting this all wrong. It seems to me it all happened a long time ago.' She murmured to herself, 'Was it your poor child?' She wondered. Was it she who had just said that or was it somebody else said it to her?

The sister was back again.

'Your address,' she said, 'Miss—Miss Cowley, or is it Mrs Cowley? Did you ask about a child?'

'Was it your poor child? Did somebody say that to me or am I saying it to them?'

'I think I should sleep a little if I were you now, dear,' said the sister.

She went away and took the information she had obtained to the proper place.

'She seems to have come to herself, Doctor,' she remarked, 'and she says her name is Prudence Cowley. But she doesn't seem to remember her address. She said something about a child.'

'Oh well,' said the doctor, with his usual casual air, 'we'll give her another twenty-four hours or so. She's coming round from the concussion quite nicely.'

Tommy fumbled with his latchkey. Before he could use it the door came open and Albert stood in the open aperture.

'Well,' said Tommy, 'is she back?'

Albert slowly shook his head.

'No word from her, no telephone message, no letters waiting—no telegrams?'

'Nothing I tell you, sir. Nothing whatever. And nothing from anyone else either. They're lying low—but they've got her. That's what I think. They've got her.'

'What the devil do you mean—they've got her?' said Tommy. 'The things you read. Who've got her?'

'Well, you know what I mean. The gang.'

'What gang?'

'One of those gangs with flick knives maybe. Or an international one.'

'Stop talking rubbish,' said Tommy. 'D'you know what I think?'

Albert looked inquiringly at him.

'I think it's extremely inconsiderate of her not to send us word of some kind,' said Tommy.

'Oh,' said Albert, 'well, I see what you mean. I suppose you *could* put it that way. If it makes you happier,' he added rather unfortunately. He removed the parcel from Tommy's arms. 'I see you brought that picture back,' he said.

'Yes, I've brought the bloody picture back,' said Tommy. 'A fat lot of use it's been.'

'You haven't learnt anything from it?'

'That's not quite true,' said Tommy. 'I *have* learnt something from it but whether what I've learnt is going to be any use to me I don't know.' He added, 'Dr Murray didn't ring up, I suppose, or Miss Packard from Sunny Ridge Nursing Home? Nothing like that?'

'Nobody's rung up except the greengrocer to say he's got some nice aubergines. He knows the missus is fond of aubergines. He always lets her know. But I told him she wasn't available just now.' He added, 'I've got a chicken for your dinner.'

'It's extraordinary that you can never think of anything but chickens,' said Tommy, unkindly.

'It's what they call a *poussin* this time,' said Albert. 'Skinny,' he added.

'It'll do,' said Tommy.

The telephone rang. Tommy was out of his seat and had rushed to it in a moment.

'Hallo... hallo?'

A faint and far-away voice spoke. 'Mr Thomas Beresford? Can you accept a personal call from Invergashly?'

'Yes.'

'Hold the line, please.'

Tommy waited. His excitement was calming down. He had to wait some time. Then a voice he knew, crisp and capable, sounded. The voice of his daughter.

'Hallo, is that you, Pop?'

'Deborah!'

'Yes. Why are you sounding so breathless, have you been running?'

Daughters, Tommy thought, were always critical.

'I wheeze a bit in my old age,' he said. 'How are you, Deborah?'

'Oh, I'm all right. Look here, Dad, I saw something in the paper. Perhaps you've seen it too. I wondered about it. Something about someone who had had an accident and was in hospital.'

'Well? I don't think I saw anything of that kind. I mean, not to notice it in any way. Why?'

'Well it—it didn't sound too bad. I supposed it was a car accident or something like that. It mentioned that the woman, whoever it was—an elderly woman—gave her name as Prudence Cowley but they were unable to find her address.'

'Prudence Cowley? You mean—'

'Well yes. I only—well—I only wondered. That *is* Mother's name, isn't it? I mean it was her name.'

'Of course.'

'I always forget about the Prudence. I mean we've never thought of her as Prudence, you and I, or Derek either.'

'No,' said Tommy. 'No. It's not the kind of Christian name one would associate much with your mother.'

'No, I know it isn't. I just thought it was—rather odd. You don't think it might be some relation of hers?'

'I suppose it might be. Where was this?'

'Hospital at Market Basing, I think it said. They wanted to know more about her, I gather. I just wondered—well, I know it's awfully silly, there must be quantities of people called Cowley and quantities of people called Prudence. But I thought I'd just ring up and find out. Make sure, I mean, that Mother was at home and all right and all that.'

'I see,' said Tommy. 'Yes, I see.'

'Well, go on, Pop, is she at home?'

'No,' said Tommy, 'she isn't at home and I don't know either whether she is all right or not.'

'What do you mean?' said Deborah. 'What's Mother been doing? I suppose you've been up in London with that hush-hush utterly secret idiotic survival from past days, jawing with all the old boys.'

'You're quite right,' said Tommy. 'I got back from that yesterday evening.'

'And you found Mother away—or did you know she was away? Come on, Pop, tell me about it. You're worried. I know when you're worried well enough. What's Mother been doing? She's been up to something, hasn't she? I wish at her age she'd learn to sit quiet and not do things.'

'She's been worried,' said Tommy. 'Worried about something that happened in connection with your Great-aunt Ada's death.'

'What sort of thing?'

'Well, something that one of the patients at the nursing home said to her. She got worried about this old lady. She started talking a good deal and your mother was worried about some of the things she said. And so, when we went to look through Aunt Ada's things we suggested talking to this old lady and it seems she'd left rather suddenly.'

'Well, that seems quite natural, doesn't it?'

'Some of her relatives came and fetched her away.'

'It still seems quite natural,' said Deborah. 'Why did Mother get the wind up?'

'She got it into her head,' said Tommy, 'that something might have happened to this old lady.'

'I see.'

'Not to put too fine a point on it, as the saying goes, she seems to have disappeared. All in quite a natural way. I mean, vouched for by lawyers and banks and all that. Only—we haven't been able to find out where she is.'

'You mean Mother's gone off to look for her somewhere?'

'Yes. And she didn't come back when she said she was coming back, two days ago.'

'And haven't you heard from her?'

'No.'

'I wish to goodness you could look after Mother properly,' said Deborah, severely.

'None of us have ever been able to look after her properly,' said Tommy. 'Not you either, Deborah, if it comes to that. It's the same way she went off in the war and did a lot of things that she'd no business to be doing.'

'But it's different now. I mean, she's quite *old*. She ought to sit at home and take care of herself. I suppose she's been getting bored. That's at the bottom of it all.'

'Market Basing Hospital, did you say?' said Tommy.

'Melfordshire. It's about an hour or an hour and a half from London, I think, by train.'

'That's it,' said Tommy. 'And there's a village near Market Basing called Sutton Chancellor.'

'What's that got to do with it?' said Deborah.

'It's too long to go into now,' said Tommy. 'It has to do with a picture painted of a house near a bridge by a canal.'

'I don't think I can hear you very well,' said Deborah. 'What are you talking about?'

'Never mind,' said Tommy. 'I'm going to ring up Market Basing Hospital and find out a few things. I've a feeling that it's your mother, all right. People, if they've had concussion, you know, often remember things first that happened when they were a child, and only get slowly to the present. She's gone back to her maiden name. She may have been in a car accident, but I shouldn't be surprised if somebody hadn't given her a conk on the head. It's the sort of thing that happens to your mother. She gets into things. I'll let you know what I find out.'

Forty minutes later, Tommy Beresford glanced at his wrist watch and breathed a sigh of utter weariness, as he replaced the receiver with a final clang on the telephone rest. Albert made an appearance.

'What about your dinner, sir?' he demanded. 'You haven't eaten a thing, and I'm sorry to say I forgot about that chicken—Burnt to a cinder.'

'I don't want anything to eat,' said Tommy. 'What I want is a drink. Bring me a double whisky.'

'Coming, sir,' said Albert.

A few moments later he brought the required refreshment to where Tommy had slumped down in the worn but comfortable chair reserved for his special use.

'And now, I suppose,' said Tommy, 'you want to hear everything.'

'Matter of fact, sir,' said Albert in a slightly apologetic tone, 'I know most of it. You see, seeing as it was a question of the missus and all that, I took the liberty of lifting up the extension in the bedroom. I didn't think you'd mind, sir, not as it was the missus.'

'I don't blame you,' said Tommy. 'Actually, I'm grateful to you. If I had to start explaining—'

'Got on to everyone, didn't you? The hospital and the doctor and the matron.'

'No need to go over it all again,' said Tommy.

'Market Basing Hospital,' said Albert. 'Never breathed a word of that, she didn't. Never left it behind as an address or anything like that.'

'She didn't intend it to be her address,' said Tommy. 'As far as I can make out she was probably coshed on the head in an out of the way spot somewhere. Someone took her along in a car and dumped her at the side of the road somewhere, to be picked up as an ordinary hit and run.' He added, 'Call me at six-thirty tomorrow morning. I want to get an early start.'

'I'm sorry about your chicken getting burnt up again in the oven. I only put it in to keep warm and forgot about it.'

'Never mind chickens,' said Tommy. 'I've always thought they were very silly birds, running under cars and clucking about. Bury the corpse tomorrow morning and give it a good funeral.'

'She's not at death's door or anything, is she, sir?' asked Albert.

'Subdue your melodramatic fancies,' said Tommy. 'If you'd done any proper listening you'd have heard that she's come nicely to herself again, knows who she is or was and where she is and they've sworn to keep her there waiting for me until I arrive to take charge of her again. On no account is she to be allowed to slip out by herself and go off again doing some more tomfool detective work.'

'Talking of detective work,' said Albert, and hesitated with a slight cough.

'I don't particularly want to talk about it,' said Tommy. 'Forget it, Albert. Teach yourself bookkeeping or window-box gardening or something.'

'Well, I was just thinking—I mean, as a matter of clues—'

'Well, what about clues?'

'I've been thinking.'

'That's where all the trouble in life comes from. Thinking.'

'Clues,' said Albert again. 'That picture, for instance. That's a clue, isn't it?'

Tommy observed that Albert had hung the picture of the house by the canal up on the wall.

'If that picture's a clue to something, what do you think it's a clue to?' He blushed slightly at the inelegancy of the phrase he had just coined. 'I mean—what's it all about? It ought to mean something. What I was thinking of,' said Albert, 'if you'll excuse me mentioning it—'

'Go ahead, Albert.'

'What I was thinking of was that desk.'

'Desk?'

'Yes. The one that came by the furniture removers with the little table and the two chairs and the other things. Family property, it was, you said?'

'It belonged to my Aunt Ada,' said Tommy.

'Well, that's what I meant, sir. That's the sort of place where you find clues. In old desks. Antiques.'

'Possibly,' said Tommy.

'It wasn't my business, I know, and I suppose I really oughtn't to have gone messing about with it, but while you were away, sir, I couldn't help it. I had to go and have a look.'

'What—a look into the desk?'

'Yes, just to see if there might be a clue there. You see, desks like that, they have secret drawers.'

'Possibly,' said Tommy.

'Well, there you are. There might be a clue there, hidden. Shut up in the secret drawer.'

'It's an agreeable idea,' said Tommy. 'But there's no reason as far as I know for my Aunt Ada to hide things away in secret drawers.'

'You never know with old ladies. They like tucking things away. Like jackdaws, they are, or magpies. I forget which it is. There might be a secret will in it or something written in invisible ink or a treasure. Where you'd find some hidden treasure.'

'I'm sorry, Albert, but I think I'm going to have to disappoint you. I'm pretty sure there's nothing of that kind in that nice old family desk which once belonged to my Uncle William. Another man who turned crusty in his old age besides being stone deaf and having a very bad temper.'

'What I thought is,' said Albert, 'it wouldn't do any harm to look, would it?' He added virtuously, 'It needed cleaning out anyway. You know how old things are with old ladies. They don't turn them out much—not when they're rheumatic and find it hard to get about.'

Tommy paused for a moment or two. He remembered that Tuppence and he had looked quickly through the drawers of the desk, had put their contents such as they were in two large envelopes and removed a few skeins of wool, two cardigans, a black velvet stole and three fine pillow-cases from the lower drawers which they had placed with other clothing and odds and ends for disposal. They had also looked through such papers as there had been in the envelopes after their return home with them. There had been nothing there of particular interest.

'We looked through the contents, Albert,' he said. 'Spent a couple of evenings really. One or two quite interesting old letters, some recipes for boiling ham, some other recipes for preserving fruit, some ration books and coupons and things dating back to the war. There was nothing of any interest.'

'Oh, that,' said Albert, 'but that's just papers and things, as you might say. Just ordinary go and come what everybody gets holed up in desks and drawers and things. I mean real secret stuff. When I was a boy, you know, I did six months with an antique dealer—helping him fake up things as often as not. But I got to know about secret drawers that way. They usually run to the same pattern. Three or four well-known kinds and they vary it now and then. Don't you think, sir, you ought to have a look? I mean, I didn't like to go it meself with you not here. I would have been presuming.' He looked at Tommy with the air of a pleading dog.

'Come on, Albert,' said Tommy, giving in. 'Let's go and presume.'

'A very nice piece of furniture,' thought Tommy, as he stood by Albert's side, surveying this specimen of his inheritance from Aunt Ada. 'Nicely kept, beautiful old polish on it, showing the good workmanship and craftsmanship of days gone by.'

'Well, Albert,' he said, 'go ahead. This is your bit of fun. But don't go and strain it.'

'Oh, I was ever so careful. I didn't crack it, or slip knives into it or anything like that. First of all we let down the front and put it on these two slab things that pull out. That's right, you see, the flap comes down this way and that's where the old lady used to sit. Nice little mother-of-pearl blotting case your Aunt Ada had. It was in the left-hand drawer.'

'There are these two things,' said Tommy.

He drew out two delicate pilastered shallow vertical drawers.

'Oh, them, sir. You can push papers in them, but there's nothing really secret about them. The most usual place is to open the little middle cupboard—and then at the bottom of it usually there's a little depression and you slide the bottom out and there's a space. But there's other ways and places. This desk is the kind that has a kind of well underneath.'

'That's not very secret either, is it? You just slide back a panel—'

'The point is, it looks as though you'd found all there was to find. You push back the panel, there's the cavity and you can put a good many things in there that you want to keep a bit from being pawed over and all that. But that's not all, as you might say. Because you see, here there's a little piece of wood in front, like a little ledge. And you can pull that up, you see.'

'Yes,' said Tommy, 'yes, I can see that. You pull that up.'

'And you've got a secret cavity here, just behind the middle lock.'

'But there's nothing in it.'

'No,' said Albert, 'it looks disappointing. But if you slip your hand into that cavity and you wiggle it along either to the left or the right, there are two little thin drawers, one each side. There's a little semi-circle cut out of the top, and you can hook your finger over that—and pull gently towards you—' During these remarks Albert seemed to be getting his wrist in what was almost a contortionist position. 'Sometimes they stick a little. Wait—wait—here she comes.'

Albert's hooked forefinger drew something towards him from inside. He clawed it gently forward until the narrow small drawer showed in the opening. He hooked it out and laid it before Tommy, with the air of a dog bringing his bone to his master.

'Now wait a minute, sir. There's something in here, something wrapped up in a long thin envelope. Now we'll do the other side.'

He changed hands and resumed his contortionist clawings. Presently a second drawer was brought to light and was laid beside the first one.

'There's something in here, too,' said Albert. 'Another sealed-up envelope that someone's hidden here one time or another. I've not tried to open either of them—I wouldn't do such a thing.' His voice was virtuous in the extreme. 'I left that to you—But what I say is—they may be *clues*—'

Together he and Tommy extracted the contents of the dusty drawers. Tommy took out first a sealed envelope rolled up lengthways with an elastic band round it. The elastic band parted as soon as it was touched.

'Looks valuable,' said Albert.

Tommy glanced at the envelope. It bore the superscription 'Confidential'.

'There you are,' said Albert. '"Confidential". It's a clue.'

Tommy extracted the contents of the envelope. In a faded handwriting, and very scratchy handwriting at that, there was a half-sheet of notepaper. Tommy turned it this way and that and Albert leaned over his shoulder, breathing heavily.

'Mrs MacDonald's recipe for Salmon Cream,' Tommy read. 'Given to me as a special favour. Take 2 pounds of middle cut of salmon, 1 pint of Jersey cream, a wine-glass of brandy and a fresh cucumber.' He broke off. 'I'm sorry, Albert, it's a clue which will lead us to good cookery, no doubt.'

Albert uttered sounds indicative of disgust and disappointment.

'Never mind,' said Tommy. 'Here's another one to try.'

The next sealed envelope did not appear to be one of quite such antiquity. It had two pale grey wax seals affixed to it, each bearing a representation of a wild rose.

'Pretty,' said Tommy, 'rather fanciful for Aunt Ada. How to cook a beef steak pie, I expect.'

Tommy ripped open the envelope. He raised his eyebrows. Ten carefully folded five-pound notes fell out.

'Nice thin ones,' said Tommy. 'They're the old ones. You know, the kind we used to have in the war. Decent paper. Probably aren't legal tender nowadays.'

'Money!' said Albert. 'What she want all that money for?'

'Oh, that's an old lady's nest egg,' said Tommy. 'Aunt Ada always had a nest egg. Years ago she told me that every woman should always have fifty pounds in five-pound notes with her in case of what she called emergencies.'

'Well, I suppose it'll still come in handy,' said Albert.

'I don't suppose they're absolutely obsolete. I think you can make some arrangement to change them at a bank.'

'There's another one still,' said Albert. 'The one from the other drawer—'

The next was bulkier. There seemed to be more inside it and it had three large important-looking red seals. On the outside was written in the same spiky hand 'In the event of my death, this envelope should be sent unopened to my solicitor, Mr Rockbury of Rockbury & Tomkins, or to my nephew Thomas Beresford. Not to be opened by any unauthorized person.'

There were several sheets of closely written paper. The handwriting was bad, very spiky and here and there somewhat illegible. Tommy read it aloud with some difficulty.

> *'I, Ada Maria Fanshawe, am writing down here certain matters which have come to my knowledge and which have been told me by people who are residing in this nursing home called Sunny Ridge. I cannot vouch for any of this information being correct but there seems to be some reason to believe that suspicious—possibly criminal—activities are taking place here or have taken place here. Elizabeth Moody, a foolish woman, but not I think untruthful, declares that she has recognized here a well-known criminal. There may be a poisoner at work among us. I myself prefer to keep an open mind, but I shall remain watchful. I propose to write down here any facts that come to my knowledge. The whole thing may be a mare's nest. Either my solicitor or my nephew Thomas Beresford, is asked to make full investigation.'*

'There,' said Albert triumphantly—'Told you so! It's a CLUE!'

BOOK 4

Here is a Church and here is the Steeple Open the Doors and there are the People

CHAPTER 14

Exercise in Thinking

'I suppose what we ought to do is think,' said Tuppence.

After a glad reunion in the hospital, Tuppence had eventually been honourably discharged. The faithful pair were now comparing notes together in the sitting-room of the best suite in The Lamb and Flag at Market Basing.

'You leave thinking alone,' said Tommy. 'You know what that doctor told you before he let you go. No worries, no mental exertion, very little physical activity—take everything easy.'

'What else am I doing now?' demanded Tuppence. 'I've got my feet up, haven't I, and my head on two cushions? And as for thinking, thinking isn't necessarily mental exertion. I'm not doing mathematics, or studying economics, or adding up the household accounts. Thinking is just resting comfortably, and leaving one's mind open in case something interesting or important should just come floating in. Anyway, wouldn't you rather I did a little thinking with my feet up and my head on cushions, rather than go in for action again?'

'I certainly don't want you going in for action again,' said Tommy. 'That's *out*. You understand? Physically, Tuppence, you will remain quiescent. If possible, I shan't let you out of my sight because I don't trust you.'

'All right,' said Tuppence. 'Lecture ends. Now let's think. Think together. Pay no attention to what doctors have said to you. If you knew as much as I do about doctors—'

'Never mind about the doctors,' said Tommy, 'you do as *I* tell you.'

'All right. I've no wish at present for physical activity, I assure you. The point is that we've got to compare notes. We've got hold of a lot of things. It's as bad as a village jumble sale.'

'What do you mean by things?'

'Well, facts. All sorts of facts. Far too many facts. And not only facts—Hearsay, suggestions, legends, gossip. The whole thing is like a bran tub with different kinds of parcels wrapped up and shoved down in the sawdust.'

'Sawdust is right,' said Tommy.

'I don't quite know whether you're being insulting or modest,' said Tuppence. 'Anyway, you do agree with me, don't you? We've got far too *much* of everything. There are wrong things and right things, and important things and unimportant things and they're all mixed up together. We don't know where to start.'

'I do,' said Tommy.

'All right,' said Tuppence. 'Where are you starting?'

'I'm starting with your being coshed on the head,' said Tommy.

Tuppence considered a moment. 'I don't see really that that's a starting point. I mean, it's the last thing that happened, not the first.'

'It's the first in my mind,' said Tommy. 'I won't have people coshing my wife. And it's a *real* point to start from. It's not imagination. It's a *real* thing that *really* happened.'

'I couldn't agree with you more,' said Tuppence. 'It really happened and it happened to me, and I'm not forgetting it. I've been thinking about it—Since I regained the power of thought, that is.'

'Have you any idea as to who did it?'

'Unfortunately, no. I was bending down over a gravestone and whoosh!'

'Who could it have been?'

'I suppose it must have been somebody in Sutton Chancellor. And yet that seems so unlikely. I've hardly spoken to anyone.'

'The vicar?'

'It couldn't have been the vicar,' said Tuppence. 'First because he's a nice old boy. And secondly because he wouldn't have been nearly strong enough. And thirdly because he's got very asthmatic breathing. He couldn't possibly have crept up behind me without my hearing him.'

'Then if you count the vicar out—'

'Don't you?'

'Well,' said Tommy, 'yes, I do. As you know, I've been to see him and talked to him. He's been a vicar here for years and everyone knows him. I suppose a fiend incarnate *could* put on a show of being a kindly vicar, but not for more than about a week or so at the outside, I'd say. Not for about ten or twelve years.'

'Well, then,' said Tuppence, 'the next suspect would be Miss Bligh. Nellie Bligh. Though heaven knows why. She can't have thought I was trying to steal a tombstone.'

'Do you feel it might have been her?'

'Well, I don't really. Of course, she's *competent*. If she wanted to follow me and see what I was doing, and conk me, she'd make a success of it. And like the vicar, she was there—on the spot—She was in Sutton Chancellor, popping in and out of her house to do this and that, and she could have caught sight of me in the churchyard, come up behind me on tiptoe out of curiosity, seen me examining a grave, objected to my doing so for some particular reason, and hit me with one of the church metal flower vases or anything else handy. But don't ask me *why*. There seems no possible reason.'

'Who next, Tuppence? Mrs Cockerell, if that's her name?'

'Mrs Copleigh,' said Tuppence. 'No, it wouldn't be Mrs Copleigh.'

'Now why are you so sure of that? She lives in Sutton Chancellor, she could have seen you go out of the house and she could have followed you.'

'Oh yes, yes, but she talks too much,' said Tuppence.

'I don't see where talking too much comes into it.'

'If you'd listened to her a whole evening as I did,' said Tuppence, 'you'd realize that anyone who talks as much as she does, non-stop in a constant flow, could not possibly be a woman of action as well! She couldn't have come up anywhere near me without talking at the top of her voice as she came.'

Tommy considered this.

'All right,' he said. 'You have good judgement in that kind of thing, Tuppence. Wash out Mrs Copleigh. Who else is there?'

'Amos Perry,' said Tuppence. 'That's the man who lives at the Canal House. (I have to call it the Canal House because it's got so many other odd names. And it was called that originally.) The husband of the friendly witch. There's something a bit queer about him. He's a bit simple minded and he's a big powerful man, and he could cosh anyone on the head if he wanted to, and I even think it's possible in certain circumstances he might want to—though I don't exactly know why he should want to cosh *me*. He's a better possibility really than Miss Bligh who seems to me just one of those tiresome, efficient women who go about running parishes and poking their noses into things. Not at all the type who would get up to the point of physical attack, except for some wildly emotional reason.' She added, with a slight shiver, 'You know, I felt frightened of Amos Perry the first time I saw him. He was showing me his garden. I felt suddenly that I—well, that I wouldn't like to get on the wrong side of him—or meet him in a dark road at night. I felt he was a man that wouldn't often want to be violent but who could be violent if something took him that way.'

'All right,' said Tommy. 'Amos Perry. Number one.'

'And there's his wife,' said Tuppence slowly. 'The friendly witch. She was nice and I liked her—I don't want it to be her—I don't think it *was* her, but she's mixed up in things, I think... Things that have to do with that house. That's another point, you see, Tommy—We don't know what the important thing is in all this—I've begun to wonder whether everything doesn't circulate round that *house*—whether the *house* isn't the central point. The picture—That picture does mean something, doesn't it, Tommy? It must, I think.'

'Yes,' said Tommy, 'I think it must.'

'I came here trying to find Mrs Lancaster—but nobody here seems to have heard of her. I've been wondering whether I got things the wrong way round—that Mrs Lancaster was in danger (because I'm still sure of that) *because she owned that picture*. I don't think *she* was ever in Sutton Chancellor—but she was either given, or she bought, a picture of a house here. And that picture *means* something—is in some way a menace to someone.'

'Mrs Cocoa—Mrs Moody—told Aunt Ada that she recognized someone at Sunny Ridge—someone connected with "criminal activities". I think the criminal activities are connected with the picture and with the house by the canal, and a child who perhaps was killed there.'

'Aunt Ada admired Mrs Lancaster's picture—and Mrs Lancaster gave it to her—and perhaps she talked about it—where she got it, or who had given it to her, and where the house was—'

'Mrs Moody was bumped off because she definitely recognized someone who had been "connected with criminal activities".'

'Tell me again about your conversation with Dr Murray,' said Tuppence. 'After telling you about Mrs Cocoa, he went on to talk about certain types of killers, giving examples of real life cases. One was a woman who ran a nursing home for elderly patients—I remember reading about it vaguely, though I can't remember the woman's name. But the idea was that they made over what money they had to her, and then they lived there until they died, well fed and looked after, and without any money worries. And they *were* very happy—only they usually died well within a year—quite peacefully in their sleep. And at last people began to notice. She was tried and convicted of murder—But had no conscience pangs and protested that what she had done was really a kindness to the old dears.'

'Yes. That's right,' said Tommy. 'I can't remember the name of the woman now.'

'Well, never mind about that,' said Tuppence. 'And then he cited another case. A case of a woman, a domestic worker or a cook or a housekeeper. She used to go into service into different families. Sometimes nothing happened, I believe, and sometimes it was a kind of mass poisoning. Food poisoning, it was supposed to be. All with quite reasonable symptoms. Some people recovering.'

'She used to prepare sandwiches,' said Tommy, 'and make them up into packets and send them out for picnics with them. She was very nice and very devoted and she used to get, if it was a mass poisoning, some of the symptoms and signs herself. Probably exaggerating their effect. Then she'd go away after that and she'd take another place, in quite a different part of England. It went on for some years.'

'That's right, yes. Nobody, I believe, has ever been able to understand *why* she did it. Did she get a sort of addiction for it—a sort of habit of it? Was it fun for her? Nobody really ever knew. She never seems to have had any personal malice for any of the people whose deaths she seems to have caused. Bit wrong in the top storey?'

'Yes. I think she must have been, though I suppose one of the trick cyclists would probably do a great deal of analysis and find out it had all something to do with a canary of a family she'd known years and years ago as a child who had given her a shock or upset her or something. But anyway, that's the sort of thing it was.'

'The third one was queerer still,' said Tommy. 'A French woman. A woman who'd suffered terribly from the loss of her husband and her child. She was brokenhearted and she was an angel of mercy.'

'That's right,' said Tuppence, 'I remember. They called her the angel of whatever the village was. *Givon* or something like that. She went to all the neighbours and nursed them when they were ill. Particularly she used to go to children when they were ill. She nursed them devotedly. But sooner or later, after apparently a slight recovery, they grew much worse and died. She spent hours crying and went to the funeral crying and everybody said they wouldn't know what they'd have done without the angel who'd nursed their darlings and done everything she could.'

'Why do you want to go over all this again, Tuppence?'

'Because I wondered if Dr Murray had a reason for mentioning them.'

'You mean he connected—'

'I think he connected up three classical cases that are well known, and tried them on, as it were, like a glove, to see if they fitted anyone at Sunny Ridge. I think in a way any of them might have fitted. Miss Packard would fit in with the first one. The efficient matron of a Home.'

'You really have got your knife into that woman. I always liked her.'

'I daresay people *have* liked murderers,' said Tuppence very reasonably. 'It's like swindlers and confidence tricks-men who always look so honest and seem so honest. I daresay murderers all seem very nice and particularly soft-hearted. That sort of thing. Anyway, Miss Packard *is* very efficient and she has all the means to hand whereby she could produce a nice natural death without suspicion. And only someone like Mrs Cocoa would be likely to suspect her. Mrs Cocoa might suspect her because she's a bit batty herself and can understand batty people, or she might have come across her somewhere before.'

'I don't think Miss Packard would profit financially by any of her elderly inmates' deaths.'

'You don't know,' said Tuppence. 'It would be a cleverer way to do it, *not* to benefit from all of them. Just get one or two of them, perhaps, rich ones, to leave you a lot of money, but to always have some deaths that were quite natural as well, and where you didn't get anything. So you see I think that Dr Murray might, just *might*, have cast a glance at Miss Packard and said to himself, "Nonsense, I'm imagining things." But all the same the thought stuck in his mind. The second case he mentioned would fit with a domestic worker, or cook, or even some kind of hospital nurse. Somebody employed in the place, a middle-aged reliable woman, but who was batty in that particular way. Perhaps used to have little grudges, dislikes for some of the patients there. We can't go guessing at that because I don't think we know anyone well enough—'

'And the third one?'

'The third one's more difficult,' Tuppence admitted. 'Someone devoted. Dedicated.'

'Perhaps he just added that for good measure,' said Tommy. He added, 'I wonder about that Irish nurse.'

'The nice one we gave the fur stole to?'

'Yes, the nice one Aunt Ada liked. The very sympathetic one. She seemed so fond of everyone, so sorry if they died. She was very worried when she spoke to us, wasn't she? You said so—she was leaving, and she didn't really tell us why.'

'I suppose she might have been a rather neurotic type. Nurses aren't supposed to be too sympathetic. It's bad for patients. They are told to be cool and efficient and inspire confidence.'

'Nurse Beresford speaking,' said Tommy, and grinned.

'But to come back to the picture,' said Tuppence. 'If we just concentrate on the picture. Because I think it's very interesting what you told me about Mrs Boscowan, when you went to see her. She sounds—she sounds *interesting*.'

'She was interesting,' said Tommy. 'Quite the most interesting person I think we've come across in this unusual business. The sort of person who seems to *know* things, but not by thinking about them. It was as though she knew something about this place that I didn't, and that perhaps you don't. But she knows *something*.'

'It was odd what she said about the boat,' said Tuppence. 'That the picture hadn't had a boat originally. Why do you think it's got a boat now?'

'Oh,' said Tommy, 'I don't know.'

'Was there any name painted on the boat? I don't remember seeing one—but then I never looked at it very closely.'

'It's got *Waterlily* on it.'

'A very appropriate name for a boat—what does that remind me of?'

'I've no idea.'

'And she was quite positive that her husband didn't paint that boat—He could have put it in afterwards.'

'She says *not*—she was very definite.'

'Of course,' said Tuppence, 'there's another possibility we haven't gone into. About my coshing, I mean—the outsider—somebody perhaps who followed me here from Market Basing that day to see what I was up to. Because I'd been there asking all those questions. Going into all those house agents. Blodget & Burgess and all the rest of them. They put me off about the house. They were evasive. More evasive than would be natural. It was the same sort of evasion as we had when we were trying to find out where Mrs Lancaster had gone. Lawyers and banks, an owner who can't be communicated with because he's abroad. The same sort of *pattern*. They send someone to follow my car, they want to see what I am doing, and in due course I am coshed. Which brings us,' said Tuppence, 'to the gravestone in the churchyard. Why didn't anyone want me to look at old gravestones? They were all pulled about anyway—a group of boys, I should say, who'd got bored with wrecking telephone boxes, and went into the churchyard to have some fun and sacrilege behind the church.'

'You say there were painted words—or roughly carved words?'

'Yes—done with a chisel, I should think. Someone who gave it up as a bad job.

'The name—Lily Waters—and the age—seven years old. That was done properly—and then the other bits of words—It looked like "Whosoever…" and then "offend least of these"—and—"Millstone"—'

'Sounds familiar.'

'It should do. It's definitely biblical—but done by someone who wasn't quite sure what the words he wanted to remember were—'

'Very odd—the whole thing.'

'And why anyone should object—I was only trying to help the vicar—and the poor man who was trying to find his lost child—There we are—back to the lost child motif again—Mrs Lancaster talked about a poor child walled up behind a fireplace, and Mrs Copleigh chattered about walled-up nuns and murdered children, and a mother who killed a baby, and a lover, and an illegitimate baby, and a suicide—It's all old tales and gossip and hearsay and legends, mixed up in the most glorious kind of hasty pudding! All the same, Tommy, there was one actual *fact*—not just hearsay or legend—'

'You mean?'

'I mean that in the chimney of this Canal House, this old rag doll fell out—A child's doll. It had been there a very, very long time, all covered with soot and rubble—'

'Pity we haven't got it,' said Tommy.

'I *have*,' said Tuppence. She spoke triumphantly.

'You brought it away with you?'

'Yes. It startled me, you know. I thought I'd like to take it and examine it. Nobody wanted it or anything. I should imagine the Perrys would just have thrown it into the ashcan straight away. I've got it here.'

She rose from her sofa, went to her suitcase, rummaged a little and then brought out something wrapped in newspaper.

'Here you are, Tommy, have a look.'

With some curiosity Tommy unwrapped the newspaper. He took out carefully the wreck of a child's doll. Its limp arms and legs hung down, faint festoons of clothing dropped off as he touched them. The body seemed made of a very thin suède leather sewn up over a body that had once been plump with sawdust and now was sagging because here and there the sawdust had escaped. As Tommy handled it, and he was quite gentle in his touch, the body suddenly disintegrated, flapping over in a great wound from which there poured out a cupful of sawdust and with it small pebbles that ran to and fro about the floor. Tommy went round picking them up carefully.

'Good Lord,' he said to himself, 'Good Lord!'

'How odd,' Tuppence said, 'it's full of pebbles. Is that a bit of the chimney disintegrating, do you think? The plaster or something crumbling away?'

'No,' said Tommy. 'These pebbles were *inside* the body.'

He had gathered them up now carefully, he poked his finger into the carcase of the doll and a few more pebbles fell out. He took them over to the window and turned them over in his hand. Tuppence watched him with uncomprehending eyes.

'It's a funny idea, stuffing a doll with pebbles,' she said.

'Well, they're not exactly the usual kind of pebbles,' said Tommy. 'There was a very good reason for it, I should imagine.'

'What do you mean?'

'Have a look at them. Handle a few.'

She took some wonderingly from his hand.

'They're nothing but pebbles,' she said. 'Some are rather large and some small. Why are you so excited?'

'Because, Tuppence, I'm beginning to understand things. Those aren't pebbles, my dear girl, they're *diamonds*.'

CHAPTER 15

Evening at the Vicarage

'Diamonds!' Tuppence gasped.

Looking from him to the pebbles she still held in her hand, she said:

'These dusty-looking things, *diamonds*?'

Tommy nodded.

'It's beginning to make sense now, you see, Tuppence. It ties up. The Canal House. The picture. You wait until Ivor Smith hears about that doll. He's got a bouquet waiting for you already, Tuppence—'

'What for?'

'For helping to round up a big criminal gang!'

'You and your Ivor Smith! I suppose that's where you've been all this last week, abandoning me in my last days of convalescence in that dreary hospital—just when I wanted brilliant conversation and a lot of cheering up.'

'I came in visiting hours practically every evening.'

'You didn't tell me much.'

'I was warned by that dragon of a sister not to excite

you. But Ivor himself is coming here the day after tomorrow, and we've got a little social evening laid on at the vicarage.'

'Who's coming?'

'Mrs Boscowan, one of the big local landowners, your friend Miss Nellie Bligh, the vicar, of course, you and I—'

'And Mr Ivor Smith—what's his real name?'

'As far as I know, it's Ivor Smith.'

'You are always so cautious—' Tuppence laughed suddenly.

'What's amusing you?'

'I was just thinking that I'd like to have seen you and Albert discovering secret drawers in Aunt Ada's desk.'

'All the credit goes to Albert. He positively delivered a lecture on the subject. He learnt all about it in his youth from an antique dealer.'

'Fancy your Aunt Ada really leaving a secret document like that, all done up with seals all over. She didn't actually know anything, but she was ready to believe there was somebody in Sunny Ridge who was dangerous. I wonder if she knew it was Miss Packard.'

'That's only your idea.'

'It's a very good idea if it's a criminal gang we're looking for. They'd need a place like Sunny Ridge, respectable and well run, with a competent criminal to run it. Someone properly qualified to have access to drugs whenever she needed them. And by accepting any deaths that occurred as quite natural, it would influence a doctor to think they were quite all right.'

'You've got it all taped out, but actually the real reason you started to suspect Miss Packard was because you didn't like her teeth—'

'The better to eat you with,' said Tuppence meditatively. 'I'll tell you something else, Tommy—Supposing this picture—the picture of the Canal House—*never belonged to Mrs Lancaster at all—*'

'But we know it did.' Tommy stared at her.

'No, we don't. We only know that Miss Packard said so—It was Miss Packard who said that Mrs Lancaster gave it to Aunt Ada.'

'But why should—' Tommy stopped—

'Perhaps that's why Mrs Lancaster was taken away—so that she shouldn't tell us that the picture didn't belong to her, and that she didn't give it to Aunt Ada.'

'I think that's a very far-fetched idea.'

'Perhaps—But the picture was painted in Sutton Chancellor—The house in the picture is a house in Sutton Chancellor—We've reason to believe that that house is—or was—used as one of their hidey-holes by a criminal association—Mr Eccles is believed to be the man behind this gang. Mr Eccles was the man responsible for sending Mrs Johnson to remove Mrs Lancaster. I don't believe Mrs Lancaster was ever in Sutton Chancellor, or was ever in the Canal House, or had a picture of it—though I think she heard someone at Sunny Ridge talk about it—Mrs Cocoa perhaps? So she started chattering, and that was dangerous, so she had to be removed. And one day I shall find her! Mark my words, Tommy.'

'The Quest of Mrs Thomas Beresford.'

*

'You look remarkably well, if I may say so, Mrs Tommy,' said Mr Ivor Smith.

'I'm feeling perfectly well again,' said Tuppence. 'Silly of me to let myself get knocked out, I suppose.'

'You deserve a medal—Especially for this doll business. How you get on to these things, I don't know!'

'She's the perfect terrier,' said Tommy. 'Puts her nose down on the trail and off she goes.'

'You're not keeping me out of this party tonight,' said Tuppence suspiciously.

'Certainly not. A certain amount of things, you know, have been cleared up. I can't tell you how grateful I am to you two. We were getting *somewhere*, mind you, with this remarkably clever association of criminals who have been responsible for a stupendous amount of robberies over the last five or six years. As I told Tommy when he came to ask me if I knew anything about our clever legal gentleman, Mr Eccles, we've had our suspicions of him for a long time but he's not the man you'll easily get evidence against. Too careful by far. He practises as a solicitor—an ordinary genuine business with perfectly genuine clients.

'As I told Tommy, one of the important points has been this chain of houses. Genuine respectable houses with quite genuine respectable people living in them, living there for a short time—then leaving.

'Now, thanks to you, Mrs Tommy, and your investigation of chimneys and dead birds, we've found quite certainly one of those houses. The house where a particular amount of the spoil was concealed. It's been quite a clever system, you know, getting jewels or various things of that kind changed into packets of rough diamonds, hiding them, and then when the time comes they are flown abroad, or taken abroad in fishing boats, when all the hue and cry about one particular robbery has died down.'

'What about the Perrys? Are they—I hope they're not—mixed up in it?'

'One can't be sure,' said Mr Smith. 'No, one can't be sure. It seems likely to me that Mrs Perry, at least, knows something, or certainly knew something once.'

'Do you mean she really is one of the criminals?'

'It mightn't be that. It might be, you know, that they had a hold on her.'

'What sort of hold?'

'Well, you'll keep this confidential, I know you can hold your tongue in these things, but the local police have always had the idea that the husband, Amos Perry, might just possibly have been the man who was responsible for a wave of child murders a good many years ago. He is not fully competent mentally. The medical opinion was that he *might* quite easily have had a compulsion to do away with children. There was never any direct evidence, but his wife was perhaps overanxious to provide him always with adequate alibis. If so, you see, that might give a gang of unscrupulous people a hold on her and they may have put her in as tenant of part of a house where they knew she'd keep her mouth shut. They may really have had some form of damaging evidence against her husband. You met them—what do you feel about them both, Mrs Tommy?'

'I liked *her*,' said Tuppence. 'I think she was—well, as I say I summed her up as a friendly witch, given to white magic but not black.'

'What about him?'

'I was frightened of him,' said Tuppence. 'Not all the time. Just once or twice. He seemed suddenly to go big and terrifying. Just for a minute or two. I couldn't think what I was frightened of, but I was frightened. I suppose, as you say, I felt that he wasn't quite right in his head.'

'A lot of people are like that,' said Mr Smith. 'And very often they're not dangerous at all. But you can't tell, and you can't be sure.'

'What are we going to do at the vicarage tonight?'

'Ask some questions. See a few people. Find out things that may give us a little more of the information we need.'

'Will Major Waters be there? The man who wrote to the vicar about his child?'

'There doesn't seem to be any such person! There was a coffin buried where the old gravestone had been removed—a child's coffin, lead lined—And it was full of loot. Jewels and gold objects from a burglary near St Albans. The letter to the vicar was with the object of finding out what had happened to the grave. The local lads' sabotage had messed things up.'

'I am so deeply sorry, my dear,' said the vicar, coming to meet Tuppence with both hands outstretched. 'Yes, indeed, my dear, I have been so terribly upset that this should happen to you when you have been so kind. When you were doing this to help me. I really felt—yes, indeed I have, that it was all my fault. I shouldn't have let you go poking among gravestones, though really we had no reason to believe—no reason at all—that some band of young hooligans—'

'Now don't disturb yourself, Vicar,' said Miss Bligh, suddenly appearing at his elbow. 'Mrs Beresford knows, I'm sure, that it was nothing to do with *you*. It was indeed extremely kind of her to offer to help, but it's all over now, and she's quite well again. Aren't you, Mrs Beresford?'

'Certainly,' said Tuppence, faintly annoyed, however, that Miss Bligh should answer for her health so confidently.

'Come and sit down here and have a cushion behind your back,' said Miss Bligh.

'I don't need a cushion,' said Tuppence, refusing to accept the chair that Miss Bligh was officiously pulling forward. Instead, she sat down in an upright and exceedingly uncomfortable chair on the other side of the fireplace.

There was a sharp rap on the front door and everyone in the room jumped. Miss Bligh hurried out.

'Don't worry, Vicar,' she said. 'I'll go.'

'Please, if you will be so kind.'

There were low voices outside in the hall, then Miss Bligh came back shepherding a big woman in a brocade shift, and behind her a very tall thin man, a man of cadaverous appearance. Tuppence stared at him. A black cloak was round his shoulders, and his thin gaunt face was like the face from another century. He might have come, Tuppence thought, straight out of an El Greco canvas.

'I'm very pleased to see you,' said the vicar, and turned. 'May I introduce Sir Philip Starke, Mr and Mrs Beresford. Mr Ivor Smith. Ah! Mrs Boscowan. I've not seen you for many, many years—Mr and Mrs Beresford.'

'I've met Mr Beresford,' said Mrs Boscowan. She looked at Tuppence. 'How do you do,' she said. 'I'm glad to meet you. I heard you'd had an accident.'

'Yes. I'm all right again now.'

The introductions completed, Tuppence sat back in her chair. Tiredness swept over her as it seemed to do rather more frequently than formerly, which she said to herself was possibly a result of concussion. Sitting quietly, her eyes half closed, she was nevertheless scrutinizing everyone in the room with close attention. She was not listening to the conversation, she was only looking. She had a feeling that a few of the characters in the drama—the drama in which she had unwittingly involved herself—were assembled here as they might be in a dramatic scene. Things were drawing together, forming themselves into a compact nucleus. With the coming of Sir Philip Starke and Mrs Boscowan it was as though two hitherto unrevealed characters were suddenly presenting themselves. They had been there all along, as it were, outside the circle, but now they had come inside. They were somehow concerned, implicated. They had come here this evening—why, she wondered? Had someone summoned them? Ivor Smith? Had he commanded their presence, or only gently demanded it? Or were they perhaps as strange to him as they were to her? She thought to herself: 'It all began in Sunny Ridge, but Sunny Ridge isn't the real heart of the matter. That was, had always been, here, in Sutton Chancellor. Things had happened here. Not very lately, almost certainly not lately. Long ago. Things which had nothing to do with Mrs Lancaster—but Mrs Lancaster had become unknowingly involved. So where was Mrs Lancaster now?'

A little cold shiver passed over Tuppence.

'I think,' thought Tuppence, 'I think perhaps she's *dead...*'

If so, Tuppence felt, she herself had failed. She had set out on her quest worried about Mrs Lancaster, feeling that Mrs Lancaster was threatened with some danger and she had resolved to find Mrs Lancaster, protect her.

'And if she isn't dead,' thought Tuppence, 'I'll still do it!'

Sutton Chancellor... That was where the beginning of something meaningful and dangerous had happened. The house with the canal was part of it. Perhaps it was the centre of it all, or was it Sutton Chancellor itself? A place where people had lived, had come to, had left, had run away, had vanished, had disappeared and reappeared. Like Sir Philip Starke.

Without turning her head Tuppence's eyes went to Sir Philip Starke. She knew nothing about him except what Mrs Copleigh had poured out in the course of her monologue on the general inhabitants. A quiet man, a learned man, a botanist, an industrialist, or at least one who owned a big stake in industry. Therefore a rich man—and a man who loved children. There she was, back at it. Children again. The house by the canal and the bird in the chimney, and out of the chimney had fallen a child's doll, shoved up there by someone. A child's doll that held within its skin a handful of diamonds—the proceeds of crime. This was one of the headquarters of a big criminal undertaking. But there had been crimes more sinister than robberies. Mrs Copleigh had said 'I always fancied myself as *he* might have done it.'

Sir Philip Starke. A murderer? Behind her half-closed eyelids, Tuppence studied him with the knowledge clearly in her mind that she was studying him to find out if he fitted in any way with her conception of a murderer—and a child murderer at that.

How old was he, she wondered. Seventy at least, perhaps older. A worn ascetic face. Yes, definitely ascetic. Very definitely a tortured face. Those large dark eyes. El Greco eyes. The emaciated body.

He had come here this evening, why, she wondered? Her eyes went on to Miss Bligh. Sitting a little restlessly in her chair, occasionally moving to push a table nearer someone, to offer a cushion, to move the position of the cigarette box or matches. Restless, ill at ease. She was looking at Philip Starke. Every time she relaxed, her eyes went to him.

'Doglike devotion,' thought Tuppence. 'I think she must have been in love with him once. I think in a way perhaps she still is. You don't stop being in love with anyone because you get old. People like Derek and Deborah think you do. They can't imagine anyone who isn't young being in love. But I think she—I think she is still in love with him, hopelessly, devotedly in love. Didn't someone say—was it Mrs Copleigh or the vicar who had said, that Miss Bligh had been his secretary as a young woman, that she still looked after his affairs here?

'Well,' thought Tuppence, 'it's natural enough. Secretaries often fall in love with their bosses. So say Gertrude Bligh had loved Philip Starke. Was that a useful fact at all? Had Miss Bligh known or suspected that behind Philip Starke's calm ascetic personality there ran a horrifying thread of madness? *So fond of children always*.'

'Too fond of children, I thought,' Mrs Copleigh had said.

Things did take you like that. Perhaps that was a reason for his looking so tortured.

'Unless one is a pathologist or a psychiatrist or something, one doesn't know anything about mad murderers,' thought Tuppence. '*Why* do they want to kill children? What gives them that urge? Are they sorry about it afterwards? Are they disgusted, are they desperately unhappy, are they terrified?'

At that moment she noticed that his gaze had fallen on her. His eyes met hers and seemed to leave some message.

'You are thinking about me,' those eyes said. 'Yes, it's true what you are thinking. I am a haunted man.'

Yes, that described him exactly—He was a haunted man.

She wrenched her eyes away. Her gaze went to the vicar. She liked the vicar. He was a dear. Did he know anything? He might, Tuppence thought, or he might be living in the middle of some evil tangle that he never even suspected. Things happened all round him, perhaps, but he wouldn't know about them, because he had that rather disturbing quality of innocence.

Mrs Boscowan? But Mrs Boscowan was difficult to know anything about. A middle-aged woman, a personality, as Tommy had said, but that didn't express enough. As though

Tuppence had summoned her, Mrs Boscowan rose suddenly to her feet.

'Do you mind if I go upstairs and have a wash?' she said.

'Oh! of course.' Miss Bligh jumped to her feet. 'I'll take you up, shall I, Vicar?'

'I know my way perfectly,' said Mrs Boscowan. 'Don't bother—Mrs Beresford?'

Tuppence jumped slightly.

'I'll show you,' said Mrs Boscowan, 'where things are. Come with me.'

Tuppence got up as obediently as a child. She did not describe it so to herself. But she knew that she had been summoned and when Mrs Boscowan summoned, you obeyed.

By then Mrs Boscowan was through the door to the hall and Tuppence had followed her. Mrs Boscowan started up the stairs—Tuppence came up behind her.

'The spare room is at the top of the stairs,' said Mrs Boscowan. 'It's always kept ready. It has a bathroom leading out of it.'

She opened the door at the top of the stairs, went through, switched on the light and Tuppence followed her in.

'I'm very glad to have found you here,' said Mrs Boscowan. 'I hoped I should. I was worried about you. Did your husband tell you?'

'I gathered you'd said something,' said Tuppence.

'Yes, I was worried.' She closed the door behind them, shutting them, as it were, into a private place of private consultation. 'Have you felt at all,' said Emma Boscowan, 'that Sutton Chancellor is a dangerous place?'

'It's been dangerous for me,' said Tuppence.

'Yes, I know. It's lucky it wasn't worse, but then—yes, I think I can understand that.'

'You know something,' said Tuppence. 'You know something about all this, don't you?'

'In a way,' said Emma Boscowan, 'in a way I do, and in a way I don't. One has instincts, feelings, you know. When they turn out to be right, it's worrying. This whole criminal gang business, it seems so extraordinary. It doesn't seem to have anything to do with—' She stopped abruptly.

'I mean, it's just one of those things that are going on—that have always gone on really. But they're very well organized now, like businesses. There's nothing really dangerous, you know, not about the criminal part of it. It's the *other*. It's knowing just where the danger is and how to guard against it. You must be careful, Mrs Beresford, you really must. You're one of those people who rush into things and it wouldn't be safe to do that. Not here.'

Tuppence said slowly, 'My old aunt—or rather Tommy's old aunt, she wasn't mine—someone told her in the nursing home where she died—that there was a killer.'

Emma nodded her head slowly.

'There were two deaths in that nursing home,' said Tuppence, 'and the doctor isn't satisfied about them.'

'Is that what started you off?'

'No,' said Tuppence, 'it was before that.'

'If you have time,' said Emma Boscowan, 'will you tell

me very quickly—as quickly as you can because someone may interrupt us—just what happened at that nursing home or old ladies' home or whatever it was, to start you off?'

'Yes, I can tell you very quickly,' said Tuppence. She proceeded to do so.

'I see,' said Emma Boscowan. 'And you don't know where this old lady, this Mrs Lancaster, is now?'

'No, I don't.'

'Do you think she's dead?'

'I think she—might be.'

'Because she knew something?'

'Yes. She knew about something. Some murder. Some child perhaps who was killed.'

'I think you've gone wrong there,' said Mrs Boscowan. 'I think the child got mixed up in it and perhaps she got it mixed up. Your old lady, I mean. She got the child mixed up with something else, some other kind of killing.'

'I suppose it's possible. Old people do get mixed up. But there *was* a child murderer loose here, wasn't there? Or so the woman I lodged with here said.'

'There were several child murders in this part of the country, yes. But that was a good long time ago, you know. I'm not sure. The vicar wouldn't know. He wasn't there then. But Miss Bligh was. Yes, yes, she must have been here. She must have been a fairly young girl then.'

'I suppose so.'

Tuppence said, 'Has she always been in love with Sir Philip Starke?'

'You saw that, did you? Yes, I think so. Completely devoted beyond idolatry. We noticed it when we first came here, William and I.'

'What made you come here? Did you live in the Canal House?'

'No, we never lived there. He liked to paint it. He painted it several times. What's happened to the picture your husband showed me?'

'He brought it home again,' said Tuppence. 'He told me what you said about the boat—that your husband didn't paint it—the boat called *Waterlily*—'

'Yes. It wasn't painted by my husband. When I last saw the picture there was no boat there. Somebody painted it in.'

'And called it *Waterlily*—And a man who didn't exist, Major *Waters*—wrote about a child's grave—a child called Lilian—but there was no child buried in that grave, only a child's coffin, full of the proceeds of a big robbery. The painting of the boat must have been a message—a message to say where the loot was hidden—It all seems to tie up with crime...'

'It seems to, yes—But one can't be sure what—'

Emma Boscowan broke off abruptly. She said quickly, 'She's coming up to find us. Go into the bathroom—'

'Who?'

'Nellie Bligh. Pop into the bathroom—bolt the door.'

'She's just a busybody,' said Tuppence, disappearing into the bathroom.

'Something a little more than that,' said Mrs Boscowan.

Miss Bligh opened the door and came in, brisk and helpful.

'Oh, I hope you found everything you wanted?' she said. 'There were fresh towels and soap, I hope? Mrs Copleigh comes in to look after the vicar, but I really have to see she does things properly.'

Mrs Boscowan and Miss Bligh went downstairs together. Tuppence joined them just as they reached the drawing-room door. Sir Philip Starke rose as she came into the room, rearranged her chair and sat down beside her.

'Is that the way you like it, Mrs Beresford?'

'Yes, thank you,' said Tuppence. 'It's very comfortable.'

'I'm sorry to hear—' his voice had a vague charm to it, though it had some elements of a ghostlike voice, far-away, lacking in resonance, yet with a curious depth—'about your accident,' he said. 'It's so sad nowadays—all the accidents there are.'

His eyes were wandering over her face and she thought to herself, 'He's making just as much a study of me as I made of him.' She gave a sharp half-glance at Tommy, but Tommy was talking to Emma Boscowan.

'What made you come to Sutton Chancellor in the first place, Mrs Beresford?'

'Oh, we're looking for a house in the country in a vague sort of way,' said Tuppence. 'My husband was away from home attending some congress or other and I thought I'd have a tour round a likely part of the countryside—just to see what there was going, and the kind of price one would have to pay, you know.'

'I hear you went and looked at the house by the canal bridge?'

'Yes, I did. I believe I'd once noticed it from the train. It's a very attractive-looking house—from the outside.'

'Yes. I should imagine, though, that even the outside needs a great deal doing to it, to the roof and things like that. Not so attractive on the wrong side, is it?'

'No, it seems to me a curious way to divide up a house.'

'Oh well,' said Philip Starke, 'people have different ideas, don't they?'

'You never lived in it, did you?' asked Tuppence.

'No, no, indeed. My house was burnt down many years ago. There's part of it left still. I expect you've seen it or had it pointed out to you. It's above this vicarage, you know, a bit up the hill. At least what they call a hill in this part of the world. It was never much to boast of. My father built it way back in 1890 or so. A proud mansion. Gothic overlays, a touch of Balmoral. Our architects nowadays rather admire that kind of thing again, though actually forty years ago it was shuddered at. It had everything a so-called gentleman's house ought to have.' His voice was gently ironic. 'A billiard room, a morning room, ladies' parlour, colossal dining-room, a ballroom, about fourteen bedrooms, and once had—or so I should imagine—a staff of fourteen servants to look after it.'

'You sound as though you never liked it much yourself.'

'I never did. I was a disappointment to my father. He was a very successful industrialist. He hoped I would follow in his footsteps. I didn't. He treated me very well. He gave me a large income, or allowance—as it used to be called—and let me go my own way.'

'I heard you were a botanist.'

'Well, that was one of my great relaxations. I used to go looking for wild flowers, especially in the Balkans. Have you ever been to the Balkans looking for wild flowers? It's a wonderful place for them.'

'It sounds very attractive. Then you used to come back and live here?'

'I haven't lived here for a great many years now. In fact, I've never been back to live here since my wife died.'

'Oh,' said Tuppence, slightly embarrassed. 'Oh, I'm—I'm sorry.'

'It's quite a long time ago now. She died before the war. In 1938. She was a very beautiful woman,' he said.

'Do you have pictures of her in your house here still?'

'Oh no, the house is empty. All the furniture, pictures and things were sent away to be stored. There's just a bedroom and an office and a sitting-room where my agent comes, or I come if I have to come down here and see to any estate business.'

'It's never been sold?'

'No. There's some talk of having a development of the land there. I don't know. Not that I have any feeling for it. My father hoped that he was starting a kind of feudal domain. I was to succeed him and my children were to succeed me and so on and so on and so on.' He paused a minute and said then, 'But Julia and I never had any children.'

'Oh,' said Tuppence softly, 'I see.'

'So there's nothing to come here for. In fact I hardly ever do. Anything that needs to be done here Nellie Bligh does for me.' He smiled over at her. 'She's been the most wonderful secretary. She still attends to my business affairs or anything of that kind.'

'You never come here and yet you don't want to sell it?' said Tuppence.

'There's a very good reason why not,' said Philip Starke.

A faint smile passed over the austere features.

'Perhaps after all I do inherit some of my father's business sense. The land, you know, is improving enormously in value. It's a better investment than money would be, if I sold it. Appreciates every day. Some day, who knows, we'll have a grand new dormitory town built on that land.'

'Then you'll be rich?'

'Then I'll be an even richer man than I am at present,' said Sir Philip. 'And I'm quite rich enough.'

'What do you do most of the time?'

'I travel, and I have interests in London. I have a picture gallery there. I'm by way of being an art dealer. All those things are interesting. They occupy one's time—till the moment when the hand is laid on your shoulder which says "Depart".'

'Don't,' said Tuppence. 'That sounds—it gives me the shivers.'

'It needn't give you the shivers. I think you're going to have a long life, Mrs Beresford, and a very happy one.'

'Well, I'm very happy at present,' said Tuppence. 'I suppose I shall get all the aches and pains and troubles that old people do get. Deaf and blind and arthritis and a few other things.'

'You probably won't mind them as much as you think you will. If I may say so, without being rude, you and your husband seem to have a very happy life together.'

'Oh, we have,' said Tuppence. 'I suppose really,' she said, 'there's nothing in life like being happily married, is there?'

A moment later she wished she had not uttered these words. When she looked at the man opposite her, who she felt had grieved for so many years and indeed might still be grieving for the loss of a very much loved wife, she felt even more angry with herself.

CHAPTER 16

The Morning After

It was the morning after the party.

Ivor Smith and Tommy paused in their conversation and looked at each other, then they looked at Tuppence. Tuppence was staring into the grate. Her mind looked far away.

'Where have we got to?' said Tommy.

With a sigh Tuppence came back from where her thoughts had been wandering, and looked at the two men.

'It seems all tied up still to me,' she said. 'The party last night? What was it for? What did it all mean?' She looked at Ivor Smith. 'I suppose it meant something to you two. You know where we are?'

'I wouldn't go as far as that,' said Ivor. 'We're not all after the same thing, are we?'

'Not quite,' said Tuppence.

The men both looked at her inquiringly.

'All right,' said Tuppence. 'I'm a woman with an obsession. *I want to find Mrs Lancaster*. I want to be sure that she's all right.'

'You want to find Mrs Johnson first,' said Tommy. 'You'll never find Mrs Lancaster till you find Mrs Johnson.'

'Mrs Johnson,' said Tuppence. 'Yes, I wonder—But I suppose none of that part of it interests you,' she said to Ivor Smith.

'Oh it does, Mrs Tommy, it does very much.'

'What about Mr Eccles?'

Ivor smiled. 'I think,' he said, 'that retribution might be overtaking Mr Eccles shortly. Still, I wouldn't bank on it. He's a man who covers his tracks with incredible ingenuity. So much so, that one imagines that there aren't really any tracks at all.' He added thoughtfully under his breath, 'A great administrator. A great planner.'

'Last night—' began Tuppence, and hesitated—'Can I ask questions?'

'You can ask them,' Tommy told her. 'But don't bank on getting any satisfactory answers from old Ivor here.'

'Sir Philip Starke,' said Tuppence—'Where does he come in? He doesn't seem to fit as a likely criminal—unless he was the kind that—'

She stopped, hastily biting off a reference to Mrs Copleigh's wilder suppositions as to child murderers—

'Sir Philip Starke comes in as a very valuable source of information,' said Ivor Smith. 'He's the biggest landowner in these parts—and in other parts of England as well.'

'In Cumberland?'

Ivor Smith looked at Tuppence sharply. 'Cumberland? Why do you mention Cumberland? What do you know about Cumberland, Mrs Tommy?'

'Nothing,' said Tuppence. 'For some reason or other it just came into my head.' She frowned and looked perplexed. 'And a red and white striped rose on the side of a house—one of those old-fashioned roses.'

She shook her head.

'Does Sir Philip Starke own the Canal House?'

'He owns the land—He owns most of the land hereabouts.'

'Yes, he said so last night.'

'Through him, we've learned a good deal about leases and tenancies that have been cleverly obscured through legal complexities—'

'Those house agents I went to see in the Market Square—Is there something phony about them, or did I imagine it?'

'You didn't imagine it. We're going to pay them a visit this morning. We are going to ask some rather awkward questions.'

'Good,' said Tuppence.

'We're doing quite nicely. We've cleared up the big post office robbery of 1965, and the Albury Cross robberies, and the Irish Mail train business. We've found some of the loot. Clever places they manufactured in these houses. A new bath installed in one, a service flat made in another—a couple of its rooms a little smaller than they ought to have been thereby providing for an interesting recess. Oh yes, we've found out a great deal.'

'But what about the *people*?' said Tuppence. 'I mean the people who thought of it, or ran it—apart from Mr Eccles, I mean. There must have been others who knew something.'

'Oh yes. There were a couple of men—one who ran a night club, conveniently just off the M1. Happy Hamish they used to call him. Slippery as an eel. And a woman they called Killer Kate—but that was a long time ago—one of our more interesting criminals. A beautiful girl, but her mental balance was doubtful. They eased her out—she might have become a danger to them. They were a strictly business concern—in it for loot—not for murder.'

'And was the Canal House one of their hideaway places?'

'At one time, Ladymead, they called it then. It's had a lot of different names in its time.'

'Just to make things more difficult, I suppose,' said Tuppence. 'Ladymead. I wonder if that ties up with some particular thing.'

'What should it tie up with?'

'Well, it doesn't really,' said Tuppence. 'It just started off another hare in my mind, if you know what I mean. The trouble is,' she added, 'I don't really know what I mean myself now. The picture, too. Boscowan painted the picture and then somebody else painted a boat into it, with a name on the boat—'

'Tiger Lily.'

'No, *Waterlily*. And his wife says that he didn't paint the boat.'

'Would she know?'

'I expect she would. If you were married to a painter, and especially if you were an artist yourself, I think you'd know if it was a different style of painting. She's rather frightening, I think,' said Tuppence.

'Who—Mrs Boscowan?'

'Yes. If you know what I mean, powerful. Rather overwhelming.'

'Possibly. Yes.'

'She knows things,' said Tuppence, 'but I'm not sure that she knows them because she knows them, if you know what I mean.'

'I don't,' said Tommy firmly.

'Well, I mean, there's one way of knowing things. The other way is that you sort of feel them.'

'That's rather the way you go in for, Tuppence.'

'You can say what you like,' said Tuppence, apparently following her own track of thought, 'the whole thing ties up round Sutton Chancellor. Round Ladymead, or Canal House or whatever you like to call it. And all the people who lived there, now and in past times. Some things I think might go back a long way.'

'You're thinking of Mrs Copleigh.'

'On the whole,' said Tuppence, 'I think Mrs Copleigh just put in a lot of things which have made everything more difficult. I think she's got all her times and dates mixed up too.'

'People do,' said Tommy, 'in the country.'

'I know that,' said Tuppence, 'I was brought up in a country vicarage, after all. They date things by events, they don't date them by years. They don't say "that happened in 1930" or "that happened in 1925" or things like that. They say "that happened the year after the old mill burned down" or "that happened after the lightning struck the big oak and killed Farmer James" or "that was the year we had the polio epidemic". So naturally, of course, the things they do remember don't go in any particular sequence. Everything's very difficult,' she added. 'There are just bits poking up here and there, if you know what I mean. Of course the point is,' said Tuppence with the air of someone who suddenly makes an important discovery, 'the trouble is that I'm old myself.'

'You are eternally young,' said Ivor gallantly.

'Don't be daft,' said Tuppence, scathingly. 'I'm old because I remember things that same way. I've gone back to being primitive in my aids to memory.'

She got up and walked round the room.

'This is an annoying kind of hotel,' she said.

She went through the door into her bedroom and came back again shaking her head.

'No Bible,' she said.

'Bible?'

'Yes. You know, in old-fashioned hotels, they've always got a Gideon Bible by your bed. I suppose so that you can get saved any moment of the day or night. Well, they don't have that here.'

'Do you want a Bible?'

'Well, I do rather. I was brought up properly and I used to know my Bible quite well, as any good clergyman's daughter should. But now, you see, one rather forgets. Especially as they don't read the lessons properly any more in churches. They give you some new version where all the wording, I suppose, is technically right and a proper translation, but sounds nothing like it used to. While you two go to the house agents, I shall drive into Sutton Chancellor,' she added.

'What for? I forbid you,' said Tommy.

'Nonsense—I'm not going to sleuth. I shall just go into the church and look at the Bible. If it's some modern version, I shall go and ask the vicar, he'll have a Bible, won't he? The proper kind, I mean. Authorized Version.'

'What do you want the Authorized Version for?'

'I just want to refresh my memory over those words that were scratched on the child's tombstone... They interested me.'

'It's all very well—but I don't trust you, Tuppence—don't trust you not to get into trouble once you're out of my sight.'

'I give you my word I'm not going to prowl about in graveyards any more. The church on a sunny morning and the vicar's study—that's all—what could be more harmless?'

Tommy looked at his wife doubtfully and gave in.

Having left her car by the lych-gate at Sutton Chancellor, Tuppence looked round her carefully before entering the church precincts. She had the natural distrust of one who has suffered grievous bodily harm in a certain geographical spot. There did not on this occasion seem to be any possible assailants lurking behind the tombstones.

She went into the church, where an elderly woman was on her knees polishing some brasses. Tuppence tiptoed up to the lectern and made a tentative examination of the volume that rested there. The woman cleaning the brasses looked up with a disapproving glance.

'I'm not going to steal it,' said Tuppence reassuringly, and carefully closing it again, she tiptoed out of the church.

She would have liked to examine the spot where the recent excavations had taken place, but that she had undertaken on no account to do.

'*Whosoever shall offend*,' she murmured to herself. 'It might mean that, but if so it would have to be someone—'

She drove the car the short distance to the vicarage, got out and went up the path to the front door. She rang but could hear no tinkle from inside. 'Bell's broken, I expect,' said Tuppence, knowing the habits of vicarage bells. She pushed the door and it responded to her touch.

She stood inside in the hall. On the hall table a large envelope with a foreign stamp took up a good deal of space. It bore the printed legend of a Missionary Society in Africa.

'I'm glad I'm not a missionary,' thought Tuppence.

Behind that vague thought, there lay something else, something connected with some hall table somewhere, something that she ought to remember… Flowers? Leaves? Some letter or parcel?

At that moment the vicar came out from the door on the left.

'Oh,' he said. 'Do you want me? I—oh, it's Mrs Beresford, isn't it?'

'Quite right,' said Tuppence. 'What I really came to ask you was whether by any chance you had a Bible.'

'Bible,' said the vicar, looking rather unexpectedly doubtful. 'A Bible.'

'I thought it likely that you might have,' said Tuppence.

'Of course, of course,' said the vicar. 'As a matter of fact, I suppose I've got several. I've got a Greek Testament,' he said hopefully. 'That's not what you want, I suppose?'

'No,' said Tuppence. 'I want,' she said firmly, 'the Authorized Version.'

'Oh dear,' said the vicar. 'Of course, there must be several in the house. Yes, several. We don't use that version in the church now, I'm sorry to say. One has to fall in with the bishop's ideas, you know, and the bishop is very keen on modernization, for young people and all that. A pity, I think. I have so many books in my library here that some of them, you know, get pushed behind the others. But I *think* I can find you what you want. I *think* so. If not, we'll ask Miss Bligh. She's here somewhere looking out the vases for the children who arrange their wild flowers for the Children's Corner in the church.' He left Tuppence in the hall and went back into the room where he had come from.

Tuppence did not follow him. She remained in the hall, frowning and thinking. She looked up suddenly as the door at the end of the hall opened and Miss Bligh came through it. She was holding up a very heavy metal vase.

Several things clicked together in Tuppence's head.

'Of course,' said Tuppence, '*of course*.'

'Oh, can I help—I—oh, it's Mrs Beresford.'

'Yes,' said Tuppence, and added, 'And *it's Mrs Johnson, isn't it*?'

The heavy vase fell to the floor. Tuppence stooped and picked it up. She stood weighing it in her hand. 'Quite a handy weapon,' she said. She put it down. 'Just the thing to cosh anyone with from behind,' she said—'That's what you did to me, didn't you, *Mrs Johnson*.'

'I—I—what did you say? I—I—I never—'

But Tuppence had no need to stay longer. She had seen the effect of her words. At the second mention of Mrs Johnson, Miss Bligh had given herself away in an unmistakable fashion. She was shaking and panic-stricken.

'There was a letter on your hall table the other day,' said Tuppence, 'addressed to a Mrs Yorke at an address in Cumberland. That's where you took her, isn't it, Mrs Johnson, when you took her away from Sunny Ridge? That's where she is now. Mrs Yorke or Mrs Lancaster—you used either name—York and Lancaster like the striped red and white rose in the Perrys' garden—'

She turned swiftly and went out of the house leaving Miss Bligh in the hall, still supporting herself on the stair rail, her mouth open, staring after her. Tuppence ran down the path to the gate, jumped into her car and drove away. She looked back towards the front door, but no one emerged. Tuppence drove past the church and back towards Market Basing, but suddenly changed her mind. She turned the car, drove back the way she had come, and took the left-hand road leading to the Canal House bridge. She abandoned the car, looked over the gate to see if either of the Perrys were in the garden, but there was no sign of them. She went through the gate and up the path to the back door. That was closed too and the windows were shut.

Tuppence felt annoyed. Perhaps Alice Perry had gone to Market Basing to shop. She particularly wanted to see Alice Perry. Tuppence knocked at the door, rapping first gently then loudly. Nobody answered. She turned the handle but the door did not give. It was locked. She stood there, undecided.

There were some questions she wanted badly to ask Alice Perry. Possibly Mrs Perry might be in Sutton Chancellor. She might go back there. The difficulty of Canal House was that there never seemed to be anyone in sight and hardly any traffic came over the bridge. There was no one to ask where the Perrys might be this morning.

CHAPTER 17

Mrs Lancaster

Tuppence stood there frowning, and then, suddenly, quite unexpectedly, the door opened. Tuppence drew back a step and gasped. The person confronting her was the last person in the world she expected to see. In the doorway, dressed exactly the same as she had been at Sunny Ridge, and smiling the same way with that air of vague amiability, was Mrs Lancaster in person.

'Oh,' said Tuppence.

'Good morning. Were you wanting Mrs Perry?' said Mrs Lancaster. 'It's market day, you know. So lucky I was able to let you in. I couldn't find the key for some time. I think it must be a duplicate anyway, don't you? But do come in. Perhaps you'd like a cup of tea or something.'

Like one in a dream, Tuppence crossed the threshold. Mrs Lancaster, still retaining the gracious air of a hostess, led Tuppence along into the sitting-room.

'Do sit down,' she said. 'I'm afraid I don't know where all the cups and things are. I've only been here a day or two. Now—let me see… But—surely—I've met you before, haven't I?'

'Yes,' said Tuppence, 'when you were at Sunny Ridge.'

'Sunny Ridge, now, Sunny Ridge. That seems to remind me of something. Oh, of course, dear Miss Packard. Yes, a very nice place.'

'You left it in rather a hurry, didn't you?' said Tuppence.

'People are so very bossy,' said Mrs Lancaster. 'They hurry you so. They don't give you time to *arrange* things or *pack* properly or *anything*. Kindly meant, I'm sure. Of course, I'm very fond of dear Nellie Bligh, but she's a very masterful kind of woman. I sometimes think,' Mrs Lancaster added, bending forward to Tuppence, 'I sometimes think, you know, that she is not quite—' she tapped her forehead significantly. 'Of course it *does* happen. Especially to spinsters. Unmarried women, you know. Very given to good works and all that but they take very odd fancies sometimes. Curates suffer a great deal. They seem to think sometimes, these women, that the curate has made them an offer of marriage but really he never thought of doing anything of the kind. Oh yes, poor Nellie. So sensible in some ways. She's been wonderful in the parish here. And she was always a first-class secretary, I believe. But all the same she has some very curious ideas at times. Like taking me away at a moment's notice from dear Sunny Ridge, and then up to Cumberland—a very bleak house, and, again quite suddenly, bringing me here—'

'Are you living here?' said Tuppence.

'Well, if you can *call* it that. It's a very peculiar arrangement altogether. I've only been here two days.'

'Before that, you were at Rosetrellis Court, in Cumberland—'

'Yes, I believe that was the name of it. Not such a pretty name as Sunny Ridge, do you think? In fact I never really settled down, if you know what I mean. And it wasn't nearly as well run. The service wasn't as good and they had a very inferior brand of coffee. Still, I was getting used to things and I had found one or two interesting acquaintances there. One of them who knew an aunt of mine quite well years ago in India. It's so nice, you know, when you find *connections*.'

'It must be,' said Tuppence.

Mrs Lancaster continued cheerfully.

'Now let me see, you came to Sunny Ridge, but not to stay, I think. I think you came to see one of the guests there.'

'My husband's aunt,' said Tuppence, 'Miss Fanshawe.'

'Oh yes. Yes of course. I remember now. And wasn't there something about a child of yours behind the chimney piece?'

'No,' said Tuppence, 'no, it wasn't my child.'

'But that's why you've come here, isn't it? They've had trouble with a chimney here. A bird got into it, I understand. This place wants repairing. I don't like being here at *all*. No, not at all and I shall tell Nellie so as soon as I see her.'

'You're lodging with Mrs Perry?'

'Well, in a way I am, and in a way I'm not. I think I could trust you with a secret, couldn't I?'

'Oh yes,' said Tuppence, 'you can trust me.'

'Well, I'm not really here at all. I mean not in this part of the house. This is the Perrys' part of the house.' She leaned forward. 'There's another one, you know, if you go upstairs. Come with me. I'll take you.'

Tuppence rose. She felt that she was in rather a crazy kind of dream.

'I'll just lock the door first, it's safer,' said Mrs Lancaster.

She led Tuppence up a rather narrow staircase to the first floor. She took her through a double bedroom with signs of occupation—presumably the Perrys' room—and through a door leading out of that into another room next door. It contained a washstand and a tall wardrobe of maple wood. Nothing else. Mrs Lancaster went to the maple wardrobe, fumbled at the back of it, then with sudden ease pushed it aside. There seemed to be castors on the wardrobe and it rolled out from the wall easily enough. Behind the wardrobe there was, rather strangely, Tuppence thought, a grate. Over the mantelpiece there was a mirror with a small shelf under the mirror on which were china figures of birds.

To Tuppence's astonishment Mrs Lancaster seized the bird in the middle of the mantelshelf and gave it a sharp pull. Apparently the bird was stuck to the mantelpiece. In fact, by a swift touch Tuppence perceived that all the birds were firmly fastened down. But as a result of Mrs Lancaster's action there was a click and the whole mantelpiece came away from the wall and swung forward.

'Clever, isn't it?' said Mrs Lancaster. 'It was done a long time ago, you know, when they altered the house. The priest's hole, you know, they used to call this room but I don't think it was really a priest's hole. No, nothing to do with priests. I've never thought so. Come through. This is where I live now.'

She gave another push. The wall in front of her also swung back and a minute or two later they were in a large attractive-looking room with windows that gave out on the canal and the hill opposite.

'A lovely room, isn't it?' said Mrs Lancaster. 'Such a lovely view. I always liked it. I lived here for a time as a girl, you know.'

'Oh, I see.'

'Not a lucky house,' said Mrs Lancaster. 'No, they always said it wasn't a lucky house. I think, you know,' she added, 'I think I'll shut up this again. One can't be too careful, can one?'

She stretched out a hand and pushed the door they had come through back again. There was a sharp click as the mechanism swung into place.

'I suppose,' said Tuppence, 'that this was one of the alterations they made to the house when they wanted to use it as a hiding place.'

'They did a lot of alterations,' said Mrs Lancaster. 'Sit down, do. Do you like a high chair or a low one? I like a high one myself. I'm rather rheumatic, you know. I suppose you thought there might have been a child's body there,' added Mrs Lancaster. 'An absurd idea really, don't you think so?'

'Yes, perhaps.'

'Cops and robbers,' said Mrs Lancaster, with an indulgent air. 'One is so foolish when one is young, you know. All that sort of thing. Gangs—big robberies—it has such an appeal for one when one is young. One thinks being a gunman's moll would be the most wonderful thing in the world. I thought so once. Believe me—' she leaned forward and tapped Tuppence on the knee '—believe me, *it's not true*. It isn't really. I thought so once, but one wants more than that, you know. There's no thrill really in just stealing things and getting away with it. It needs good organization, of course.'

'You mean Mrs Johnson or Miss Bligh—whichever you call her—'

'Well, of course, she's always Nellie Bligh to me. But for some reason or other—to facilitate things, she says—she calls herself Mrs Johnson now and then. But she's never been married, you know. Oh no. She's a regular spinster.'

A sound of knocking came to them from below.

'Dear me,' said Mrs Lancaster, 'that must be the Perrys back again. I'd no idea they were going to be back so soon.'

The knocking went on.

'Perhaps we ought to let them in,' suggested Tuppence.

'No, dear, we won't do that,' said Mrs Lancaster. 'I can't stand people always interfering. We're having such a nice little talk up here, aren't we? I think we'll just stay up here—oh dear, now they're calling under the window. Just look out and see who it is.'

Tuppence went to the window.

'It's Mr Perry,' she said.

From below, Mr Perry shouted,

'Julia! Julia!'

'Impertinence,' said Mrs Lancaster. 'I don't allow people like Amos Perry to call me by my Christian name. No, indeed. Don't worry, dear,' she added, 'we're quite safe here. And we can have a nice little talk. I'll tell you all about myself—I've really had a very interesting life—Eventful—Sometimes I think I ought to write it down. I was mixed up, you see. I was a wild girl, and I was mixed up with—well, really just a common gang of criminals. No other word for it. Some of them *very* undesirable people. Mind you, there *were* nice people among them. Quite good class.'

'Miss Bligh?'

'No, no, Miss Bligh never had anything to do with crime. Not Nellie Bligh. Oh no, she's very churchy, you know. Religious. All that. But there are different ways of religion. Perhaps you know that, do you?'

'I suppose there are a lot of different sects,' Tuppence suggested.

'Yes, there have to be, for ordinary people. But there are others besides ordinary people. There are some special ones, under special commands. There are special legions. Do you understand what I mean, my dear?'

'I don't think I do,' said Tuppence. 'Don't you think we ought to let the Perrys into their own house? They're getting rather upset—'

'No, we're not going to let the Perrys in. Not till—well, not till I've told you all about it. You mustn't be frightened, my dear. It's all quite—quite natural, quite harmless. There's no pain of any kind. It'll be just like going to sleep. Nothing worse.'

Tuppence stared at her, then she jumped up and went towards the door in the wall.

'You can't get out that way,' said Mrs Lancaster. 'You don't know where the catch is. It's not where you think it is at all. Only I know that. I know all the secrets of this place. I lived here with the criminals when I was a girl until I went away from them all and got salvation. Special salvation. That's what was given to me—to expiate my sin—The child, you know—I killed it. I was a dancer—I didn't want a child—Over there, on the wall—that's my picture—as a dancer—'

Tuppence followed the pointing finger. On the wall hung an oil painting, full length, of a girl in a costume of white satin leaves with the legend 'Waterlily'.

'Waterlily was one of my best roles. Everyone said so.'

Tuppence came back slowly and sat down. She stared at Mrs Lancaster. As she did so words repeated in her head. Words heard at Sunny Ridge. '*Was it your poor child*?' She had been frightened then, frightened. She was frightened now. She was as yet not quite sure what she was frightened of, but the same fear was there. Looking at that benignant face, that kindly smile.

'I had to obey the commands given me—There have to be agents of destruction. I was appointed to that. I accepted my appointment. They go free of sin, you see. I mean, the children went free of sin. They were not old enough to sin. So I sent them to Glory as I was appointed to do. Still innocent. Still not knowing evil. You can see what a great honour it was to be chosen. To be one of the specially chosen. I always loved children. I had none of my own. That was very cruel, wasn't it, or it seemed cruel. But it was retribution really for what I'd done. You know perhaps what I'd done.'

'No,' said Tuppence.

'Oh, you seem to know so much. I thought perhaps you'd know that too. There was a doctor. I went to him. I was only seventeen then and I was frightened. He said it would be all right to have the child taken away so that nobody would ever know. But it wasn't all right, you see. I began to have dreams. I had dreams that the child was always there, asking me why it had never had life. The child told me it wanted companions. It was a girl, you know. Yes, I'm sure it was a girl. She came and she wanted other children. Then I got the command. *I* couldn't have any children. I'd married and I thought I'd have children, then my husband wanted children passionately but the children never came, because I was cursed, you see. You understand that, don't you? But there was a way, a way to atone. To atone for what I'd done. What I'd done was murder, wasn't it, and you could only atone for murder with other murders, because the other murders wouldn't be really murders, they would be *sacrifices*. They would be offered up. You do see the difference, don't you? The children went to keep my child company. Children of different ages but young. The command would come and then—' she leaned forward and touched Tuppence '—it was such a happy thing to do. You understand that, don't you? It was so happy to release them so that they'd never know sin like I knew sin. I couldn't tell anyone, of course, nobody was ever to know. That was the thing I had to be sure about. But there were people sometimes who got to know or to suspect. Then of course—well, I mean it had to be death for them too, so that *I* should be safe. So I've always been quite safe. You understand, don't you?'

'Not—not quite.'

'But you do *know*. That's why you came here, isn't it? You knew. You knew the day I asked you at Sunny Ridge. I saw by your face. I said "Was it your poor child?" I thought you'd come, perhaps because you were a mother. One of those whose children I'd killed. I hoped you'd come back another time and then we'd have a glass of milk together. It was usually milk. Sometimes cocoa. Anyone who knew about me.'

She moved slowly across the room and opened a cupboard in a corner of the room.

'Mrs Moody—' said Tuppence, 'was she one?'

'Oh, you know about her—she wasn't a mother—she'd been a dresser at the theatre. She recognized me so she had to go.' Turning suddenly she came towards Tuppence holding a glass of milk and smiling persuasively.

'Drink it up,' she said. 'Just drink it up.'

Tuppence sat silent for a moment, then she leapt to her feet and rushed to the window. Catching up a chair, she crashed the glass. She leaned her head out and screamed:

'Help! Help!'

Mrs Lancaster laughed. She put the glass of milk down on a table and leant back in her chair and laughed.

'How stupid you are. Who do you think will come? Who do you think *can* come? They'd have to break down doors, they'd have to get through that wall and by that time—there are other things, you know. It needn't be milk.

Milk is the easy way. Milk and cocoa and even tea. For little Mrs Moody I put it in cocoa—she loved cocoa.'

'The morphia? How did you get it?'

'Oh, that was easy. A man I lived with years ago—he had cancer—the doctor gave me supplies for him—to keep in my charge—other drugs too—I said later that they'd all been thrown away—but I kept them, and other drugs and sedatives too—I thought they might come in useful some day—and they did—I've still got a supply—I never take anything of the kind myself—I don't believe in it.' She pushed the glass of milk towards Tuppence—'Drink it up, it's much the easiest way. The other way—the trouble is, I can't be sure just where I put it.'

She got up from her chair and began walking round the room.

'Where *did* I put it? Where did I? I forget everything now I'm getting old.'

Tuppence yelled again. 'Help!' but the canal bank was empty still. Mrs Lancaster was still wandering round the room.

'I thought—I certainly thought—oh, of course, in my knitting bag.'

Tuppence turned from the window. Mrs Lancaster was coming towards her.

'What a silly woman you are,' said Mrs Lancaster, 'to want it this way.'

Her left arm shot out and she caught Tuppence's shoulder. Her right hand came from behind her back. In it was a long thin stiletto blade. Tuppence struggled. She thought, 'I can stop her easily. Easily. She's an old woman. Feeble. She can't—'

Suddenly in a cold tide of fear she thought, 'But *I'm* an old woman too. I'm not as strong as I think myself. I'm not as strong as she is. Her hands, her grasp, her fingers. I suppose because she's mad and mad people, I've always heard, are strong.'

The gleaming blade was approaching near her. Tuppence screamed. Down below she heard shouts and blows. Blows now on the doors as though someone were trying to force the doors or windows. 'But they'll never get through,' thought Tuppence. 'They'll never get through this trick doorway here. Not unless they know the mechanism.'

She struggled fiercely. She was still managing to hold Mrs Lancaster away from her. But the other was the bigger woman. A big strong woman. Her face was still smiling but it no longer had the benignant look. It had the look now of someone enjoying herself.

'Killer Kate,' said Tuppence.

'You know my nickname? Yes, but I've sublimated that. I've become a killer of the Lord. It's the Lord's will that I should kill you. So that makes it all right. You do see that, don't you? You see, it makes it all right.'

Tuppence was pressed now against the side of a big chair. With one arm Mrs Lancaster held her against the chair, and the pressure increased—no further recoil was possible. In Mrs Lancaster's right hand the sharp steel of the stiletto approached.

Tuppence thought, 'I mustn't panic—I mustn't panic—' But following that came with sharp insistence, '*But what can I do*?' To struggle was unavailing.

Fear came then—the same sharp fear of which she had the first indication in Sunny Ridge—

'*Is it your poor child*?'

That had been the first warning—but she had misunderstood it—she had not known it was a warning.

Her eyes watched the approaching steel but strangely enough it was not the gleaming metal and its menace that frightened her into a state of paralysis; it was the face above it—it was the smiling benignant face of Mrs Lancaster—smiling happily, contentedly—a woman pursuing her appointed task, with gentle reasonableness.

'She doesn't *look* mad,' thought Tuppence—'That's what's so awful—Of course she doesn't because in her own mind she's sane. She's a perfectly normal, reasonable human being—that's what she *thinks*—Oh Tommy, Tommy, what have I got myself into this time?'

Dizziness and limpness submerged her. Her muscles relaxed—somewhere there was a great crash of broken glass. It swept her away, into darkness and unconsciousness.

'That's better—you're coming round—drink this, Mrs Beresford.'

A glass pressed against her lips—she resisted fiercely—Poisoned milk—who had said that once—something about 'poisoned milk'? She wouldn't drink poisoned milk... No, not milk—quite a different smell—

She relaxed, her lips opened—she sipped—

'Brandy,' said Tuppence with recognition.

'Quite right! Go on—drink some more—'

Tuppence sipped again. She leaned back against cushions, surveyed her surroundings. The top of a ladder showed through the window. In front of the window there was a mass of broken glass on the floor.

'I heard the glass break.'

She pushed away the brandy glass and her eyes followed up the hand and arm to the face of the man who had been holding it.

'El Greco,' said Tuppence.

'I beg your pardon.'

'It doesn't matter.'

She looked round the room.

'Where is she—Mrs Lancaster, I mean?'

'She's—resting—in the next room—'

'I see.' But she wasn't sure that she did see. She would see better presently. Just now only one idea would come at a time—

'Sir Philip Starke.' She said it slowly and doubtfully. 'That's right?'

'Yes—Why did you say El Greco?'

'Suffering.'

'I beg your pardon.'

'The picture—In Toledo—Or in the Prado—I thought so a long time ago—no, not very long ago—' She thought about it—made a discovery—'Last night. A party—At the vicarage—'

'You're doing fine,' he said encouragingly.

It seemed very natural, somehow, to be sitting here, in this room with broken glass on the floor, talking to this man—with the dark agonized face—

'I made a mistake—at Sunny Ridge. I was all wrong about her—I was afraid, then—a—wave of fear—But I got it wrong—I wasn't afraid of *her*—I was afraid *for* her—I thought something was going to happen to her—I wanted to protect her—to save her—I—' She looked doubtfully at him. 'Do you understand? Or does it sound silly?'

'Nobody understands better than I do—nobody in this world.'

Tuppence stared at him—frowning.

'Who—who was she? I mean Mrs Lancaster—Mrs Yorke—that's not real—that's just taken from a rose tree—who was she—herself?'

Philip Starke said harshly:

'*Who was she? Herself? The real one, the true one*
Who was she—with God's Sign upon her brow?'

'Did you ever read *Peer Gynt*, Mrs Beresford?'

He went to the window. He stood there a moment, looking out—Then he turned abruptly.

'She was my wife, God help me.'

'Your wife—But she died—the tablet in the church—'

'She died abroad—that was the story I circulated—And I put up a tablet to her memory in the church. People don't like to ask too many questions of a bereaved widower. I didn't go on living here.'

'Some people said she had left you.'

'That made an acceptable story, too.'

'You took her away when you found out—about the children—'

'So you know about the children?'

'She told me—It seemed—unbelievable.'

'Most of the time she was quite normal—no one would have guessed. But the police were beginning to suspect—I had to act—I had to save her—to protect her—You understand—can you understand—in the very least?'

'Yes,' said Tuppence, 'I can understand quite well.'

'She was—so lovely once—' His voice broke a little. 'You see her—there,' he pointed to the painting on the wall. 'Waterlily—She was a wild girl—always. Her mother was the last of the Warrenders—an old family—inbred—Helen Warrender—ran away from home. She took up with a bad lot—a gaolbird—her daughter went on the stage—she trained as a dancer—Waterlily was her most popular role—then she took up with a criminal gang—for excitement—purely to get a kick out of it—She was always being disappointed—

'When she married me, she had finished with all that—she wanted to settle down—to live quietly—a family life—with children. I was rich—I could give her all the things she wanted. But we had no children. It was a sorrow to both of us. She began to have obsessions of guilt—Perhaps she had always been slightly unbalanced—I don't know—What do causes matter?—She was—'

He made a despairing gesture.

'I loved her—I always loved her—no matter what she was—what she did—I wanted her safe—to keep her safe—not shut up—a prisoner for life, eating her heart out. And we did keep her safe—for many many years.'

'We?'

'Nellie—my dear faithful Nellie Bligh. My dear Nellie Bligh. She was wonderful—planned and arranged it all. The Homes for the Elderly—every comfort and luxury. And no temptations—*no children*—keep children out of her way—It seemed to work—these homes were in faraway places—Cumberland—North Wales—no one was likely to recognize her—or so we thought. It was on Mr Eccles's advice—a very shrewd lawyer—his charges were high—but I relied on him.'

'Blackmail?' suggested Tuppence.

'I never thought of it like that. He was a friend, and an adviser—'

'Who painted the boat in the picture—the boat called *Waterlily*?'

'I did. It pleased her. She remembered her triumph on the stage. It was one of Boscowan's pictures. She liked his pictures. Then, one day, she wrote a name in black pigment on the bridge—the name of a dead child—So I painted a boat to hide it and labelled the boat *Waterlily*—'

The door in the wall swung open—The friendly witch came through it.

She looked at Tuppence and from Tuppence to Philip Starke.

'All right again?' she said in a matter-of-fact way.

'Yes,' said Tuppence. The nice thing about the friendly witch, she saw, was that there wasn't going to be any fuss.

'Your husband's down below, waiting in the car. I said I'd bring you down to him—if that's the way you want it?'

'That's the way I want it,' said Tuppence.

'I thought you would.' She looked towards the door into the bedroom. 'Is she—in there?'

'Yes,' said Philip Starke.

Mrs Perry went to the bedroom. She came out again—

'I see—' She looked at him inquiringly.

'She offered Mrs Beresford a glass of milk—Mrs Beresford didn't want it.'

'And so, I suppose, she drank it herself?'

He hesitated.

'Yes.'

'Dr Mortimer will be along later,' said Mrs Perry.

She came to help Tuppence to her feet, but Tuppence rose unaided.

'I'm not hurt,' she said. 'It was just shock—I'm quite all right now.'

She stood facing Philip Starke—neither of them seemed to have anything to say. Mrs Perry stood by the door in the wall.

Tuppence spoke at last.

'There is nothing I can do, is there?' she said, but it was hardly a question.

'Only one thing—It was Nellie Bligh who struck you down in the churchyard that day.'

Tuppence nodded.

'I've realized it must have been.'

'She lost her head. She thought you were on the track of her, of our, secret. She—I'm bitterly remorseful for the terrible strain I've subjected her to all these long years. It's been more than any woman ought to be asked to bear—'

'She loved you very much, I suppose,' said Tuppence. 'But I don't think we'll go on looking for any Mrs Johnson, if that is what you want to ask *us* not to do.'

'Thank you—I'm very grateful.'

There was another silence. Mrs Perry waited patiently. Tuppence looked round her. She went to the broken window and looked at the peaceful canal down below.

'I don't suppose I shall ever see this house again. I'm looking at it very hard, so that I shall be able to remember it.'

'Do you want to remember it?'

'Yes, I do. Someone said to me that it was a house that had been put to the wrong use. I know what they meant now.'

He looked at her questioningly, but did not speak.

'Who sent you here to find me?' asked Tuppence.

'Emma Boscowan.'

'I thought so.'

She joined the friendly witch and they went through the secret door and on down.

A house for lovers, Emma Boscowan had said to Tuppence. Well, that was how she was leaving it—in the possession of two lovers—one dead and one who suffered and lived—

She went out through the door to where Tommy and the car were waiting.

She said goodbye to the friendly witch. She got into the car.

'Tuppence,' said Tommy.

'I know,' said Tuppence.

'Don't do it again,' said Tommy. 'Don't ever do it again.'

'I won't.'

'That's what you say now, but you will.'

'No, I shan't. I'm too old.'

Tommy pressed the starter. They drove off.

'Poor Nellie Bligh,' said Tuppence.

'Why do you say that?'

'So terribly in love with Philip Starke. Doing all those things for him all those years—such a lot of wasted doglike devotion.'

'Nonsense!' said Tommy. 'I expect she's enjoyed every minute of it. Some women do.'

'Heartless brute,' said Tuppence.

'Where do you want to go—The Lamb and Flag at Market Basing?'

'No,' said Tuppence. 'I want to go home. HOME, Thomas. And stay there.'

'Amen to that,' said Mr Beresford. '*And if Albert welcomes us with a charred chicken, I'll kill him*!'

The *Agatha Christie* Collection

THE MISS MARPLE MYSTERIES

Join the legendary spinster sleuth from St Mary Mead in solving murders far and wide.

The Murder at the Vicarage
The Thirteen Problems
The Body in the Library
The Moving Finger
A Murder is Announced
They Do It With Mirrors
A Pocket Full of Rye
4.50 from Paddington
The Mirror Crack'd from Side to Side
A Caribbean Mystery
At Bertram's Hotel
Nemesis
Sleeping Murder
Miss Marple's Final Cases

THE TOMMY & TUPPENCE MYSTERIES

Jump on board with the entertaining crime-solving couple from Young Adventurers Ltd.

The Secret Adversary
Partners in Crime
N or M?
By the Pricking of My Thumbs
Postern of Fate